RAVE RE...
MARY ANN MITCHELL!

"Mary Ann Mitchell writes expressionistic hallucinations
in which fascination, Eros, and dread play out elaborate masques."
—Michael Marano, author of *Dawn Song*

"Mary Ann Mitchell is definitely someone to watch."
—Ed Gorman, author of *The Dark Fantastic*

SIPS ⊕F BL⊕⊕D

"Mitchell casts a spell with her prose to make it all come out unique.
A compelling read."
—*Hellnotes*

"Mitchell is able to write without the stuffiness that puffs out
the majority of modern vampire novels and given the chance she can
turn on the gruesome as good as anyone."
—*Masters of Terror*

"Gut-churning good. I haven't read a vampire novel
this 3-D in quite some time."
—*The Midwest Book Review*

"Rich in imagery and sympathetic characters, *Sips of Blood* is a fast-paced
and intriguing tale that vampire fans are sure to enjoy."
—*Painted Rock Reviews*

DRAWN +⊕ +HE GRAVE

"Mitchell knows how to set a mood, and how to sustain this eerie novel."
—*Mystery Scene*

THE VAMPIRE'S COFFIN

Cracking sounds of the wood echoed in the room. Cecelia worked quickly and sensed that Michael was almost by her side. Several of the panels in the coffin's lid gave way, and she ripped them apart and flung the pieces across the room.

The smell was horrid, but she wouldn't stop. Finally she was able to rip off a large slab of the lid. Michael vomited onto the floor, his candle threw eerie waves of light as his body shook. Large portions of what looked like adipose fat shimmered in the light, glinting with its swarm of maggots seeking darkness, burying themselves deeper into the flesh.

Catching his breath, Michael turned to peer into the coffin.

"It's alive!" he said.

She looked down at the face, which was gaunt and almost featureless in its decay. The eyes took in the invaders' presence. What should have been a mouth opened and revealed a number of sharp oversized teeth. A hand dripping flesh reached for Cecelia. . . .

MARY ANN MITCHELL

CATHEDRAL OF VAMPIRES

LEISURE BOOKS NEW YORK CITY

A LEISURE BOOK®

June 2002

Published by

Dorchester Publishing Co., Inc.
276 Fifth Avenue
New York, NY 10001

ISBN 0-8439-5023-4

The name "Leisure Books" and the stylized "L" with design are trademarks of Dorchester Publishing Co., Inc.

Printed in the United States of America.

Visit us on the web at www.dorchesterpub.com.

CATHEDRAL OF VAMPIRES

"*At the moment a novel of mine is being printed, but it is a work too immoral to be sent to so pious and so decent a man as yourself. I needed money, my publisher said that he wanted it well spiced, and I gave it to him to fit to plague the devil himself. It is called* Justine, or Good Conduct Well Chastised. *Burn it and do not read it, if perchance it falls into your hands. I am disclaiming the authorship. . . .*"

—MARQUIS DE SADE, *writing to his friend and lawyer on June 12, 1791*

Chapter One

Justin stood naked in front of his mother's crypt. His body, soaked in blood, shimmered in the moonlight. The shine of his muscles rising and falling with the catch of each breath seemed to grow more intense. He didn't move toward Cecelia. He waited for her to take him. He waited for Cecelia to open her arms in invitation.

Cecelia wept to see his beauty. Her mouth watered and her body tensed. She could reach out and touch him. Reach out and caress his beautiful face dripping with his gift.

She hadn't fed for longer than she could remember. When had her tongue last pressed against the clotted scarlet drink that nourished her body? The definition of his body cast shadows over the rouge blood, cast shadows that invited her to explore, in-

2

vited her to cling to him to satisfy her lust.

Her hand reached out to touch his body, but he did not feel clammy the way she had expected. Instead his flesh was satin. She took a deep breath to catch his scent, but it was not there. Again she stole big breaths of air. Finally she opened her mouth and drank in air, hoping to find it tinged with a sweet, coppery salt. But no.

Frustrated, she used both hands to push hard against his chest, losing the feel of him as he fell away and her casket lid flew open.

Opening her eyes, she saw a fractured light fixture dangling from the paint-starved ceiling. This had been home to Wil and Keith long ago when they had been human, she thought. She remembered Keith as a grumpy old man who had been transformed into a crippled vampire. Instead of coming out of his vampiric sleep a whole man, he had become an invalid dependent on his son, Wil, to push him around in a wheelchair. The fool of a son did his father's bidding even though his father had always been distant to his only child, blaming him for his mother's death while she was in labor. Now as vampires they wandered the world. Souls lost and bound to the earth.

She placed her hands on each side of the coffin and brought herself up to a seated position. Looking around the room, she knew Justin's body smeared in blood had only been a half-dream. A vision that frequently came to her upon awakening. Sometimes she found herself calling out his name, wanting him to be there, praying that he could take away the pain.

Cecelia climbed out of the coffin. Birds chirped outside the window, reminding her of the solitary state in which she existed. The sun was going down, but there still would be at least another hour of daylight. She was loneliest in daylight when she couldn't hide.

From a dresser she took a silk lace-trimmed shawl and covered her head and shoulders. The rest of her body was swathed in a simple white cotton top and pants. At the door to her bedroom she stopped to listen for Justin. He walked lightly and moved with such gentleness that he barely disturbed the air around him. Opening the door, she caught no hint of his scent or of his movements.

He had said that he would find her father. Tell her how her father lived without the wife and daughter he had loved. Perhaps Justin would even speak to her father and bring back sentences in her father's own cadence. Maybe she could smile again at the sound of Daddy's words.

Cecelia left the room and the house to visit the willow tree under which Wil had buried her mother, his first vampire kill. Her naked feet crushed grass and weeds and insects that wandered in the wrong territory.

The tree appeared to dip lower upon her approach, unable to offer anything more than regret. She sat under the tree. The grass on the ground was spotty with large bald areas totally devoid of life.

"Mommy," she whispered, wanting to rest in her mother's arms once again. A breeze touched Cecelia's cheek, and she pulled the shawl lower over her face. She didn't want her mother pandering to her needs and vices. "Only your arms surrounding me like I was a child again."

Justin called her name as his long legs stretched in a steady gait. She looked toward him, anticipating the solace he would bring in the guise of her father's life.

He stopped in front of her and took off the dark glasses that hid his emerald eyes. She watched as they clouded over into a darker, murkier color.

"I went to the house where you once lived. The house has been sold to a young couple with an infant. They bought the place months ago from an elderly man. A broken man, they said. A man they were sure looked far older than his true years. He sold at a low price, saying that he wanted the house to shine again with the happiness a family brings. They have no idea where he went. It seems he was burdened with the need to retain the past, and to vanquish it."

"If I were to return to him, what do you think he would do?"

"Cecelia, you know you cannot. He would think himself either mad or haunted. Never would he believe that you were really within reach."

Cecelia nodded her head.

"And Sade's old house?"

"Burned down like the one in San Francisco."

San Francisco, the place she had lived with the historical Marquis de Sade. His vampire blood allowed him to continue his brutal tortures and rapes. Sade had taken her from this small New York town, promising a fancy, luxurious life. In truth, she found degradation and isolation as one of his vampire followers.

"He destroyed anything that could be traced to him, except for me. And he'll be sorry one day, Justin, that he didn't take the time to find me."

As Cecelia began to rise Justin reached out a hand to steady her. She grabbed onto his hand with a firmness that forced her to feel the sharp bones in his fingers and the scaled flesh that covered them. Fingers that had been used to stake his own mother, forcing her to lie in her coffin, awaiting her half-breed son's ultimate judgment.

"Why don't we bring your mother here? We could live in this abandoned house."

"No, Cecelia. You are a ghost to most of the people who live in this town. Regular feedings have revived your beauty."

He was right; even her hair had grown back, and the tattoos had started to fade. She had removed the decorations from her flesh and the piercings had begun to close.

"What do I do, Justin?"

He stared at her; his eyes had lightened to emerald green once again. He had pushed his flaxen hair back behind his ears, and the sculpted features of his face seduced her. Do we hide in our passions?

she wondered. Obsess about each other's body until sated? But I could never be satisfied with you, Justin. I would want more with each quiver of flesh.

"You are beautiful, Justin. Even your eyes. They want me."

He would not stalk her. He would allow her to choose the time. He stood waiting, as in her half-dream. Only this time he was dressed in tight jeans and a black muscle shirt that clutched his chest.

"How do you control your desires, Justin? Do you ever take what you want?"

"I took my mother's life."

"That's only temporary. You yank the stake from her heart and she's back." Cecelia moved closer to rest her breasts against his chest. "Have you ever had a woman, Justin?"

"The women I have had slept deeply," he said, and turned away to return to the house.

What did he mean? she wondered. She was tempted to call out to him but knew he would never answer her questions. Questions she had asked him so many times. Was he afraid she would die from his overwrought passion? She had survived the Marquis de Sade; certainly Justin couldn't reach the same heights of wicked pleasure that Sade had pursued.

Chapter Two

Justin had been eager to visit the cemetery. He had been the one to open the iron gates and lead Cecelia down the gravel path. Cecelia needed to visit her own grave. Had anything mournful been written on the tombstone? Shortly they would know.

As they got closer to her family's plot she grew excited, fidgety, and pushed her way in front of Justin. He fell back, knowing she would be disappointed.

"Over there," she yelled as she approached a thick chain-link fence. Her grave was cordoned off from the rest of the family's, and there was no tombstone.

"Why?" she asked.

"When the caretaker reported seeing two dead bodies and your grave empty, I'm sure it caused much gossip. Without a body, why should there be a tombstone?" Justin watched Cecelia relive the bloody scene in her mind. Her eyes flashed and her shoulders shook.

"This is where my vampire life began, Justin. I awoke to Sade offering me the blood of a stranger, an unkempt man who smelled bad and tasted foul."

"Is this necessary, Cecelia?"

"Sade killed two men here, then rushed off to answer the call of his precious Liliana. He always loved her, Justin. Loved her too much. That love will destroy him."

Uneasy, Justin looked back over his shoulder. He sensed people who needed peace. He could bring comfort and oblivion to them. He moved away from Cecelia and wandered toward the old section of the cemetery. He saw hints of shadows melting behind old tombstones and weary, decaying trees. When he attempted to follow, they moved quickly away from him. Their stench made his eyes water, and he collected the rags that dropped from their mutant bodies.

These were the undead he had heard of. The ones who hunger for blood but don't understand from where the desire stems. Mindless, some called them. But they were aware. Their trickery was simplistically minimal. They freaked at the sight of live bodies and feasted on the dead. Fear drove them from the memories of their own lives. They were keen enough to fear the living but not to understand why.

Justin wished for flowers to spread among them. A lily, a rose, a carnation, to prove that they were

9

remembered. Decayed bramble lay at his feet. He reached out to touch trees spotted and peeling with disease. The bark crumbled in his hand, leaving a brown unwholesome ash. The bodies of the mutants disintegrated like the nature surrounding them. Flesh bruised and split. Bones fractured and poked out from the skin. No repair could be made to their bodies as they clung to the idea of existence.

"Let me help you," he called out to the shadows that pulled steadily back from him. The farther they withdrew, the worse their stench became. He walked into waves of odor that now smelled of fear and aggression.

A shadow stumbled, seeking footing among the layers of mulch that covered the ground. Justin almost touched the mutant, but the creature's snarl weakened Justin's resolve. The fleeing mutant went down on all fours, like the animal it had become.

Justin heard the explosive chittering of the shadows, heard the beat of their escape in the breeze that lightly stroked his own body.

He moved forward, never wondering what might be following him.

Chapter Three

Justin was right; there was no reason to stand here and relive the nightmare of her death.

Cecelia turned and saw only tilting headstones, chipped mausoleums, stone statues posed as if they were guardians, and tired crosses sinking into the earth. Where had Justin gone? she wondered.

She retraced her steps down the gravel path.

"Let me help you." Justin's voice came from the old section of the cemetery. He thinks he brings peace, but he couldn't, she knew.

Without calling to him, she scrambled over the ancient debris that covered the old section of the cemetery. Whispers of movement forced her to pause. Were they surrounding her? She hissed and spat as an animal would. The sounds of the movements around her dimmed as the mutants moved away from her.

Justin began singing in a high-pitched voice.

> *"All Christian men, give ear a while to me.*
> *How I am plung'd in pain but cannot die;*
> *I liv'd a life the like did none before,*
> *Forsaking Christ, and I am damn'd therefore."*

She followed the song until she viewed Justin under a bald, ancient tree. Within the tree's arms a mutant sat, staring down on Justin's flaxen hair. The starved mutant crouched almost as if in prayer; folding its long, clawlike fingers, it seemed to ask for God's assistance. A branch shivered under the mutant's weight but did not break. Peeled flesh upon its scarred head lifted in the evening breeze.

Mesmerized, she watched as the mutant fell upon Justin's shoulders, sinking its teeth into the exposed portion of Justin's right arm. A faint cry came from Justin's lips, but no call for help. They scuffled, rolling in and out of the moonlight. Even in the dark she could see how Justin fought. His eyes glowed, his mouth tightened into a grimace, and his legs entwined with the thing's bones. Another mutant lunged out of the shadow, and she could see that a third was not far behind.

Now she ran, feeling the heat of the fight and smelling Justin's blood and fear. A scrawny arm reached out to grab her hair, and Cecelia was thrown off-balance. She fell upon a bed of dead leaves and immediately kicked her pursuer in the chest. The mutant fell backward, a deep impression caving in its chest. It ran, and the others quickly followed, except for one. Justin held on to that one, a mangled doll with its tendons raw and gleaming. Its hair fell onto its face and its clothes fell limply about what little flesh it still retained. Justin cuddled it as if it were a baby. Frozen in silence, with confusion reflected in its watering eyes, the thing did not move.

Cecelia approached Justin.

"She is an innocent," pronounced Justin.

"An innocent who almost ripped your arm off," Cecelia said, kicking dust at the injured mutant.

"Please, she is frightened."

"And she wasn't scaring the hell out of you just a few minutes ago." Cecelia kneeled next to Justin. The smell of his blood captured her attention. His right arm dripping blood brought back her dreams of him waiting for her to have her fill of him.

"You and she share the same hunger," Justin said.

Cecelia looked into his emerald eyes and saw a strange spite that she had never seen in him before.

"I haven't attacked you yet."

"You're biding your time," he answered.

The mutant's body jerked, and Cecelia could see that with his bare hands Justin had detached the thing's head from its body. She took the head from him.

"She died young. Look, her hair hadn't even started to turn gray yet." She spread threads of hair across her knees. "Her nose has been bitten. A chunk of flesh is missing. Did you do that, Justin?"

He didn't answer. She knew he hadn't.

"Will we take her home with us? We could start a fine collection of skulls. This one we could set in the front window to scare the murderers and thieves away. Our very own scarecrow."

"Don't mock her, Cecelia. We will bury her deep in the ground, the head separate from the body. But not in hallowed ground."

"Just outside the gates?"

He shook his head. "On the property where we are staying."

"Not next to my mother."

"No. Someplace dark, where the sun will never find her."

"It doesn't matter anymore, does it?"

"I don't want her to suffer an eternal burning."

"Hey, Justin. Wake up! She's burning in hell as we speak. The devil is probably branding her with his own pitchfork. And we can't hear her screams because we don't want to."

"I would think you would gain a certain pleasure from her screams. How often have you heard someone plead for mercy?"

"After a while you don't hear words, only irritating noises that have to be stifled. Sade brought men to me. Many men. Every man thought he had found his own personal love slave. My orifices were open, my skin cold, my voice trapped in my throat. But I was never the one in danger. Soon they learned about the wrath a slave can wield, when their blood dripped down my gullet. I hated those men, Justin. I hated them all because of their weakness. They spread my legs and thought I was easy. Each one died gripped tightly between my thighs."

"You've never truly been able to love a man," Justin said.

"I love you." She smiled, but as she did, she could feel the hardness tightening the muscles in her face.

"Maybe you will someday," he replied.

Chapter Four

Days later, Cecelia found Justin in the cemetery again. He had laid out pieces of cloth on a smooth rock. A breeze caught one of the strips, forcing him to give chase. Cecelia watched, noting the care Justin took with the bits of cloth. He attempted to match some pieces; others he placed inside a pocket of his jacket.

"Those things are falling apart bit by bit," said Cecelia.

"They don't understand that I can help them."

"You mean the way you helped your mother by staking her in her coffin?"

"We all want peace, Cecelia."

Cecelia doubted the savages in the cemetery wanted anything but something to eat.

"I'm going back to San Francisco to retrieve the skull Sade kept so secret inside his coffin," she announced. "There must be some special power in that skull for him to have guarded it so closely."

"His mother-in-law despised Sade. That is why he destroyed her," Justin said.

"Then why keep her skull so close? Unless he fears the possibility of her return. She was a vampire; perhaps there's a way for her to return. We can leave—"

"I'm not going. There is nothing for me to do in that city. But here I am needed. I can sense the desperation."

"What about visiting your mother's coffin?"

"You'll do that for me." He looked at her with a slight smile. "That is where you hid the skull, isn't it?"

"I didn't think your mother would notice the company."

"I will stay here and ease as much pain as I can." His emerald eyes defied her.

"You'll be here when I get back?" she asked.

"I have much work to do here, Cecelia. I won't be running off so soon."

"Would my child be as pathetic as you are?" she asked.

"Your child was lucky."

"Don't dare say she was lucky. She was a baby. Small, helpless. Wrapped in a pale cotton blanket and tucked into an antique cradle when Sade took her life. He killed his own love."

"He was protecting the child from herself and from the sins the world would force her to commit. I live in hiding behind dark glasses and a shy demeanor because the pain of revealing myself as half-vampire and half-human would be more than I could handle."

Justin rose from the ground and faced Cecelia in defiance of her increasing anger.

"I too would have killed your baby, Cecelia. You have no right to force life where it should not exist."

"She belonged to me."

"And what of the human father? Would he have wanted the baby to live? Was he ever present in her life?"

"I didn't need him anymore. I cast him aside as soon as I sensed that I was pregnant."

"Another man you hated?" he asked, tilting his head to the side.

Cecelia shook her head.

"No, I pitied him. He was only a boy, easily controlled. He still lived with his mother and with whatever strange men she brought home with her."

"Would you have wanted that life for your little one?"

"I wouldn't have brought men home like that. When I needed to feed, I would have left the house." She threw her shoulders back and defied Justin's stare.

"How would you have fed the baby?"

"You know the answer to that."

"Small mice and rats. Perhaps for a special treat a kitten just birthed in an alley."

"That is how vampires live. Besides, when she got older, like you, she could have made her own decision about what she'd eat."

"Breast milk could have kept her alive. But your breasts were dry, weren't they, Cecelia?"

A wind whistled between Justin and Cecelia. She found herself touching her breasts. Never to be a mother who could suckle her young, she reminded herself.

"Sade stole a lot from me, Justin. I mean to get even. That's why I must get the skull. I know it has some sort of power that he dreads; that's why he kept it so close to him. If I could bring back Marie's soul, she would know what to do."

"Haven't you had enough of trying to bring vampires back to life, Cecelia? Let the poor woman's soul rest."

"Neither of us will rest until we gain retribution. I'll go alone and leave you here with these 'things.' Watch that they don't trap you some night, because I want you whole when I get back."

Justin reached out and touched a hand to her hair. She felt his heat pass into her cold body.

"I don't want to lie between your legs, Cecelia. I want to reach inside your head and clean away all the crud that starves your brain. All the crud that keeps you from thinking rationally."

19

"I'm sure you wouldn't turn away a little flesh as an appetizer." She cocked her head, and her right hand meshed with his fingers still threading through her hair. Her blue eyes attempted to stare him down, but he remained passionless.

"I would willingly take you, Cecelia, but that isn't what you need. I would destroy you, and you would never realize your ultimate dream."

Cecelia laughed and began stripping off her clothes.

"Destroy me then, Justin. Here in the cemetery where I belong. And when you're finished with me, bury me in that empty plot that lies chained off from all the others."

Naked, Cecelia began to undress Justin. She opened the buttons of his shirt and marveled at how well-defined his flesh was. Slowly she lowered the shirt down his shoulders and over his arms. He stood still, allowing her to use him. With one hand she unsnapped his jeans and lowered the zipper. She spread her arms so that she could touch the sides of his slim hips. She drew the jeans down far enough to see that he truly was erect and ready for her.

"This is not what you want, Cecelia," he said.

Cecelia raised her hands and began to shout.

"How the hell do you know what I want? How do you know what these beasts who live in this cemetery want? Maybe they don't want peace, Justin. Perhaps they need to get even. To rip the guts from the empty shells buried here."

She took several steps backward and twirled around.

"Come out and tell him what you want. Don't let him decide for you, because he doesn't have a clue." She stopped and stared into Justin's eyes. "He wants to make right what isn't wrong. He wants to play God. That's it, isn't it? Standing there with that hard-on, you don't look like any god I was taught to worship. No, you look like the men who jacked off while watching others fucking."

She saw him grimace.

"Wait, I've offended you. Let me correct myself. Jacked off while watching others *make love*. You do believe in love, don't you? A fleshly love that goes beyond simply giving people peace. There's nothing peaceful about getting off, Justin. We have to strain our bodies for our pleasures. Peace and pleasure aren't the same."

"If you want me, get down on your knees and take me."

"I've played at this before." She dropped to her knees directly in front of him. "You can't shame me. You don't even come close to being Sade's equal."

"I don't want to be compared to the man who ruined you." Justin pulled his jeans over his erection and slid the zipper closed.

"And what are you going to do, Justin? Mend me?"

She watched him turn his back on her and walk away, leaving his shirt lying on the ground. She watched the luscious whiteness of his flesh bob in and out of sight as he wove between the trees. His back muscles flexed seductively in the night.

Cecelia reached out and grabbed his shirt and wrapped it around her shoulders.

Chapter Five

Justin wandered the house alone. Cecelia had left to set her vengeance in motion. A vengeance that could never bring her peace. If Sade were dead, what would she have to live for? With both her child and her lover out of reach, she had no one to whom she could cling. Justin was only her tool, a gift that came to her without prayer. He had come to offer solace when she had nothing. He remembered her soft flesh, covering a youth's body containing a harpy's soul. Sometimes she laughed as a girl would, sometimes she cried as an innocent would, sometimes she expressed a warm caring. The last was the oddest mood, because she didn't want to care about anyone, not even herself. Yet there had been hours she would sit next to Justin reading and reaching for him more than occasionally to make sure he kept her company.

She would miss him on this trip, but only as a child longing for her teddy bear. What did he expect of her? A physical love that should never bear fruit into a third soul? She had borne a child to a boy for a man. All he offered was himself as a man-child who couldn't even risk setting his mother totally free.

Rows of glass birds were shelved on the wall in front of him. Birds painted many colors, with hints of swollen feathers, sharp beaks, and legs glued to tin pedestals. The species' names appeared in bold gothic lettering, marking each bird as one of God's typical creatures. Old-man ornaments, he thought. Dust leaded down each bird, fixed to a certain spot, to a prison. Even soap and water couldn't give these birds freedom. They weren't real. Justin wasn't real and couldn't ask for a life of freedom.

Alone he drifted from room to room, noting the owner's idiosyncrasies and passions. The blood-spattered mattress in the main bedroom spoke to Justin of strife and pain. Sheets with small holes where fingernails had dug in and split the material lay in bundles on the floor. He looked at the blood-stained walls that no one had ever cleaned. He turned a full circle, imagining the terrors the room had witnessed. No more. Now the room remained quiet, with sunlight daring to brighten such a sad place.

From the window he could see the willow tree, waving its arms like a dancer performing a strange ballet. He had noted previously that neither bird nor beast nor insect climbed the trunk of that tree. The branches offered no protection for skittering squirrels. The leaves turned brown and fell without feeding any insect. Why? he wondered. Was it because Cecelia's mother was interred at its base? A new Judas tree, perhaps, only lacking the small purple flowers that had attracted the informer. Weeping silently, the tree waved its arms in invitation, but all were wise enough to fend off the tree's seduction. Including himself, Justin thought, as he turned his back on the window and gazed again at the room.

Would Cecelia return to this misery, or would she flee with the skull to Paris, to her lover?

Justin would miss her. He would bleed for her if she asked. But he never would hear the request come from her lips. Sometimes he dreamed of her gently taking her feed from him. The spinning ecstasy of her teeth meshing their bodies and souls together made him close his eyes. But only for a moment.

Others spoke to him of their writhing pain. Souls closer, within reach. He thought of the nearby cemetery. The confused eyes of the mutants stared back at him in his mind. Their numbers never seemed to diminish, his work forever before him. He cursed his cross and started for the front door.

Chapter Six

At the San Francisco cemetery Cecelia walked between the mausoleums and tombstones with the prideful but weakened steps of a widow. The half-moon played at her white dress, casting a blue hue to the long skirt that skimmed the soil.

She had thought about bringing flowers to continue Justin's tradition but nixed the idea when she remembered what a fool he had appeared to be that night when she first met him. He had offered her a flower. One of the many flowers he reserved for the dead.

Justin's family mausoleum could be seen a few yards away from where she stood. The semirusted door, still protected by marble spirals, stood closed. As she reached the door, she put out a hand and grabbed the handle firmly. She took several breaths of fresh air before forcing the door open. It squawked its reproval as she stepped into the mausoleum.

Death hung in the air, ancient, judgmental, and angry because she had cheated it. The humid air clotted her throat and she coughed. In front of her lay the coffin containing Justin's staked mother. The gloss of the wood appeared dulled and the painting beneath the lid was stained.

When her hands touched the lid, her fingers tingled with a spirit that had not been inside that coffin before. Invigorated, Cecelia threw back the lid. Empty. The quilted satin enfolded not a body, not a skull. Merely air. An air that reeked of decay and something she didn't recognize. The sweetness of flowers? No, she thought. Not fruit, not honey. The odor bore an ethereal sweetness that knew no earthly comparison.

She spun around to take in every corner of the room. Only Justin's blanket, meager pile of clothes, and recorder lay in one corner, left behind when they'd had to flee, returning to New York for her home soil.

Justin's mother must be out hunting, she thought. But how did she regain her strength? Who had dared to rip the stake from the woman's heart? She turned to the portrait and fingered the stains. Blood, she realized. Cecelia could not tell whether the blood came from a victim or from the predator herself.

Cecelia did not care whether the woman walked again as long as she gave her back the skull. Sade's mother-in-law's skull.

Must she wait until almost daybreak, or would the woman bring her prey back to her nest? Unlikely the woman would bring her feed back, Cecelia realized after another search of the mausoleum. The only bloodstain in the room was on the portrait. The vampire kept her cave neat.

"A visitor. I'm so glad to meet you. You are the only one of my own kind that I've met since . . . regaining my health."

Cecelia turned to the doorway where the woman in the portrait stood. She had changed from the seventeenth-century gown she had worn. A slinky black dress curved into her hips and sprouted out again across a substantial bust. Her black stockings whispered as she walked closer to Cecelia.

"I don't know you. However, I sense a whiff of familiarity. Masculine in nature, and you are certainly not that. It's someone who made you."

"No. You probably sense your son. We've traveled together."

"I have no son. Two daughters lie in peace, but no son."

"You must know Justin." Cecelia began to panic, thinking herself tricked by a man she had dared to trust.

"I know more Judases than Justins." The woman looked inside her coffin.

28

"I didn't change anything. I was just looking for something that belongs to me," Cecelia clarified.

"You think I possess this 'something'?" The woman waved her hands in the air, conjuring but failing to make anything appear.

"I left it with you in the coffin."

The woman looked back inside the coffin.

"I've taken nothing out except myself." The woman shrugged and took a step backward to reappraise her intruder. "Pretty," she said and smiled politely.

Suddenly the smile sagged and the eyes burned. The woman rushed forward and grasped hold of Cecelia's arms.

"I know that smell. It's been a long time since I've had to tolerate it. Is he here?" Warily she glanced around the room.

"Who?" The woman was strong and certainly would bruise Cecelia's arms.

"Louis. The fop who ruined my daughters and brought about this life . . . I so enjoy."

Cecelia's guard instantly came up.

"If you enjoy your life so much, why be angry at the one who gave it to you?"

"Because he still exists. I smell him in your blood. He's left his mark on your body," the woman said, brushing her thumb across a faded tattoo on Cecelia's right arm.

"The tattoo was something I chose." Cecelia raised her chin.

"He certainly marked your flesh and warped your mind. That is what he does."

"Who is this person you're talking about?" Cecelia asked.

"My son-in-law. The marquis. Louis Sade."

"Then you're not Justin's mother, but you *have* taken her body. You are Marie."

"A younger and therefore more attractive version of what I used to be. I always hated having been turned vampire in my sixties. The horrid wrinkles, the sagging breasts, and the white streaks that crossed my rounded stomach. Hmmm. You are even younger and prettier," the woman noted.

"And not staked and vulnerable to your invasion."

The woman laughed.

"Yes, it was easy to pierce a defenseless body, but how frustrating to lie with a piece of wood sticking out of your chest. My life bubbled inside her husk and still she sleeps, because I have buried her spirit deep and will never release it."

"How did you get the stake out of your heart?"

"I've always been a seducer of men, you know," the woman said in a hushed voice. "I can make a man kneel on shards of glass and beg me to whip the shit out of him. I've had men beg me to take their blood even when I was sated. Mostly younger men." The woman primped and wrapped a single dark curl around her finger.

"While lying in a grave it is hard to seduce a man," Cecelia dared to remind the woman.

"They came to me. Three boys, late teens or early twenties. They came to commit mischief. An accessible mausoleum is such an enticement to boys that age. Especially when they wear black and make believe they are more than what they are.

"They were here to despoil the dead. How cruel! Totally helpless, I lay within the confines of this vulnerable body.

"When the lid was raised, I could see their faces peering down at me. Frightful, drunken faces. Wild with youth and ignorant in their mortality."

The woman closed her eyes and drifted on with her story.

"They were gleeful to find the likes of a grade-B movie within their grasp. A stake in the heart, moldy old-fashioned clothing, and papery-thin flesh that flaked badly in crevices. Like at the edges of the mouth," she said, bringing her hands up to her face but not touching her skin. She opened her eyes.

"What wonderful entertainment I was for the boys. They spent at least an hour scaring each other and passing a cheap bottle of booze. Two of these boys attempted to pitch the third in with me. At that point I did worry about the fragility of the body I was in. My original frame was hardy and withstood quite a bit, except for fire."

"The scorched skull that I put into the coffin," Cecelia said.

"And from where did you get my skull, child?"

"You haven't finished your story yet. How did you manage to have the stake taken from your heart?"

"The boy, the one his friends wanted to sleep with me, brushed against the stake and in panic grabbed hold of the wood, yanking it out in order to beat off his comrades.

"It didn't take long," Marie hissed. "I felt the flush of existence sweeping through my body. My borrowed body. It was like a cold wave hitting my body. The tension left after the wave drifted off. The muscles complied with my thoughts. Flexibility returned to the joints. I was famished and found myself standing in front of my dinner."

Marie laughed and spun around several times, obviously enjoying the feel of her body.

"The boys scuffled with each other for the door. And one by one I disabled them. Didn't kill them immediately; I like my food fresh. Ah! It was a banquet. Better than anything I had tasted in life."

"And you disposed of the bodies?" Cecelia asked.

"That is what the Bay is for. Now, child, answer my question: How did you obtain my skull?"

"I took it from Sade."

"In a fair fight, no doubt."

"Don't make fun of me. You owe your existence to me."

Marie nodded and waited.

"I stole into his room while he was away and destroyed his coffin. I tossed it out the window. It shattered on the ground, and then I mixed his soil with California soil and ripped out the satin lining. That's when I found the skull. He kept it by his feet." Cecelia looked straight at Marie, awaiting a reaction.

Marie brought a hand to her breast and stared down at the cement floor.

"You are brave, child. I would have said foolish, except here you are in front of me." She raised her head and looked at Cecelia. "You survive his wrath. I must now ask if he still haunts our lives."

"I assume he immediately went back to France in order to be reunited with his own soil."

"We must be off to Paris, then. I've missed my country so much. I was driven out just like a common witch, but those who could remember me are no more. You'll love Paris."

"How do you know he'll go there?"

"That will merely be our starting point, child."

"Cecelia."

Marie smiled and acknowledged the name.

"We have to go to New York first. Justin is waiting."

"Who the hell is Justin? You kept saying I was his mother."

"The woman whose body you're in was his mother."

"My. Will this upset him? Does he believe his mother traipsed this city for victims?"

"No."

"He knew she was staked?"

"He staked her," Cecelia answered.

"Then he must have a terrible temper. I love men like that. It is so easy to break them."

Chapter Seven

Justin had spent days and nights in the cemetery, not bothering to return home. He fasted to make his senses keener. The clothing he wore had picked up the mutants' own scent. They were always with him, even when he was alone.

He had managed to free several souls from the agony of this world, but they had been ancient and barely able to walk. The others moved faster and never let him near. They knew his goal.

On this day a small child, not more than five or six, had been playing a game of hide-and-seek with him. The child would cry out to get his attention and then would escape with a fleet motion that was almost a blur.

Justin sat on the boundary that divided the old cemetery from the new. He picked up a number of

34

fallen twigs and branches and began designing a doll, a stick figure that could entice a young one. He twined vines around the pieces, binding them together in a simple human shape. He used leaves and pebbles to make its clothes. Caveman clothes, he thought, as the attire took on a certain fashion. He covered the head with wisps of grass, combining dried bits with fresh to shade the hair around the face.

A stick flew into his right hand but didn't disturb the figure. The child was back. Justin looked around him. The boy or girl, Justin did not know which, hid.

"You may have the doll if you want it," Justin called.

A small battered face peeked out from behind a tree. Poor thing had to fight hard for its food in competition with stronger adult mutants, Justin thought.

"Shall I name the doll for you? Perhaps I could list some names and you could nod at your favorite?"

The child stretched out its neck; whether in interest or curiosity, Justin didn't know. However, he began a list of names, some from the Bible, some made up inside his head. The child made no response until the word "Priscilla" shaped Justin's lips.

"Priscilla. Do you know a Priscilla? Is that your name?" Justin asked. He watched the child step out into full view. "Come take the doll. Take Priscilla."

The child appeared to be confused but took several steps toward Justin, stopping just out of reach.

Justin placed the doll on the ground and stood to take several steps backward.

The child had been so quick before that Justin had never really been able to see the details of her face and body. Now the horror of the mutant life crouched before him, crawling toward the twig-and-stick doll. The skin on the child's arms and legs had bite marks in various stages of rot. The newer ones glistened under the moon. The older ones lay dry and shredded.

Justin knew that the mutants took part in feeding frenzies when a fresh corpse was interred in the cemetery. He had already witnessed two interments and what had followed. After the bones had been picked clean, the mutants reburied the bones, either in respect or more likely burying the bones the way dogs did. He found it difficult to assess their intelligence. If they understood speech, he hadn't been able to get them to respond. Until now. He looked down at the child, cautiously reaching out to take the doll.

She looked up at Justin, the face a parody of a child's; the complexion very pale, the eyes lost in a distant stare, with sparks of color only hinted at in the ravished sockets. The nose and lips pulsated as if constantly taking in the odors and tastes of the surroundings. The small chin, almost gone in decay, quivered in time with the lips.

He watched as the child stretched out her blackened tongue to lick the surface of the doll.

Was it a smile or a smirk that twisted the innocent's lips? he wondered.

Justin squatted down. "Do you like the doll? I made it specially for you, Priscilla." He dared to guess the child's name.

The child caressed the doll in her shattered arms and rocked back and forth, moaning and crying dry tears.

"You miss your mother, don't you? I have a mother, too. She held me and lullabied me when I was as young as you. My mother is like you, and yet not the same. I tried to bring her peace but couldn't make it final. Limbo is her home now, because I'm not brave enough to be completely alone. I am ashamed." He felt his face dampen with tears.

The child reached out toward Justin, watching the tears leave shiny streaks on his face. Justin cried freely.

Suddenly the child became angry, ripping the doll apart, shoving fistfuls of leaves from the skirt and grass from the hair into her mouth. The child finally bit down on the sticks, and Justin saw several teeth come free from her gums.

Justin jumped to his feet and rushed the child, quickly turning the tiny neck until her body fell away to the ground.

He would bury Priscilla near the others he had destroyed, but he would bury the head separate from the body. Deep in the ground, Priscilla wouldn't have to fight anymore. Priscilla would rest for the first time in how many years? From the rags that hung on the child's limp body, Justin guessed it may have been at least a hundred years.

Justin's face was dry now. His movements were solemn but not sad, his steps hardly burdened by the weight of the child's husk. His mind was directed toward a single goal that vanquished all the pain.

Chapter Eight

"I think you should wait outside the house until I can explain what happened to Justin," Cecelia said to Marie.

"Maybe I should go in with you and give him a thrill. Mommy's back, badder than ever. Do you suppose he would run to my arms? Is he attractive? You haven't described him to me."

"You're his mother," Cecelia said, aghast at the implication.

"Hmmm. He could make love to two women at the same time. A little incest with a lot of raunchy sex." Marie smiled. Her eyes seemed to peer off into a distant daydream.

"Please, try to be kind to him." Cecelia wondered whether she should have gone off with this woman and left Justin to his twisted plans. Selfishly, she had returned for Justin because of the uneasiness she felt in the presence of this woman.

"If he's had to survive as half-vampire, half-human, he can't be too soft-shelled," said Marie.

"If anything, what he is has made him more sensitive."

"I know this house. Sensitive has never lived here. The old man was a bastard and his son . . . ah! His son." Marie smiled. "I wonder where his son is." Marie climbed the steps to the house. Cecelia waited at the foot of the stairs.

"I smell death," Marie said. "Tainted blood and death. Can't you smell it, Cecelia?"

My own mother's death, Cecelia thought. She knew the trail of blood in the house, having followed it on several occasions.

Marie put her hand on the doorknob and twisted. The door opened invitingly wide.

"Anyone home?" she called.

Cecelia ran up the steps and pushed Marie out of the way.

"Justin," Cecelia called and was almost relieved when no one answered. "Justin," she called again, walking slowly from room to room. When she returned to the living room, she saw Marie making herself comfortable on the couch.

"Maybe he became tired of waiting for you, Cecelia. Or has he?" Marie faced the front window and leaned forward. "Shoulder-length hair and a not-too-slender body with a terribly sexy gait. In charge. That is the aura he sends out."

Cecelia ran to the front door to greet Justin. He carried a child-size mutant in his arms.

"You're not taking that thing in this house," she yelled, calling attention to herself.

Justin stopped for a split second and looked at her. He continued walking toward the house and gently placed the mutant husk on the ground before climbing the steps.

"You've come back," he said.

"I have a surprise."

"Sade is here?" he asked.

"No. I found Marie."

"Her skull, you mean."

"No. She has a body now. Only . . . she's borrowing your mother's body."

He stood inches from her, not comprehending. He carried the scent of the cemetery's residents, an odor that caused Cecelia to gag.

"My mother?"

Cecelia sensed a breeze flow by her.

"Son." Marie stood next to Cecelia with arms wide open.

Cecelia reached out to touch Justin, but he stepped too far back, almost falling down the stairs.

"Oh, don't look sullen. I'm not your mother, exactly. She does live inside me, though. I feel her tremors from time to time. Now, for instance. I think she recognizes that you are present. Why does she want to flee from you, Justin?"

"You can't have my mother."

41

"Why not? You were wasting a good body inside that coffin. A body that I desperately needed."

"I can make you sleep again," he said.

Marie gave him a fetching smile and then swung her arm in a wide arc, knocking him backwards down the flight of stairs.

Cecelia saw his eyes turn a muddy color and raced down the steps to quietly speak to him. Her hands rested on his shoulders as she squatted.

"I need this woman, Justin. She can help me find Sade. She can help me destroy him," she whispered. "Destroy her and you can never get your mother back. You heard her say that she could sense your mother inside her."

"I should have destroyed Mother long ago. I should never have taken this kind of chance."

"Keep her alive awhile longer for me, please. I will always have to run from Sade unless I find him first."

"You betrayed me, Cecelia."

"I never knew this would happen. I only wanted a safe place for the skull. A place where Sade could never find it."

"Boy!" yelled out Marie. "Never threaten me or your mother. I'll protect us with everything I can, even if it should mean killing you.

"We must be off to Paris soon. Money! Did that dirty old man leave any money?" She reentered the house.

"I'll help you after we find Sade. I promise," Cecelia said to Justin.

"What will you do?"

"I don't know, but . . ."

"That woman is wicked. Perhaps she is worse than Sade," he said. "And she will taunt you with the information she has about Sade, then join him in defeating you."

"Ridiculous. He destroyed her body, Justin. He trapped her in an eternal limbo."

"That you helped her escape." The resentment in Justin's voice hurt Cecelia.

"So did you! You left your mother staked and helpless in that mausoleum. I didn't see you stay to guard her. I didn't even hear you complain when you surreptitiously caught me hiding the skull. None of us knew this would be the consequence. But then, she wasn't my mother. I know my mother sleeps in her grave."

"You know what a man told you, Cecelia, and how often have men been honest with you?"

"This one was. It pained him to tell me the truth. Guilt forced him into revealing what he and his father had done. I will never forgive him, and he knows that. He had nothing to gain by telling a lie. She rests under that willow tree, Justin. I swear I'll help you put your own mother at rest too. I know how important it is to you."

"And for you finding Sade is imperative?"

Cecelia nodded. "He will kill me if he has the opportunity."

"He can't kill you, Cecelia. He can only give you rest."

"Damn!" Cecelia stood. "What if I enjoy being what I am? What if your mother had been happy with her life? Don't judge, Justin. Listen to what we say."

Justin looked at the child. His muddy eyes turned a shiny emerald.

"You all want rest, Cecelia. All of you."

"I'm not a monster in a cemetery, Justin. I don't rip apart corpses because I don't know what else to do." Cecelia walked over to the husk on the ground. "It's small. Do you suppose the child knew what it wanted? Did you ask permission, Justin? Did it beg you to destroy it? You may not be God's messenger. You may be the devil's."

Chapter Nine

"What is that thing he's burying?" Marie stood by the bedroom window and called to Cecelia in the hallway.

"It's a mutant," Cecelia said. "He finds them in the local cemetery. They're vampires turned into animals. They eat the dead."

"How sickening. Why did he bring it here?"

"It's part of his quest," Cecelia said, drawing closer to the window. "Look at him. Have you ever seen anyone work so hard to bury a stranger?"

"Only when one's own life depended on it." Marie turned away from the window and glared at the walls. She hadn't been able to leave the room since she had set foot in it. The memories it held jolted her mind out of the semi-fog it had been in since reawakening in the mausoleum. Blood spotted the room, but not all the blood was hers. Sade must have had a killing feast here. Or perhaps it was Wil. The room secreted chaos. Whoever killed here didn't know how to drink his blood. He had scrambled for it. Wil, she thought again.

"When will my coffin arrive?" Marie asked.

"Tomorrow. We have to be careful when the coffin arrives, because I don't know what the sight of his mother's coffin will trigger in Justin."

"The hell with Justin. I need rest."

"Will the San Francisco soil serve to keep you safe?"

"This body thrives on American soil. I may not be able to return to my home soil." A headache accompanied by dizziness forced Marie to sit on the naked mattress where she had killed Wil's father.

"Will you be able to make it until tomorrow?" asked Cecelia.

"These headaches come occasionally when Justin's mother becomes frisky. I told you I couldn't find my skull. Sometimes I feel as if it seeped inside this head and wrapped itself around the skull already there."

"Maybe it has."

There was a rumble of thunder, and lightning lit up the weeping willow tree.

"Mother," Cecelia cried, running from the room.

Chapter Ten

By the time Cecelia reached the tree, several branches were on fire. She ran to the spot where she believed her mother was buried and began to stomp out the sparks that fell from the tree.

She felt a hand grab her wrist, and she was pulled back by Justin.

"Foolish. The fire can't reach your mother's body, but it can destroy you. Look at the house, Cecelia. That woman is standing at the window laughing at you. You can't trust her."

"I don't," Cecelia said. "But I need her. She knows his secret lairs."

"And you believe he will return to his old living arrangements?"

"He must. It is property he owns and can hide

away in. He doesn't know that Marie's back. Who is there to locate him besides her?"

A cloudburst erupted, and a heavy rain fell, putting out the fire. Justin and Cecelia let the water wash their bodies.

"Your mother is safe, Cecelia. She is truly dead."

"I'm so sorry, Justin. I understand your pain, but I can't let the opportunity to find Sade vanish in your mother's body." Cecelia fell onto the muddy ground. With arms spread wide, she began picking up clumps of earth while pleading with Justin to forgive her.

Did she cry? she wondered. Or did the rain author a lie?

"Have you finished burying the child?" she asked.

"A few more shovelfuls of dirt and I'll be finished."

"Then go back to the child. Finish what you've started, Justin."

She looked down at her silt-covered hands. Pressure built under her nails as the earth crept deeper into each crevice. Yet she continued to dig. Water filled up the hole every time she pulled out more earth. What would she find under the loosened soil? What did she want to find?

"Cecelia, you can't bring your mother back," Justin said. "If she rests under this tree, let her be."

The simple word *if* energized her actions. *If* would never satisfy the hunger she felt. She dug deep until she touched cloth. The rain kept hiding the texture and color of the material.

"Help me, Justin. Help me." She turned to look up at him and saw his hair hanging limply to his shoulders. His clothes seemed plastered to the contours of his body. His eyes, though, shined like precious jewels. They sparkled down at her like beacons lighting a world she couldn't completely understand.

"I need to know," she whispered, knowing that he would hear her.

He squatted next to her. "Will you be able to recognize the bones and rotted flesh as your mother's? She will never again be whole for you. Leave her here, Cecelia."

"There has to be something recognizable. Her clothes. I'll know the dress around the skeleton. I'll be able to tell you where she bought it, how much it cost, how much I hated it then and how much I love it now."

Justin helped her dig. Soon the hole was big enough to lift out Cecelia's treasure. Waterlogged, the thing seemed to fall apart in their hands. The material binding the skeleton together ripped, and Cecelia rushed to pull the split material together.

Finally a wasted body lay close to the willow tree's trunk. A hand wasn't whole. A foot remained buried in the ground. Gray hair swept across cheekbones that bled flesh in the rain.

"There's enough to know she's here," Cecelia whispered to Justin. "A ring that she never removed still sits loosely on her finger. A bit of flesh molding familiar features. One of the dresses she wore only when working, still stained in places with liquid cleaners."

"We must bury her deeper," Justin said. "This Wil did not bury her with respect."

"He only wanted her out of his sight. He was ashamed, Justin." Her hand stroked the gray hair, pulling strands back off the corpse's face. "He told me that this was his favorite tree. He thought that would make up for his crime. I want her reburied here. If he comes back someday, let him find a marker that proves his heartlessness." She looked into Justin's face. "He'll never find peace under this tree again."

Chapter Eleven

The girls bled for him under the whip and allowed their bodies to be contorted into painful positions with rope, wire, and scarves. Their flesh awash in sweat glowed under the soft whispers of candlelight. They used tongues to lick absinthe and brandy from his fingertips. Eyes closed in ecstasy when he deigned to caress their bodies. Yet he knew that most would be at Sunday mass, chaperoned by middle-aged parents who never asked questions.

Girls with dark hair that glistened under the sun's warmth. Redheads freckled in peculiar patterns that formed in answer to the sun's shine. Blondes, some with dark roots and olive skin, who luxuriated in the altering power of the sun. He had chosen one of each to satisfy himself this night. Tomorrow he might choose to dine with the family of one of these girls. A well-educated and proper gentleman, he would be welcome in any of the girls' homes. The family might even harbor hopes that he would take their child as a wife. He laughed, and the quiet one looked up at him, trying to recognize pleasure or disdain in his eyes. Madeline was the smallest of the girls. She meant to please but often stiffened when she should have relaxed into the play. Her hooded brown eyes kept constant watch. The others had floated away hours ago on the absinthe he had served liberally. Every time her red locks fell over her eyes she would toss her head back, sending the tresses flying back to rest against the pillow.

He spoke French to her in a low, soft voice that imitated a father caressing his child. Her response was always a heightened awareness. He would smile and she would wince. And when he ignored her, she became anxious. She had hardly spoken during their night of lust, merely answering questions that were asked of her. Her sharp teeth had bruised his flesh in many places, her demands always made in a passive but provocative fashion.

He had promised himself that he would take no special woman to live with him. The loss of Liliana and the betrayal of Cecelia had ended his longing to have one dear and close to him. Yet Madeline haunted him even while he rode one of the other girls. He doubted he would recognize either of the other girls on a road in the village. Their features didn't matter anymore, their bodies served only one purpose, and their voices whimpered and cried in drunken stupor.

He had tied Madeline in the tightest and most painful position. He could see the wire cutting at her white skin, drawing the blood that he so adored. He would drink of this girl, he knew, tasting her inner and outer beauty. He would leave most of her blood behind, running through her veins. He would limit the pleasure he would take of her, purposely letting her believe that she was just a village girl spawning no special feeling in his soul.

Ah! But Madeline would come to him in his fantasies, and she would play the clever maid who touched his life with beauty and rapture.

If he were mortal he would take her on a world trip, testing her in every city where they wandered. And when she bore him a child, the child would be a treasure, not a misshapen freak with half its nature devoted to death.

The remembrance of the smell of Cecelia's babe caused him to retch, and the girls accepted this as part of the sport. Not Madeline. No, she stared into his eyes and knew that he hurt. Not a physical pain, but a deeper emotion that he shared with no one in the room.

"Speak to me, Madeline, *ma fille*," he said, reaching for her lips. The pad of his left thumb skimmed her full mouth until she spread her lips and sucked in the sweetness and sourness of his flesh. He leaned sideways in order to stay inside one of the other girls while touching Madeline's bloody wrist with his tongue. He carried away a few drops on his tongue and placed them inside Madeline's mouth.

She closed her eyes and swept her tongue over his, transferring the blood.

"*Douleur et sang* are one in my world, Madeline. Are you capable of caressing them both?" he asked her.

He yanked the wire tighter around her wrists and watched as her skin gave way to the pressure. She gasped and winced. He continued to lap at her wounds.

Chapter Twelve

Cecelia felt more like a tourist than a hunter in Paris. She walked the Louvre in a day, roamed the Jardin des Tuileries, watching well-dressed gigolos introduce themselves to wealthy women, climbed Montmartre to view Sacré-Coeur, and memorized the many stores on the Avenue des Champs-Elysées. Once she visited the Place de la Bastille, recalling the memories Sade had shared, although now a gaudy opera house stood, because the Bastille had been dismantled during the French Revoulution.

Hoping to get a lead on Sade, Cecelia visited Montmartre and walked the streets of Pigalle. The flashing multicolored lights gave her a headache. The adult movie houses and cheap hotels made her shudder, remembering past trips to such places in the United States. The smell of the streetwalkers turned her stomach as the perfume and sex invaded her nose and seemed to stick to her flesh. She slipped into a lingerie and sex shop, evading the men who approached her on the street. But this proved no haven when she noticed the milling men staring at her over equipment that startled even her. The shoddily dressed proprietor asked if he could be of assistance, and Cecelia felt her eyes burn with the desire for tears. A man touched her arm as if to wake her, and she swung out her right fist in defense, sending the man into the magazine shelves. Quickly the proprietor came out from behind the counter. He demanded that she leave the store or he would call the police. Enraged, Cecelia toppled several tables on her way out, but no one dared to touch or follow her.

None of this satisfied her hunger. Where was Sade? He wouldn't remain in Paris. He would require space, a pleasant estate on which he could luxuriate in his freedom. Even he would be sickened by the city's meanest streets. But she waited for Marie to settle her financial affairs and for Justin to tire of the Cimetière du Père Lachaise, where he had found none of the mutants he needed to save.

"I don't sense them near," Justin said. "When I go to the cemetery, I feel sadness and loss, but no hate. The cemetery is surely blessed."

"Aren't most cemeteries?"

"This cemetery has banished evil."

"Yeah, and it's running around the rest of Paris. I saw a tour bus today actually nudge a policeman.

I lost track of the curses that passed between driver and policeman. Some I had never heard before."

"An opportunity, Cecelia, to enrich your French vocabulary."

He looked at her with a small weak smile.

"I can't stay in this city much longer. Sade's not here. And Marie seems to spend most of her time at fetish clubs and bordellos."

"She is searching for him."

"Bullshit! She enjoys the pain and lust of others. She's no better than Sade."

"This comes as a surprise to you, Cecelia?"

"We'll join her tonight."

"Perhaps this is her night to stay home."

"She hasn't stayed home a single night since we've been here. No, we'll dress up, and when she awakens we'll be ready."

"Personally, I shall never be ready."

Cecelia came closer to him. She knelt at his feet and placed her hands on the leather arms of the chair in which he sat.

"Do you ever wonder what she does? Wonder what she puts your mother's body through on these long evenings?"

"I know I've never seen bruises, and only the smell of death clings to the hairs covering my mother's body."

"There could be wounds you can't see. Wounds that perhaps heal before she rises the next evening. And what is she doing to others? Does she use your mother's hands to excite masochists? Her tongue?

How well does she tease with your mother's tongue, Justin? She's proud of your mother's body. Did you know she was a woman of sixty-two when Sade changed her? Sixty-two. How old was your mother when she transformed? Thirty-two, possibly?"

"My mother didn't live a life of innocence," he said.

"But did she live a life of debauchery as extreme as Marie's?"

"I never sat on my mother's knee and asked. You don't care about my mother, Cecelia. Ask me to go with you properly for the true reason."

"And what's that?"

"You're frightened. You don't trust Marie and shouldn't. You also fear going back to enjoying the very life that you speak of so distastefully. When is the last time a man coveted you? Truly wanted you, not just admired your good looks? The orgies were addictive, Cecelia. You hated what came so naturally to you."

"I ridiculed the men who engaged me." Cecelia stood. "They had no dignity by the time they left me."

"And did you?"

"Far more than you have." Cecelia closed in on the seated Justin. Her breath caught in her throat in an attempt to calm her anger. "Lay with me, Justin," she whispered in his ear. "Lay with me and know for sure whether what you say is correct."

"Children, where are you? Hidden away in this darkened room. Why?" Marie glided into the room, the charms of her body being moved and directed in the most sensual ways. "Is Cecelia trying to seduce you again, Justin? What's so special about her that makes you want to wait?" She stared intently at the younger woman. "Do you think the adventure wouldn't be as good as the fantasy? You may be right. She has the parts, but who knows how she uses them? Sometimes you do appear awkward, child."

"Cecelia. I haven't been a child since Sade first took me."

"Was he the first? How unfortunate for you! So you never had sex as a normal with a normal. Didn't miss anything. I can vouch for that."

"We're joining you tonight," Cecelia said flatly.

" 'Marie, may we join you tonight?' " Marie corrected.

"I'm tired of hearing about your financials and how wrapped in red tape they are. Do you believe that Sade will show at one of these events you attend in the evenings?"

"I hope not. He would ruin the fun I've been having."

"Cecelia and I haven't had fun waiting for you to move on Sade," said Justin.

"I've been away a long time, Justin. I wanted to reacquaint myself with French habits before entering the countryside."

"And, no doubt, make up for the time you lost after Sade destroyed you," Justin said.

"You are so insightful, Justin. I can't believe how young, how naive you are, and yet you read people so well."

59

"Enough! We go with you tonight, and if we can't locate Sade by the end of the week, we move on." Cecelia walked out of the room, knowing there was no way to enforce her words.

Chapter Thirteen

Marie brought the children with her to the gaudiest club in Paris. Red velvet drapes hung from the tall windows. The ceiling stood fifteen feet above their heads and was decorated with mythological characters painted in pastels that imitated the heavens on a cloudy day. An elaborate chandelier with many tiers hung in the center of the ceiling. Often the crystals would tinkle when articles of clothing were thrown up to catch on the varied ornamentation. Satin, silk, lace, and even cotton draped the chandelier in a multicolored rainbow of fabrics. The flooring was smooth, cold marble, with veins of green, pink, and gold flowing throughout. Wrought-iron tables and chairs in earth and moss tones speckled the floor. Mirrors had been placed between each window, reflecting the carnival look of the occupants.

Feathers, lace, and leather meshed in strange designs on bodies that were barely covered. Clientele dressed as animals scampered and hopped across the shiny floor. One woman with scalelike designs tattooed over her entire body slunk across the floor, blending sometimes with the colors of the marble. Her head had been shaved and her eyes were emphasized with the blackest of kohl. As she approached a person, her tongue would flick out to touch an ankle or a foot. Most giggled or laughed in response. One woman, surprised by the dampness of the tongue, screeched loudly.

The bar was lit up with Christmas lights, not long lines of bulbs but circular wires that made the lights look almost like bull's-eyes dangling over the sides of the bar. The cash register was made in the shape of a slot machine. Many of the drinks served looked like mistakes from a high-school chemistry class. The six foot five bartender wore his black silk shirt opened deeply in the front and had his sleeves rolled up to his elbow. His tawny flesh was covered with dark tufts of hair. His clean-shaven face showed a massive jaw, a sharp nose, heavy-lidded, smoky-dark eyes, and a lined forehead that came from knowledge and pain. The bartender's black hair was slicked back into a long ponytail. His large hands quickly snatched money from hands but never seemed to return any change.

Operatic arias blared out of the enhanced sound system. Disintegrating smoke clouds told of incense and drugs. Dried, condensed poppy juice floated through the air, making the clientele sluggish and amenable to the queries that passed through the crowd.

"Do you see anyone who needs to be saved, Justin?" asked Cecelia.

"Most are human, although I sense a deadness in this room."

"Probably us you're smelling, dear." Marie dismissed his warning with a flick of her fingers. "Shall we go over and speak with the Neanderthal behind the bar? Bartenders are so wise and so free with information for the right price. I never miss a chance at a conversation with one."

Dressed in a long, sheer gown of silky plum with expensive satiny underwear beneath, Marie swept gracefully across the room. She wore no jewelry other than a heart-shaped diamond on her left ring finger. She detested Cecelia's choice of gold skin-tight vinyl; not even leather, she had noted. Cecelia wore a gold arm bracelet that matched a gold choker around her neck. She had used flecks of sparkle powder to make the exposed skin look golden. Her eyelashes and brows were a blond that she had refused to darken or enhance. She had barely touched her lips with gloss.

The girl believes she's some sort of goddess, thought Marie, who was quite content to outshine her.

On the other hand, Justin was intriguing, with his dark glasses and all-black ensemble. His flaxen hair fell forward, teasing the women, who tried to catch a glimpse of his face.

"A Chateau d'Yquem," Marie ordered.

"One or two ounces?" asked the bartender.

"Give us the bottle. It will be for the three of us," she replied, indicating her companions, standing on either side of her. Her hand slid down her neck and inside her silk garment to touch a plump breast before pulling out money from inside her bra. "We need information also. We're looking for an older, attractive man, quite cultured, with a dominating presence. He may be alone or traveling with a female or maybe a boy, a delicate boy."

"Look within two feet of yourself in any direction and you will spy such a man."

"This one has a wonderful crown of white hair and blue eyes. Perhaps his only flaw is his height. Something like five-three or five-five. Although most won't take notice of his height, given the charm and hauteur he exudes."

"As much as I like the francs you hold in your hand, I still cannot help you . . . unless . . . A man has been ordering drinks. He looks very different from what you have described; however, he seems to be acting as valet for a gentleman seated in the far corner." The bartender took the time to point in that direction and then grasped the francs in Marie's hand.

"A greedy monster I'd so like to tame. Sad for you that I don't have the time." Marie shrugged and indicated the three empty glasses on the bar. The bartender quickly opened the Chateau d'Yquem and poured.

Lifting her glass, Marie turned to her companions.

"Children, why don't you wait here, and I'll check out this gentleman in the far corner."

"We can't even see him from here," Cecelia whispered.

"So what?"

"I think the three of us should go over."

"You, child, he will recognize immediately. And I'd rather keep Justin secret in case we need him later. Perhaps you could play with that plastic coating you have wrapped around your body. I'm sure if Justin pulled hard enough he could snap you across the room. Oh, please, Justin, not in the direction in which I am going." She smiled and pushed her way into the crowd. The last word she could hear spoken was a passionate-sounding "bitch," which she decided to ignore.

Marie didn't believe she would truly find Sade here. She already had made a tour of most of the fetish clubs in Paris and found her own pleasure in some but found Sade in none.

She spied the table the bartender had described. Naked women lounged on the laps and at the feet of well-dressed men. One man stood at attention; the valet no doubt.

She pressed closer, hoping to see the man seated in front of the valet. A hand waved in the air, and Marie stooped over in pain. Her stomach convulsed, frightening her into almost retreating. The stench of a dead man forced her to hold her breath. She knew this dead man. His scent could attract most to him, but for her it would always be repellent.

Marie fought the desire to be sick and straightened her body to its full height. She would have him pay. But would he recognize her? She carried another woman's odor. Another woman's body moved her spirit closer to Sade. Another woman's voice would seduce the reprobate. *He will not recognize me.*

Three small steps and she stood before Sade. Panic caused her hands to tremble; her bottom lip quivered.

Sade leaned back, laughing and puffing on a thick, round cigar that had obviously just been lit.

She heard the sound of a gulp come from within her throat.

Sade allowed one of the women to place her lips on the cigar, and the table mates laughed uproariously when she coughed, causing her heavy breasts to jiggle as she shimmied in the lap of a young male with golden hair and porcelain flesh.

"Perhaps you should allow me to have a taste of that cigar," Marie said. She hadn't yelled, but her voice had carried, and all at the table turned to her.

"Ah, mademoiselle, if I keep giving others a puff there will be none for me." Sade fingered the cigar, holding it high for her to see. "And then what can you give me for my pleasure?"

Marie moved forward until her thigh touched the table. He didn't know her, she kept repeating to herself.

"You're right. It's rather stubby. Too bad you don't have something far heftier to offer."

"This I offer to acquaintances," Sade said, indicating the cigar. "But I do prize my closest companions with something far more special. First prove yourself on this, mademoiselle." He passed the cigar across the table, delivering it into her delicate fingers.

She noticed that several men at the table nudged each other and grinned slyly. Marie circled the tip of the cigar with her tongue, wetting down the strongly scented tobacco leaf. At the same time, she used her other hand to finger the tops of her breasts. Leaning her head far back, she lowered the cigar into her mouth and took a deep drag. Removing the cigar, she lowered her chin and blew out smoky circles in waves.

Applause crackled the air surrounding her. Sade stood and offered his own chair to her. After seating herself, Marie could feel Sade's hands rest on her shoulders. His property, she thought.

"Which would you prefer," asked the blond young man. "Champagne or grappa? The table has been equally divided between the two. Please break the tie, and we can announce a winner."

"A winner?" she asked.

"Yes, Louis and Amelia have a bet going as to which beverage is most preferred. Amelia here"—indicating the woman seated on his lap—"has been demurring spending a weekend at Louis's estate.

And Louis has put up quite a sum of money on his side."

The asshole was always a champagne fiend, Marie recalled.

"I shall have a grappa," she pronounced clearly.

A roar went up at the table, and Louis Sade immediately presented the naked Amelia with a check.

"And which grappa shall you have?" asked the blond man.

"Is there another gamble on that?"

No, there was no further bet to settle, he informed her.

"Ah, but wait," said Sade. Marie looked up at him. "This table has been unusual in that they have all chosen the same grappa this evening. You, *ma chère*, may prove yourself unique." He smiled and gently massaged her shoulders. She reminded herself that barfing wasn't an option. "Let us wager a bet, mademoiselle. Since you have so charmingly ruined my weekend, I will give you the opportunity of taking Amelia's place. If you order what everyone else is having, then I will give you a check equal to the one I have just presented to Amelia."

The naked woman sitting in the blond man's lap held up the check so that Marie could see the amount. Marie acted impressed, but this was a bet she wanted to lose.

"Otherwise, I presume, I will be visiting your estate, monsieur. Am I right?"

Sade bent and kissed her on the cheek and whispered, "If you are mine this weekend, you will be mine forever."

All she could smell was the champagne on his breath. She pulled away from him and tried to catch a whiff of what brand of grappa lingered under the champagne scent. She almost reached out to grab a glass nearby but knew this would certainly nullify the bet. Or would it?

Quickly she reached out and took the glass in her hand, bringing the rim of the glass to her nose before the blond man took it from her hand.

"Giannola Nonino Picolit," Marie announced.

"Not fair," said the blond-haired man.

"Do you believe such a brief sniff could give her the name, monsieur?" asked Sade. "I do not. I think this dark-haired beauty simply has a taste for the best."

Marie smiled up at Sade. The egotist, she thought.

Chapter Fourteen

Sade wandered through the Maison-Alfont, where the Seine and the Marne rivers met. Daybreak was coming fast, but Sade needed to visit this neighborhood before leaving Paris for Albi. Across the water Charenton, the mental hospital in which he had supposedly died, stood with foreboding malice. The water-stained walls loomed above the rivers, which reflected the hospital's dreary stone during daylight. Under the dying moon, the hospital offered only shadows to those who dared to look. He turned away to head for a bizarre structure with spike-topped stone walls and slit-windowed turrets. Some might think it a prison, but no, this was the Ècole Nationale Vétérinaire d'Alfort, an old and still used veterinary hospital.

70

Honoré Fragonard had been the school's first director in 1776. Sade had been fascinated by the man, who used bodies rather than clay for his sculptures. Much of his work looked as if the bodies had been flayed while still alive—the movements had been so excellently duplicated. Fragonard would never share the secrets of his technique with Sade, leaving him to speculate that perhaps live bodies were used. Sade meditated on the tying up of a body in a desired position and watching the knife whittle away the flesh so that only muscle cord, blue veins, tendons, and ligaments remained. The frightful screams and spattered blood filled the artist's studio until all that remained was silence and a beautiful anatomy.

He wondered how Madeline would look revealed thusly. Her wary sight permanently shut, her body opened entirely to his uses, without the subtle hooded looks that were such a torture to him.

Ah! And what of the delight he had met this night? As hoary as her name had sounded to him, he had to admit she was a beauty. Perhaps he could find a pet name for her and eliminate Marie from both their vocabularies. He sensed that she too was a vampire, but not one he was able to recognize. Her odor was salty and earthy, as if she had been decaying for some time before being restored to her undead state. Her breath had told him that she wasn't hungry. She took what she needed and didn't suffer any guilt. A woman who could match his fierceness

71

and dominance. Truly a prize after these long months of bedding mortals.

When she had first given him her name, a chill had run up and down his dead body. Marie, his mother-in-law. And what could Cecelia be doing with Marie's skull? He hoped she had smashed the skull in anger, that it now lay in pulverized pieces on foreign soil.

Sade swung around quickly, hearing the light steps of a female. He hadn't eaten his fill yet, and this wanderer could satisfy him before he rested.

A young girl, not more than fifteen, turned onto the street where Sade stood. At first she was hesitant to continue. She almost retreated but changed her mind and kept walking. Her shoulders were pulled back in defiance of the strange man who loitered at the end of the block. Even though there was a chill in the air, she wore shorts that barely covered her crotch. She wobbled on spike heels. The leather jacket she wore had been pulled tightly around her trunk. Too much makeup caused her eyes to be red, and her hair fell in bouncy baby curls over her forehead.

Not a prostitute, Sade thought, but a girl testing her sexuality. Probably had been out with her boyfriend and had had an argument. She chose to travel in the opposite direction from her love. Possibly the girl didn't know how far away from home she had strayed while wallowing in her pugnacious snit.

Oui, come closer, Sade silently invited.

She had lost her nerve and was headed toward the curb in order to cross the street. She tripped as she stepped off the curb and caught herself on the back of a parked car. Stopping, she checked one of her heels while Sade moved closer. He heard her curse and take several intakes of breath to control the tears that were so close to the surface. Like a scared, confused rabbit she awaited Sade's approach. When he touched her arm, she faced him and offered herself to him, giving up without a sound.

Chapter Fifteen

Justin pondered the brand-new world that passed by. The barge they had taken was slow but offered plenty of time to get to know the countryside.

"They're known for their chocolates and foie gras in Albi," Marie said. "Do you eat food? I ask because I haven't seen you eat or drink anything. Do you live as a vampire or as a mortal, Justin?" Marie leaned against Justin's body, and he reflexively pulled away.

"I am neither."

"Then you don't eat or drink at all?"

"I don't steal other lives to survive."

"You must need to replenish your energy somehow, Justin."

"How long before we dock at Albi?" Justin asked.

"Soon. You know Cecelia doesn't care what happens to you. You waste your time thinking about her and hoping to be her lover. Cecelia doesn't want a lover."

"I know." Justin walked closer to the edge of the barge.

"I didn't mean to depress you to the point of jumping off the barge."

"You certainly can't bring Cecelia and myself to Sade's residence. What do you suggest we do?"

"There's a cathedral, the Place Sainte-Cécile. The cathedral is rife with secret passageways and wonderful art. I'm sure Cecelia will be able to make herself comfortable there."

"You expect us to live in a church?"

"Not you, only Cecelia. Obviously Sade would recognize her instantly. And you can be my . . . I hate to use the word *son*. Not that you aren't charming. I just don't want to be aged by your presence. Perhaps you could be my brother. What do you think?"

"I should stay with Cecelia," Justin said.

"And miss out on the fun? He has never met you, has he?"

Justin shook his head. "You're frightened of Sade. He's a man who could best you."

"I respect his power, Justin. I have also seen him weak, close to helplessness. I think with your help I will be able to bring him that low again."

"What will he think if you arrive with a man?"

Marie stepped closer to Justin.

"He'll love your latent sexuality and be happy to enhance your knowledge."

"You, madam, are using my mother's body but will never be able to control mine."

"Cecelia controls you. You let me live through your mother's body because that is what Cecelia wants. And you'll assist me, Justin, if she demands that of you."

A rat scuttled across the barge, suddenly disturbed by one of the humans peeking in the barge's cubbyholes. The rat slipped over the side of the barge, but Justin couldn't tell whether it had splashed into the water or traveled down the side of the barge to another small hole.

In the distance he could see a red brick town.

"Is that where we're going?" he asked.

"Yes, that is Albi. There's a magnificent painting of the Last Judgment in the cathedral. All flames, gaping mouths, and round, haunted eyes peering out from sooty faces. Wonderful character to the painting, almost makes me want to repent."

"And you expect Cecelia to lock herself away in that place?"

"She could march into Sade's residence and announce that she's had enough of the bastard. Only I doubt she'd gain anything by doing that. Most probably she would suffer another death much worse than the first." Marie looked into Justin's eyes and smiled. "I have experience with death, Justin. I know how cruel Sade can be when he has grown tired of allowing someone to survive. I could actually feel the ax cutting my throat and the resonance of the metal hitting the floor beneath me. When he lifted the ax I watched my own blood drip down on my face. Drops trickled into my open mouth. Even smelled the innards of my body leaking out. Finally my spirit escaped into the ugly room and floated above to watch the fire fed with parts of my body.

"I would have Sade feel, smell, and taste everything the same way I did. Only Cecelia can defeat me in this quest. She must stay away until we have the upper hand."

"... *Dance, now that you're dead, now that life and misfortune have left your flesh! Have at it! There will be no tomorrow to your celebrations, for they will be as eternal as death, so dance! Rejoice in your oblivion. You'll have no more cares or labors, since you no longer exist. No more misery for you in your nonbeing. Ah, my dead ones, dance!*"

—GUSTAVE FLAUBERT

Chapter Sixteen

Cecelia was uncertain whether Justin had hesitated to leave her or the ancient cemetery that encircled the cathedral. Certainly if there existed mutants anywhere it would be here. The rusting fence around the cemetery swayed when she leaned against it to say good-bye to Justin. He caught her in his arms before she could fall. Marie stood several feet away, sighing and tapping a boot-clad foot.

After Marie and Justin had left, the loneliness quickly settled throughout her body. Marie had arranged for Cecelia to stay with the caretaker. His house was on church property, and he had an extra room he would rent for a fee. The caretaker was an elderly man with a constant smile and stoop from old age. His hair was a glowing white, and the creases in his face seemed to be from squinting while working outdoors. He didn't talk very much, for which she was grateful. For an additional fee he would prepare three meals a day for her. Cecelia told him it was unnecessary, that she would fend for herself.

Cecelia walked through the cemetery, noting the round, molelike holes in the ground. Mel, the caretaker, certainly wasn't the best at his work, but then, given his age, Cecelia concluded his employment was really part of the cathedral's charity work.

"The graves here are very old, mademoiselle."

She turned and saw that Mel had followed along behind her.

"The engravings on quite a few of the tombstones are unreadable," she said.

"Some were never meant to be read." He came closer to her. "Many years ago there was a terrible plague, and most of those stones are in memory of the lives lost twice over."

"I don't understand."

"It was not a disease that swept through here, but the blood suckers. The living dead, you see."

"Vampires?"

Mel nodded but refused to utter the word.

"Do you think they still live in the town?"

"The Sainte-Cécile Cathedral protects us from them."

"Was the cathedral built with that purpose in mind?"

"Yes. The cathedral prevents them from roaming the countryside, seeking nourishment from the innocent."

"And I suppose on a silent, cold night one can hear the ravings of these vampires?"

"Only from within the church can you sometimes hear them scratching at the walls, throwing their bodies against the barrier, attempting to reach us, the living, again."

"Why from within the cathedral?"

"Because that is where they are trapped."

Justin should be here now, she thought. He would find this old man informative. She herself thought the caretaker to be full of superstitions.

"Would you like to see inside the cathedral? There is much beauty inside. Some think it is to hide what really lurks inside its walls. There are many statutes, and the largest Renaissance fresco in Europe. You would love Our Lady's chapel. It is so feminine and soft in comparison to much of the other architecture."

"Not right now, thank you," she said.

"The cathedral is always open. If you should need some late night a place to rejuvenate your soul, come here. I must warn you, though, that Lottie frequently walks the aisles."

"Another vampire?"

"No, a woman who must be at least a hundred. She doesn't speak. Whether she is deaf and dumb we do not know. She arrived here months ago. She changes the flowers and dusts the altars. She sleeps in a shack that had been long deserted. She shares it with the stray animals who seek shelter from bad weather. She accepts no charity from anyone, except

81

for bits of food that the townspeople leave at her door, and even that we fear she shares with the animals. I'd take her in myself. . . ." She could have sworn that the old man hesitated and blushed. "I've been a widower for many years, and the company would be good for both of us. I've invited her for dinner and prepared the most savory dishes, hoping to attract her. Sadly, she ignores me." Mel shrugged. "Perhaps she has been badly hurt by a man."

Cecelia turned from Mel before he could see the smile on her face.

"She just doesn't know what a catch you are, Mel. When I see her I'll tell her."

"Oh, but don't say that you are staying with me; she may misunderstand."

A giggle escaped Cecelia.

"Where is this shack, Mel?" She looked around and could spot nothing that looked abandoned.

"It is a good walk from here. Still, she comes every day to visit the cathedral. To visit our Lord and make him comfortable. She must be a very holy person, because no matter what the weather, I find her wandering the aisles, dusting and polishing. Strangely, I have never caught her in prayer, but I suppose that she performs in a less blatant manner. She is also humble, you see."

"You seem to think you know a lot about her, even though you two have never spoken."

"My wife has been dead many years. Now I view life from outside; therefore, I have learned to read people by their actions."

Cecelia turned and walked over to Mel and put a hand on his shoulder.

"People are deceptive. They allow you to see just enough to make you comfortable, then they'll snatch whatever you most treasure. What is your greatest treasure, Mel? Is it life? Is it the blood flowing through your veins? Many would envy that blood." She raised a hand to indicate the cathedral. "Certainly those vampires long to hold you in their arms."

"Your hand is cold, mademoiselle."

Immediately she pulled her hand away.

"It is a chilly night, and my circulation suffers, especially when I'm forced to travel without proper food or sleep."

"I invite you to dine with me. No charge. I would appreciate the company. After dinner I will see that you have the softest and warmest comforter."

"Thank you," she said, knowing that her true resting place lay in the hills where her coffin and Marie's had been hidden by Justin.

"*I love prostitution in and for itself. . . . In the very notion of prostitution there is such a complex convergence of lust and bitterness, such a frenzy of muscle and sound of gold, such a void in human relations, that the very sight of it makes one dizzy! And how much is learned there! And one is so sad! And one dreams so well of love!*

—GUSTAVE FLAUBERT, *writing to his mistress,*
Louise Colet

Chapter Seventeen

"These servants could be employed at a Playboy club," said Justin.

"Louis has always liked having beautiful people around him. That's why we're here." Marie followed the maid into the main room.

The tight leather pants and the sheer black blouse didn't correspond to what her job should entail. Her spiked heels clicked delicately on the marble floor. Her perfectly made-up face and exquisite features managed to distract Justin from her cleavage and swollen nipples.

"Did you grow up in this village?" he asked the maid.

"But no! I am from Paris, sir." She smiled and left them in the main room to wait for Sade.

"Why would an attractive girl like that want to hide away in this town?" Justin muttered to himself, but Marie felt compelled to answer.

"Because everything can be bought in Paris."

"I hurried to greet you, Marie, when they informed me you were here." Sade gave a side glance toward Justin.

"He's my brother. I didn't think you would mind if I brought him."

"Does he run errands for you, Marie? Do you feed from him?" Sade asked.

"I didn't have you fooled, Mr. Sade."

"Fooled. Neither of us are young vampires, mademoiselle. We had to recognize each other instantly, don't you think?"

Justin wondered whether they both had been stupid to come here and stay in Sade's territory. Could Sade have already pegged Marie as his mother-in-law? His sight slightly blurred, as it always did when his eye color changed.

"If you truly knew me, you wouldn't have invited me here, Mr. Sade."

"The fact that you are a vampire is only a minuscule part of what attracted me to you. It is all the hidden, playful, and hideous things about you that called. And now I find that you do not travel alone." Sade approached Justin. "Is she your parent or the other way around, monsieur?"

"I am embarrassed by your question, Mr. Sade. Do I look old enough to be his mother?"

"If you two are related, it is only by the drinking of blood, not natural birth." Before Justin could stop Sade, he reached out and pulled off Justin's glasses. "What perversion, madam, have you brought into my house! He is half vampire and half mortal."

"Mr. Sade, you've certainly seen those like this man before. Don't act so shocked. And as far as perversions go, I can't think of a greater one than the drinking of blood. A perversion we both share, Mr. Sade. Justin doesn't engage in such gross conduct, do you?"

"No, but I understand the needs of your kind and wish only to free you from your pain."

"Free me! What are you talking about, monsieur? I have no need to be freed from pain. I nurture pain," Sade said.

"He wants to serve us, Louis," Marie blurted. "If you don't mind my calling you by your first name. His mother was a vampire. Unfortunately, he was unable to keep her from destroying herself. Now he tries to serve our kind since he was unable to help her."

"Destroyed herself? In what way, monsieur?"

"She opened herself to a mortal lover who staked her and destroyed the body," Marie immediately responded.

"Why is it, mademoiselle, that you tell his story?"

"Because he would allow you to believe anything you wanted. He has no stomach for confrontation."

"Why is your speech so familiar to me, mademoiselle? I can almost picture you as someone else.

87

But if you are anything like the woman I am thinking of, I would rather keep you under watchful eyes until I know what to expect from you."

"I am no woman you've ever met. You should count yourself blessed."

"Blessings never visit vampires, mademoiselle. I'm sure you have learned that lesson."

Sade walked over to a bar filled with glasses and liquors.

"I'm sorry your visit started out badly. Let us drink together and make peace. Wine, mademoiselle, or blood?" Sade reached up and pulled a sash that was connected to a bell.

A few seconds later a muscular, middle-aged man dressed in latex entered the room.

"Blood will be fine," Marie whispered.

"You seem revolted by mademoiselle's choice, monsieur."

Justin watched as the middle-aged man knelt down before Marie. She forced him to crawl to the sofa, where she sat and scratched his neck with her long fingernail. Justin could see the uneven line marring the man's skin, but she drew no blood. She seemed enthralled by the mark she left on the man. The scratch became deeper and longer. A smirk contorted her face into a gruesome mask.

"So familiar," whispered Sade. "But how could it be, monsieur, that one who has been destroyed dares to return in another's body? Do you know, monsieur? Are you party to something beyond your own understanding?" Sade slid a delicate glass of sherry in front of Justin's nose. "It is at its peak, monsieur. I recommend it highly."

The only odor that caught in Justin's throat was that of blood. The blood that now flowed from the man's flesh. His skin in ribbons, his wounds gapping, his breath gasping, he kneeled before Marie, a slave. Marie slapped the man across the face several times, using her tongue to wipe away the blood on her upper lip. She laughed, but it didn't sound like his mother's laugh. It was a wicked, hurtful laugh that meant to demean the man kneeling before her.

"Truly, she is someone I knew before," Sade whispered into Justin's ear. "Could my nemesis be reborn, monsieur? Have you brought my destruction into this house?"

"You invited her." Justin thought a moment. "Possibly knowing who she was."

"I do not know, but I surmise who she may be. I don't believe you, monsieur; do you have any idea of the horror with which you have been traveling?"

"She stole something from me and I mean to take it back." Justin pushed the glass away from his face and heard it break when Sade let it drop onto the floor.

The crash brought Marie's attention away from the man. Justin saw her stare in fear at him and Sade. *Does she know that she has given herself away?* Justin wondered.

She stood, and the man fell in a faint to the floor.

"Am I so amusing that you can do nothing else except stare at my feeding? A private moment would have been preferred."

"Perhaps you would like to wash away that dribble trickling down your chin. I'll have the maids show you to your rooms," Sade said.

Chapter Eighteen

The caretaker's house had one dim light in the front window; the rest of the rooms were dark. Justin tapped at the window, and watched as Mel left his dinner table and moved to open the window.

"You have come back. You have missed the young one you left behind. I knew you would. She is far more gentle than the other. The other is capable of tearing your heart out."

"I have only returned temporarily. Where is Cecelia?" Justin asked.

"Cecelia," Mel called, and from an unseen side of the room Cecelia appeared.

"I need to talk to you, Cecelia."

She shrugged and left the room for the front door.

"Have you visited the church yet, Cecelia?"

"Is that why you came down here? You run around that graveyard by yourself. Mel has already taken me on the limited tour."

"No. I want to visit the cathedral. I need to, Cecelia, but I don't want to go alone."

"It's formidable. The locals call it their threatening dragon or red brick sailing vessel."

"It's a prison, Cecelia. The bars are made of air, but they're stronger than any physical material."

"Then why go in?"

"I want to know who it holds prisoner."

Justin jumped when he heard Mel loudly close the window.

"It holds vampires, Justin. From what the old man says, the town has been storing its vampires in the cathedral for centuries."

"Many of them must be insane by now."

"A good reason to stay out of the cathedral."

Justin took her hand and pulled her across the cemetery to the front steps of the cathedral.

"Marie said the art inside is a masterpiece of French Gothic. Shall we see if she has lied again?"

"Again? What happened, Justin?"

"I have seen her in her cruelty. A taste of giving pain and she hungers for more. Even Sade mocked her in her lust."

Justin started climbing the stairs, pulling Cecelia up, as if she were an anchor that couldn't be left behind.

The huge front doors emanated no warmth, no security, no forgiveness, all of which Justin expected from a church. Upon opening the door the air was immediately filled with the scent of fresh flowers and stale incense. A set of inner doors already stood ajar, allowing the visitor to immediately see the front altar. The white linens and gold accoutrements lay spread across the top of the marble altar, far from the visitor's reach.

Justin let go of Cecelia's hand, but she followed behind him anyway. He could hear her soft steps echo his own.

A round stone holy water fount stood on each side of the entrance, the water still and clear.

Justin moved to take the center aisle, but Cecelia grasped his arm.

"I'd rather take a side aisle," she whispered. "I don't want to flaunt myself in God's eyes."

Justin turned left and continued down a side aisle. His flesh sweated and his hands shook.

"Someone is calling for help. Others are screaming shouts that aren't definable. The pounding on the walls hurts my head."

He looked to the side and saw an elderly woman hiding in the shadows of a chapel.

"That woman . . ."

"She must be Lottie. Mel said she's new to the town but carefully tends to the needs of the cathedral."

"She talks to them, Cecelia. She whispers into the cracks and massages the walls with the imprint of her hand. They are all talking too fast for me to understand. But she singles out each voice and caters to them. I try to hear their words, Cecelia. I try, but the sounds get louder and more garbled the harder I try. Damn!" Justin covered his ears and swayed in his agony.

Cecelia took his arm and guided Justin back to the front steps of the cathedral.

"I heard nothing in there, Justin. But Mel claims the vampires are walled up and seeking release. Is that true?"

"I can turn all that pain into dust."

"You don't know how to reach them, and I don't think the townspeople would take to you ripping out their cathedral's walls."

"Sade must be aware. Many are probably his own children."

"From the way he treated our child . . ."

"You never had a child with Sade. A mortal placed the seed for that infant inside you. What are you trying to get even for, Cecelia? He had no ties to that baby. Why shouldn't he destroy something so deplorable and unnatural? Leave this quest to destroy Sade behind you. Leave it to Marie, who engages his interest and can linger in his sports. Run from him."

Cecelia shook her head.

"He can't destroy a part of me like that, Justin."

Chapter Nineteen

Madeline had returned to his bed. The other two women were different than last time. They weren't as pretty as he usually chose, but they were athletic.

He had placed Madeline on a throne of pillows at the foot of the bed, giving her a complete view of what was taking place. She sat stiffly, holding her knees together, as if shy or ashamed of her sex. He had allowed her to drape a single piece of lace over her shoulders; otherwise she was naked.

What the other women did to his body was unimportant. Only Madeline should watch and envy. He wanted her to long for his attentions.

Wet flesh slid against wet flesh, making the acrobatics easier. He noticed how the bottom sheet had come undone and inched its way to the center of the mattress.

One of the woman almost fell from the bed. Sade grasped her dark, oily hair in his hand and assisted her in gaining her balance. He pulled on her hair until her lips were even with his. She leaned toward him to kiss him, and he bit her lips, drawing blood. The drink spiked his desire for Madeline, and he cast the woman aside.

He rose to a seated position and circled Madeline's ankles with his hands. A woman dared to touch Madeline's flesh and he shouted at her to get away. Cross, the woman retreated. He could see how she despised the chosen flower. But neither woman dared to interfere.

He yanked on Madeline's ankles, bringing her down off the pillows and flat onto the mattress. He spread her legs apart and saw drops of lust wetting her opening. His penis strained to fill her.

"Ask me for anything, *ma* Madeline."

Her lips quivered, and he thought she would cry. Instead she screamed her command.

"Fuck me!"

Sade jammed into her. He took the lace in his hands and drew it tight around Madeline's neck. As he drove inside her, he pulled the lace tighter and heard her gasp. No scream from his flower. Her white flesh bleached into a ghostly pallor. Her lips barely moved. And the eyes—her beautiful green eyes lost sight of him and stared up toward the ceiling.

The waves came, sending his body into writhing motion. He tasted her flesh, and his hands loosened their hold.

Gasping and coughing, Madeline tried to wiggle away from him, but he held her fast. He licked the salty vapor that covered her skin and teased her breath back with his hands, pushing in and out on her chest.

Chapter Twenty

Each guest received a small cardboard box decorated with obscene drawings of couples and groups. Some of the characters had a strong resemblance to Sade. Justin attempted to pass by without accepting a box but was abruptly stopped by an overmuscled gladiator who insisted he take a box.

"Please, sir. We will be asking everyone to open his or her box soon," said a short, matronly woman. Her clothes were dowdy and did not fit in with the fancy wear the guests wore. She seemed to be a local farmer's wife who was making extra money for a special upcoming family event.

"Only one?" asked Justin, staring at the helmeted man before him.

"I'd give you another, but I'm not sure we'll have

enough for everyone," the woman said, forcing the box into Justin's hand.

Justin was tempted to offer up his box to the next person in line so they wouldn't run out of boxes, but he didn't, realizing his antagonism was directed at the gladiator and not the woman. When he accepted the box the gladiator stepped out of his way.

Justin continued down the long hall, admiring the busts and statues that lined the way. Two of the statues were carved of marble and had worn spots where guests had obviously rubbed their palms.

"They say if you smooth your palm across Diana's breast or Hercules's penis, you will have a fabulous night of lust."

Justin turned to see a small man directly behind him. Dressed in a black velvet Victorian suit and a red silk tie, he called attention to himself. He smiled, and Justin noted that the man was missing every other tooth, as if by design.

"I never pass by without touching both. Sometimes when no one is looking I go for his big toe." The man looked over both his shoulders. "Join me?" The man stooped to caress Hercules's big toe and even gave it a quick peck.

"Guess what part of the anatomy I especially love?" the man said, looking down at Justin's sneakers.

Justin chose not to answer the man and continued into the Great Hall. Here he found crowds of people already in the throes of a decadent party. On the ceiling the muses Terpsichore and Erato peeked over elaborately painted fans of church scenes. Surrounding the muses were clouds dotted with cherubs.

He felt a nudge and turned around to see the little man again.

"Sorry, so difficult to keep from running into others. All these people, and I know so few. And believe it or not, I come to the festivities here frequently."

Justin tried to move away, but the little man had grasped his arm.

"See the flowers in the vase over there? Don't know what they're called, but I've heard they're outrageously expensive. Imported from Holland. Oh, and the carpet! Pity you can't see it as a whole. The colors blend magnificently. Especially the copperhead over in the distant right corner."

"Are you telling me there are live snakes in the room?"

"No, they're woven into the fabric of the rug. So are the birds and the rabbits. Toads, too. You must be in the very center of the room to see those."

Justin pulled away from the little man.

"Wait; wouldn't you like to see the gardens? There's a charming gazebo in the very center."

"Excuse me. I'm looking for someone, and I need to make the rounds of the room to find them," Justin said.

"You didn't come alone?" the little man asked.

Justin shook his head and managed to escape.

Partially clad bodies brushed against him as he walked through the crowd to the opposite end of the room. Feeling overwhelmed by the heat and the number of bodies in the room, Justin found himself a niche built into a wall that had a colorful gouache hanging within it. The painting reflected the ostentation of Louis XIV's court. He acted the art connoisseur for several minutes until he felt brave enough to face the mob behind him.

The self-important gladiator entered the room and unsheathed his sword, almost taking off a few ears in just one sweep.

This is ridiculous, thought Justin as he tried to force his back through the wall.

The gladiator called out for everyone to hold their boxes above their heads and open the side flaps.

Quickly the room was filled with butterflies, all seeking escape.

Justin looked down at his own unopened box. He held the box at arm's length and undid the flap. Nothing came out. He shook the box gently and still nothing happened, except for a tiny object he could feel hitting the sides of the box. Looking inside, he saw a dead butterfly, the wings almost severed. He flung the box to the floor, and someone backstepped a heel, crushing the box.

He heard a woman's giggle come from his right, and he looked to see a pretty red-haired woman playing with a black and golden butterfly that flitted between the tips of her fingers. Finally the butterfly rose and landed on the tip of her nose, as if admiring the freckles that spotted her cheeks. Her giggle became a soft smile as she held her body very still.

Justin's lips turned up in an unaccustomed grin, and he removed his dark glasses.

Slowly the woman brought her right index finger up to her nose and the butterfly hopped onto it. Her delicate hand froze, and her eyes were gay with wonder.

Just beyond her, Justin could see an emaciated man moving in her direction. He wore no shirt, and his skin was flecked with scabs that almost covered his chest. He picked up speed before Justin could intercept him and blew hard on the butterfly, which rose up to the high vaulted ceiling.

The man cackled and danced his way back into the anonymity of the crowd.

Justin saw the woman's upturned chin shiver as the butterfly vanished.

"That was very cruel of him," Justin said.

The woman, just becoming aware of Justin's presence, turned toward him.

"He did that on purpose. I would have stopped him, but I was too far away. I'm sorry."

"Did you frighten the butterfly away?" she asked.

"No, I never would."

"I didn't see who did it, but if you didn't, you shouldn't say you're sorry."

"I meant—"

"I'm Madeline," the woman said, noticing his eyes. "I've never seen such green eyes. Are they contacts?"

"No." He started to replace his glasses.

"Please don't. Your eyes are beautiful."

Justin slipped the glasses inside his jacket pocket.

"Should I call you Green Eyes?" she asked.

"Justin."

"You've come down from Paris?"

"Yes, just a few days ago."

"He has so many people come from Paris. He's promised to take me someday, but I think he lies."

"Sade?"

She nodded her head. "But you are not originally from Paris."

"No, San Francisco."

She perked up. "America. I'd like to go there too."

When he laughed, she frowned.

"I don't mean to hurt your feelings, Madeline, but it sounds like you desperately want to get out of Albi."

"I read so much about the rest of the world but don't know how to reach it, nor how to act if I ever get there."

"I can take you to America tonight. At least with words," he clarified.

Marginal disappointment touched her eyes.

"Come outside with me, Justin, and fill my head with fantasies."

Chapter Twenty-one

"And it hurts here," Marie said, raising her skirt and allowing the man to kiss her inner thigh.

When he moved to cover her mound with his mouth, she yanked on his hair, forcing him to stand.

"I didn't say it hurt there, fool." Marie released the thick, dark mane and took a step back. "It's naughty to overstep your welcome. Perhaps I need to find a more compliant partner."

The swarthy man fell to his knees and kissed her naked feet. With one foot she pushed him away.

"Did I say you could kiss my feet? I didn't even tell you to kneel."

"I'm sorry, mistress. What would you have me do?" The man bowed his head abjectly.

A butterfly settled on the top of his head, flapping its wings, readying for its next flight. Marie brought her hand down to his head, hoping to snatch the butterfly. However, when she was within grasping distance, the butterfly rose into the pungent air and escaped. Irritably, she slapped the top of his head.

"You bore me with your wallowing and confusion. Either you know how to be a slave or go find yourself another teacher. My time is too precious." She spat in his face when he looked up at her.

Marie spun around, hoping to find herself a new playmate.

"You have lovely feet."

A short man in a black velvet Victorian suit and a red silk tie stood in front of her, an inch shy of her eye level.

"I doubt I'd be able to say the same for your feet, buried inside those ugly boots. What are they, SS Troop issue?"

"Exactly. My father stole them during the war."

Remembering the man at her feet, Marie looked down. "Oh, go crawl away, you insect. I have no use for you."

She turned back to the little man, and he stood grinning at her.

"Why are you missing so many teeth?"

"They were pulled by various lovers."

"Every other tooth?"

"I didn't want big gaps."

"And now what are you going to do, darling? It appears your next lover will be leaving a bigger gap somewhere in your mouth."

105

"I was thinking about starting on my nails." He stretched out his fingers so that she could see them. His nails were long and perfectly rounded, with a shimmer of a pastel pink color.

"That ensures you of ten new lovers at least. And then I suppose the toenails can go up for grabs, so to speak."

His thin brown hair was center parted, with the ends skimming his shoulders. A greasy film darkened his hair, allowing a reflection of the chandelier lights. His eyebrows were plucked and lightly shaded with pencil. His lashes were naturally long and gave his eyes a little-boy quality that the rest of his face denied.

"If I plucked one of your nails, would you be satisfied and go home?"

"Only if you used your teeth." He laughed and brought his fingertips to her lips. "Any one you want," he said.

"If my teeth dipped into you, monsieur, I would be stealing more than just your dead flesh."

His eyes shined with glee.

"Has Louis played with you?"

"Not yet, but I keep coming back in hope."

"And how do you come by your invitations?"

He grew cross and began biting his bottom lip.

"What do you do, clean the dung out of Sade's stable, so he throws you a party crumb once in a while?" Marie laughed, seeing the terror that showed on the little man's face. "I've guessed correctly, haven't I? It's probably the horses that have kicked your teeth out."

"No! I entertain some of Sade's guests who come down from Paris."

"That's exactly what I am. Entertain me, monsieur, and perhaps I will favor you with a taste of blood."

Chapter Twenty-two

Sade watched the fop, Andre, obsequiously fawn on the newest guest. The little man allowed Marie to rip open his jacket and shirt. The large safety pins piercing his nipples amused her. He scampered away for a brief while, to return with a step stool on which he stood. Marie nibbled at his nipples hard enough to draw blood from one. Languorously, she lapped at the blood. Sade moved closer to view the delight on her face. The features were not the same as his mother-in-law's, but the technique was so familiar.

He was irked by this puzzle, but more so by Madeline. His beautiful, quiet, soft Madeline, who allowed Justin to take her out to the garden. The butterflies had been Madeline's idea, and Sade had hoped that she would find some amusement in the rush of captured butterflies in the great room. He never guessed it would lead to her finding a more amusing soul.

Sade didn't like Justin. He believed the man had an invisible strength that belied the mockery Justin made of humility. Of all that had been in the room, Justin was the true survivor. Marie would never break him.

He could follow the young couple out to the garden and intrude on their solace. But Justin would be the one to win, even if Sade tempted Madeline away. Justin would leave a taste to which she would long to return. She would think of him while lying with Sade. Her dreams would take her into arms that hadn't held her close. Into the eyes of a half-breed who lives as neither mortal nor vampire. A loathsome soul who teeters on self-destruction but will never topple. Unless Sade found a way to plunge that soul into complete agony.

Chapter Twenty-three

Sade watched Madeline walk into his bedroom. She looked around the room several times. She had never been invited here alone before. Always there were one or several women already disrobed and eyeing her with jealousy.

He dropped his feet from the badly devarnished step stool. His hands gripped the leather armrests of his chair. He waited for her to come to a complete stop. *How close would she dare come?* Or did she even suspect that he had seen her with Justin?

She wore a green dress that reminded Sade of Justin's eyes. The dress reached just below her knees, and on her feet were a ratty pair of sandals. She had become too comfortable in her visits.

"*Ma* Madeline, I do hope you own another pair

of shoes. Must I order you fine new ones from Paris?"

"I'm sorry, Monsieur Sade." She removed the sandals and stood barefoot in front of him.

"You are so eager to please me, *ma chere*. Do you try this hard with anyone else?"

"I am only intimate with you, Monsieur Sade."

"Louis, *ma fille*, Louis."

She nodded her head solemnly.

Sade let go of the armrests and began rubbing his palms up and down the leather, like a cat wanting to leave its scent.

"And if I come close to you and take a deep breath, what do I smell, *ma fille*? Only my own flesh mingled within your pores? Or will there be a distraction? An odor I do not recognize? At least not as my own."

"You think I've been with someone else?" The quizzical look on her face caused Sade to grit his teeth.

"I no longer seek a mate, *ma fille*; however, I expect consistency. Can you say that nothing in your heart detracts from the feelings you have for me?"

"I am loyal to you, Louis." She pronounced his name with great care.

"You haven't been drawn to anyone else lately?" Sade stood. He watched Madeline take a hesitant step backward.

"I don't understand."

Sade reached out and placed his spread right hand

111

across her face. "What about Justin? Has he not intrigued you? At the party the other night you and he disappeared from the great room for several hours. Did you hold hands under the moonlight?" He circled her body and spoke into her left ear. "Did you two kiss? A slight peck, perhaps?" Sade kissed her delicately on her left ear. "Or was it more passionate than that? Did you grope each other's body?" He touched her breast with his free hand. "Did your tongues meet within the softness of your young mouth?" His tongue outlined her lips and continued his circle. "Show me what you did with him, Madeline. Show me now." He spun her around to face him.

"I swear we did nothing but talk. He is gentle and wouldn't take advantage."

"Were you disappointed, Madeline?" His bottom lip pouted.

"He . . ." Madeline paused. Sade could see how carefully she thought out her reply. "Yes, because his behavior confuses me. I understand your decadence, your immorality. I see it outside these walls when I walk down a street and lewd noises or comments are cast at me. I serve a base purpose for most men. But Justin only talked, and he spoke of everyday topics. My own parents could have sat with us and joined the conversation."

Sade sprawled across the canopied bed.

"Do you know what he is, Madeline?"

"A guest you invited from the States."

"Never did I or would I have invited him. He's an abomination. A trick nature played on his mother. I wonder where the poor woman is now. At first I thought Marie to be his mother, but she doesn't have the spirit of a good mother. I become more and more convinced that she's a harridan who has come back to destroy me. And yes, I believe he had a kind mother. He is too soft to have been brought up by a woman like Marie. She would have toughened him. Abused him into being forceful. You say he is gentle, but he is really soft."

"What would the difference be?"

"Soft, weak. Unable to make people hate him. He wants to please and administer to those he believes are less fortunate. Often he disappears from the estate. Where does he go, Madeline? Do you know?"

Madeline shook her head.

"He bothers me. He has too many secrets. I hate him."

Color flushed Madeline's face.

"I can't shock you, Madeline. Ah, do you worry about what I may do to him? You care, don't you? He is not mortal like you. He's a filthy hybrid."

"Why do you allow him to stay?"

"Because Marie wants him here. And I'd rather be aware of Marie's activities. Initially I thought she would join us in this bed. I presumed that she would help you to mature."

"Why not bring him to our bed?" Madeline asked.

Sade leaped forward and caught hold of Madeline's dress.

113

"Is that what you want, hussy?"

No longer meek, Madeline replied, "Yes."

Sade flung her onto the bed. "What am I to you, *ma chere?*"

"My master, and he would be *my* slave."

"What if I were he? What would you have me do?"

"I'd demand that you strip naked," she said, with more power in her voice than he had ever heard before.

Sade stripped quickly, tearing bits of cloth in his hurry.

"And now?"

"Slowly remove all my clothes, and as you do kiss and nibble on all of my flesh. Don't dare miss a spot."

Sade favored her by doing everything she said meticulously.

"Now would you have him enter you, *ma fille?*"

"No."

Stunned, Sade stared down at her until he broke into riotous laughter. "You would train him well, Madeline. But I am not your servant. It is the other way round."

He took her quickly and heard the passion in her cries. A passion driven not by him but by a calculating hybrid.

An Aged Dame

An aged dame in reverence of the dead
With care did place the scalps of men she found
Upon a hill as in a sacred bed;
But as she toil'd, she tumbl'd to the ground;
Whereat down fell the skulls within her lap,
And here, and there, they ran about the hill.
With that quoth she: No marvel is this hap
Since men alive in minds do differ still;
And as those heads in sunder down do fall,
So varied they in their opinions all.

—GEOFFREY WHITNEY

Chapter Twenty-four

"I must speak with Lottie."

"According to Mel, she doesn't speak to anyone. The locals aren't even sure whether she can hear or speak," Cecelia said.

"She can do both and much more." Justin paced the cemetery.

"There must be some lost souls out here that you can help instead of talking to walls inside the cathedral."

"I can't do it, Cecelia. I need Lottie to show me how."

"What then, Justin? You can't wring their necks unless you can reach them."

"I will bring them out. They will come to me seeking freedom from their penance. Wait!" Justin watched an elderly woman limping down the road.

Her hair was white, and her features sagged heavily from old age. The clothes she wore looked like scraps found in a garbage can. None of the colors matched; none of the articles were sized the same. As she came closer, he noticed that she had no shoes.

"Are you sure her name is Lottie?"

"It's what the locals call her. I doubt they know for sure."

"Madam," cried Justin, coming from behind the cemetery gate. "May I speak to you?"

The woman winced and turned away from him, taking the long way to the doors of the cathedral.

"Please, a few words. You see, I know there are beings walled up inside the cathedral. I can sense them, but I don't know how to contact them. You do."

The old woman whimpered as if in pain.

"I want to free them," he said.

At these words she picked up a fallen branch and began swinging it at Justin. He ducked several times until she finally caught him below his left eye, and blood flowed.

"Are you all right, Justin?" Cecelia ran to his aid; however, in the confusion she licked the blood from his face.

The old woman screeched. Dropping the branch, the woman ran at Cecelia, grabbing the girl's throat with strong, wiry hands. Her thumbs settled deep into Cecelia's throat. Justin attempted to separate the two women and found that he had to use more force than he would have wished. The old woman

117

wasn't frail. A growl came from deep within Cecelia's throat as he stepped in between the two.

"Stop, Cecelia. She thought you were going to hurt me."

"She'll know what hurt is when I rip her head from her shoulders." Cecelia's fingernails dug into Justin's arm, trying to push him out of the way.

"Let me speak to her, Cecelia. Obviously she can hear. Let me find out if she can also speak. If you wish me to continue to help, you will go join Mel in the cottage."

Cecelia spat like a cat. "You ask a lot from me, Justin."

He turned to Cecelia. "My mother is a plaything for you and Marie, and you say I ask a lot."

Cecelia rushed back inside the cemetery with hands outstretched. She sent a statue of a guardian angel plunging to the ground.

"Defiler," screamed the old woman.

Justin rounded on her as soon as he heard her speak. He reached out a hand and begged her to communicate with him. "Show me," he pleaded. "Show me how to reach those who need peace."

"They will never have peace. Their bodies will smell. Their blood will grow weak. Their minds wither. And still they will exist. He will see to that."

"Who? Who has locked them up inside the cathedral? Madam, please tell me."

"He called me here to quiet them down. They always become restless when they sense him near. I promise them things. I contain the turbulence."

"And this person pays you for your services?"

"Not with money. With blood. The blood of my baby." She lowered her voice to a whisper. "He stole my baby long ago and keeps her with him. My baby girl, only fifteen. He keeps her in this world. She was meant to die, you see. Die way too young. I couldn't have that. I couldn't bury her. She must bury me. That is the way."

"You're talking about Sade, aren't you?" Justin asked.

"Within the estate she lives in splendor."

"As a vampire." His voice was flat.

"He keeps her alive."

"He abuses anyone he gets near. Your daughter would be better off dead."

He watched tears fill the old woman's eyes.

"She is sweet and pretty. Prettier than any child I have ever seen. She never grows old. She will never die."

"And what will happen when you die?"

"He is to bury her with me. He will pierce her heart and cut her head from her shoulders and lay her in my arms."

"Then I hope you drop dead soon, old woman, for all the torture you've brought to your child."

The old woman turned away.

"One more question, please. Why did he lock the vampires inside the cathedral walls?"

"Uncontrollable. They needed to feed all the time. They killed blatantly. They killed in public. They killed even inside the cathedral. Priests and nuns died. Questions were coming from the outside. He had to do something."

"He created all these things?"

"No, they lived before him. He came here and liked the town and protected the people from them."

"And himself. He didn't want to be found out." Justin felt his lips turn up in a sneer.

"Come with me and listen to the pathetic creatures."

Justin joined the old woman, and they walked up the cathedral steps together.

"Not all were insane when he locked them away. Some were simply people he detested. Rather than kill them, he decided to punish them. But those few are also insane by now, trapped in an exitless maze. Many years ago they begged for mercy. Not anymore. Now they only want blood. Anyone's blood." She looked at Justin.

"Even yours?" he asked.

"Especially mine."

"Is that what you promise them?"

The woman shook her head. "I promise reunions with families and revenge. My blood is too sour to interest them. They know I have been working for him and almost can't stand the stink of me."

"But they like what you tell them."

"I tell them what I hear. I feed back to them their own ideas in words that sound so different from their own. They haven't found me out yet. I don't think they want to. What would they have left if they gave up on me?"

"Teach me to communicate with them."

"Why? Their pain will age you as quickly as it has me. There are open sores in me that I had long forgotten. Memories of children and loves. Days of health and confidence. Satisfaction at the end of the day. Nights when we ached and had a Lord to pray to. Now I sweep and decorate a church that means nothing to me. God doesn't want me. I have accepted that."

"He will always be there for you if you repent."

"I am sorry for nothing. I survived through all His trials without His help."

Inside the cathedral the pair walked the center aisle.

"I can hear them, madam, but I do not understand the words."

"Slow their voices down inside your mind. Force yourself to draw out each syllable. Caution; don't let them rob you of your identity. Do not imagine yourself one of them."

"If I walk closer to the wall, will that make it any easier?"

"No, I can hear them clearly now. They tell me that I bring in a blasphemy in the guise of you. What are you?"

"My father was mortal. My mother was a vampire."

"They detest your kind."

"And you?"

The old woman shrugged.

Chapter Twenty-five

"There's Cleo, my favorite. She chatters away."

"You know them by name?" Justin asked the old woman.

"I give them names. I give them existence. They no longer remember themselves as separate from the world. They are part of the miniature world in which they live. Part of the stone and brick and mortar. The warped faces carved on the walls are a reflection of them. They touch a chipped gargoyle's nose and it is their own. No mirrors separate them from their world."

"All I hear is incomprehensible rambling. Voices high-pitched, straining vocal chords," Justin said.

"Cleo, my naughty Cleo. She invites you to join her. Here, touch the wall with the flat of your palm."

Justin did, and suddenly a sultry voice was heaving whispers breathlessly inside his head. He concentrated on that voice above all others. A word would appear inside his mind and then would disappear. "Sate." "Longing." "Treasure." The words didn't form sentences. Words coming from an erratic mind making no sense, bringing no respite from his ignorance. He visualized a woman leaning over him. Naked. Her body sculpted into beautiful lines. Her face chiseled from porcelain surrounded by ringlets of blond hair. She rose and fell upon his shaft. She smiled down upon him and touched his flesh with hands blackened by age. Some would say rotted, but that wasn't the image she wanted to project. Hands simply aging with the centuries, becoming more skillful. When he removed his hand from the wall the vision vanished.

"Cleo teases," said the old woman.

"She is very beautiful."

"You haven't listened to what I've been saying. I doubt she remembers what she looked like. No, she has seen a painting or a statue and molded her flesh into that dream. Do not be deceived by promises they make. They want out, or at least you in with them, so that they will not feel so alone in their poverty of spirit."

"I would release them," Justin said.

"Why? They would spread their plague again."

"No. I wouldn't release them into this world, but into God's eternal world."

123

The old woman laughed. "They would rather stay walled inside this cathedral than to have no existence at all."

"Only because they don't know what's best for them," he replied.

The old woman came close to Justin and whispered in his left ear. "Cleo is the most vicious of those guarded by these walls. She dreams of young babes dying in her arms, mothers forced to watch, and fathers drained dry of seed so that they may never reproduce again."

"She dreams of extinction. Without future generations, she would lose her own food supply," he whispered back.

"Cleo believes herself to be death. The end that mortal man fears. She has been chosen by the Lord, or so she will tell you."

"That is what she tells you?"

"Frequently. On quiet evenings when I sit here, resting from my day, she enters my mind, attempting to win me over."

"And she will attempt to do that with me?"

"Be honest: She already has made the attempt. Wait until she makes touch real for you."

"She can't do that without being here with me."

"Oh, she can. Your fingers will tingle with her direction. You'll feel her touch your body between your legs, and you will swell with the need."

"Have you ever looked for the opening that leads to the inner sanctum of these walls?"

"I don't want to. I have no desire for that knowledge. Let them stay walled up and away from us, Justin. You can't bring them back from what they have become."

"They're still humans."

"No, Justin. Their humanity disappeared with the last drop of their blood. Now they are supernatural and cruel. You've lived closely with them; you should know."

"I lived among mutants. My mother was the only true vampire I knew." He saw lit candles flicker behind the reds and blues of the glass candle holders. "Lives are taken away every second. We fight a losing battle, and so does Cleo."

The old woman walked over to the row of candles, licked her fingertips, and put out each of the flames.

"He doesn't want them destroyed," said the old woman.

"What? Does he think of them as his own army?"

"No. As his revenge when the time comes."

Chapter Twenty-six

"Millie and Effie are two of his favorites. Calls them to his bed several times a week." The little man looked plainer now, dressed in his work clothes instead of the black velvet Victorian suit. He looked like every other laborer. Even his hair was pulled back off his shoulders, allowing him to work more efficiently.

"Andre, you will point those two girls out to me. Can you find out what night they will be at the estate?" Marie patted him on the head. He was a pet who served her main purpose in being here. A pet indebted to her for making him into what he wanted to be.

He nodded enthusiastically. "And there is Madeline. She is with him now."

"You saw her arrive?"

"Her body odor is rich, sweet. And now, thanks to you, my sense of smell is even sharper than before."

"Is she one of his favorites?"

"I think Sade fears her. When she is here he is more cautious, wary of even his own staff. Maybe she has power that I haven't recognized."

"She is his favorite, Andre. She has to be. He fears being dragged into another relationship."

"But he doesn't have relationships, Marie. He has partners who do his bidding and then go away."

"What if Madeline asked him for something?"

"The butterflies were for her."

"What?"

"The butterflies at the party. She requested them."

"Butterflies? This Madeline must be taught to think big. Her demands should equal her worth to Sade."

"I agree, Marie. I have a request to make of you."

"You wish to measure your own worth, Andre?"

"I am not so presumptuous. No, I weigh what Sade is worth to you."

"Not a cent until after the game has been played," she said.

"Money isn't what I want."

"You are a fool, Andre." She shook her head.

"I want the young man who came with you."

"He isn't mine to gift-wrap."

"You know his vulnerabilities. I want to know them too."

"So you can what?"

Andre smiled and rubbed his hands together. "I want to take advantage of him."

"Sexually, I presume. He has nothing else to offer."

"I've seen him naked," Andre said.

"Where? Certainly you haven't managed to bed him."

"Most evenings he swims down at the river. I follow. I like being close to him."

"You like tormenting yourself," she corrected.

"Could you ever doubt that?" he said with surprised glee.

She laughed and began walking away from him.

"Promise me Justin."

She stopped and turned to face Andre. "Or . . . ?"

"I don't make threats, Marie. I simply asked that you promise me Justin." The look in his eyes were deceptively humble.

"Help me to destroy Sade and I will de-talon Justin personally."

"And give him to me?"

"Yes, Andre. I certainly don't want Justin for myself." She thought of Justin's gait, the color of his eyes, his build, strong and slender. Walks down by the river in the evenings would help her think. Inspire her, even. Or satisfy her, if she was lucky.

Chapter Twenty-seven

"I don't need you to walk me all the way to my house, Louis."

Sade saw how dusk shaded the red of Madeline's hair. As it grew darker, her skin seemed to pale, her eyes dark points in the snowy allure of her face.

"I certainly don't want anything to happen to you, *ma chere*."

"You are the only thing that happens to any of us in this town."

"Not true. What nefarious secrets does the cathedral hold?"

"That is folklore."

"And I am not?" Sade smiled to himself.

"You merely attempt to copy your famous ancestor, Louis."

"And you do not think that I do a very good job. Perhaps an increased number of lashes would upgrade my status in your eyes. Should we find ourselves a quiet path?"

"I'm sorry, Louis."

He watched her lips tremble.

"I'm already late for dinner, and I promised Mother I'd be home for the birthday."

"Ah, someone is a year older. Not you, *ma petite?*"

"My younger brother."

Sade pushed back her red hair from her face.

"And you do not think they would wait an extra few minutes for your arrival?"

"I ache already, Louis. Please."

"I am so softhearted when it comes to you, *ma chere.*" His hand gripped her hair tightly. "Never tantalize me like this again, bitch. My patience is already being tested by a despicable woman who I thought would bring light into our lives. I hate being wrong. I hate being demeaned."

Her eyes were opened wide and her lips gaped in a manner that barely revealed her small white teeth.

"I like fear." He gripped her hair tighter. "I like pain." He threw her down on the ground. "Run home, *lapin*. Run to your hole and shiver quietly in your nest."

He turned his back on her and heard the leaves rustle on the ground as she picked herself up. And she did run. And he felt a certain satisfaction in knowing that he could have run faster, cutting off her escape. She had no sanctuary, no savior. Certainly not Justin.

Feeling peckish, Sade decided to walk the small streets near the cathedral. A child out beyond his curfew, a misty-eyed maid dreaming of her prince, or a prince headed to the pub. Any of these would make a fine meal, and he would drink only enough for them to forget. Dead bodies could be such a hurdle to his staying in Albi.

As if on command a woman came into view. She wore a long dark coat against the evening chill. Her fair hair was covered with a lace shawl. He would have guessed that she was either coming from or going to the cemetery. The direction she took did seem to lead to the cathedral. He followed, picking up a scent when a single breeze brushed up against the woman. His pace increased. He was eager to meet this invader because she had the smell of vampire clinging to her clothes and flesh.

First this strange woman, Marie, and now who could this be?

She passed the steps of the cathedral, and his ears rang with the roar of his ancestors. She turned once, sensing something wrong. Sade stepped into the shadow of the cathedral and caught sight of her face.

Cecelia!

She pulled the shawl up around her neck and continued on into the cemetery.

With a speed beyond her perception, Sade stood before Cecelia.

131

"*Mon amie! Mon pauvre amie!* I never thought you would follow." He reached out a hand to touch her face, and she took a step back. "What is it you want from me, Cecelia? What haven't I given to you?"

Chapter Twenty-eight

Cecelia saw the glee in Sade's eyes. His hand shook slightly from the overwhelming emotion of seeing her.

"Have you something for me, Cecelia? Something very special? I'm sure you must have carried it with you."

"No. I don't have Marie's skull anymore."

He grabbed her throat with his right hand.

"Who? Who has it, Cecelia?"

"I don't know where it is."

"You didn't lose it, Cecelia. I know you wouldn't do that. *Mon amie*, please say you have not conjured the woman back. Possibly in the guise of a tall, dark-haired beauty."

Cecelia spat at him.

His upper lip quivered with rage.

"That is what you have done, haven't you? You've brought back my damned mother-in-law. And who is this man she travels with?"

"You killed my child," she said, seeing only her own agony.

"I did not touch the infant. The old cripple, Keith, murdered your child."

"At your direction, no doubt."

"The babe is gone. Would you have me weep once again over Liliana? How many times need I suffer because of that girl? You wanted to bring her back as a half-breed to torment me. Yes, Keith murdered the babe, and in turn I ripped his body to shreds."

"She was mine." Cecelia raised her arms and let her coat fly open.

"Do not touch me, *mon amie*. My attraction to you has ended. You are worthless to me now. As worthless as that old man, Keith, after he destroyed your bastard."

"No." She lowered her arms to her sides. "You won't kill me until . . ." She hesitated, not wanting to bait Sade too much. "Until you know where your mother-in-law is."

"But I do know, and that half-breed she travels with is no danger to my safety."

"There is something about him that you fear. I can see it in your glare. I can hear it in the trembling of your voice."

"Not fear, Cecelia. Rage! He comes to steal from me."

"You stole my baby from me!" she screamed.

"No, you were attempting to steal from God. I helped her return to His breast."

"She'll never know God. No vampire will. Instead you left Liliana to lurk in limbo. I don't hear her voice anymore."

"She is finally at rest; whether it be with God or simply mingled with the molecules of the universe, she rests."

Cecelia shook her head. "Will you accept your fate when it is time for your own rest? It's coming. The quiet of the grave. No, for you there will be flames reaching high into the air, spreading your dust in the wind."

"You will never have peace, Cecelia." Sade lurched forward and grabbed her by the arms, lifting her off the ground.

She felt the pain of his hands tightening around her muscles. The night breeze tossed her hair around while he carried her to the back of the cathedral. A sheer wall of brick stood before them, and a boulder lay to the right.

Sade placed her on the ground, freeing her arms. Her blood flowed swiftly through her arms once again. He easily moved the boulder aside, and she saw a tunnel. Mesmerized, she did not fight when he brought her into the tunnel. The packed earth reminded her of her own grave. The smell made her throat tighten. And he pushed her deeper into the tunnel. By the time she had begun her fight she was

135

already pushed up against a silvery liquid wall that pulsed.

"Dream of the grave, Cecelia. Remember the beautiful casket in which you used to rest. Feel the smoothness of the wood. The coolness of the satin. It feels like your mother's womb, doesn't it? The smell of cotton lace wrapped around your body. The soft pillow on which you laid your head. Visualize it all, *mon amie*, and maybe it will give you succor in the meanest of times."

He pushed her deeper into the liquid wall. The earth that wavered around her sucked her deeper.

"No, Sade! Please! This will put me inside the cathedral. This is the entrance where you've walled up all your . . ."

"Foes, *mon amie*. You will meet people who have hated me so much that they would presume to destroy me. You will have much in common with them. And then there are those I hated only because they were aesthetically crude. Their breath smelled of vermin and human waste. Their skin crinkled and hung in detestable folds, their speech obsequious drivel meant to rally me to them."

Her hands grabbed at the liquid soil, but it slid through her fingers. She felt Sade's hand on her forehead, and a whoosh sent her deeper into the silvery soil. She heard the sucking and lapping noises of the earth as it made room for her body to pass through.

Opening her mouth, she felt the pressure of the liquid wall bar her ability to scream. Bits of the silvery brown ooze slipped into her mouth. When she tried to spit out the earth she gagged. Her own whimpering echoed around her.

She saw Sade's silver hair fall into his blue eyes, a picket fence of white threads for him to peep through. His face, contorted into a champion's smug grimace, would be the last she would see of the world. His hands were her last connection to the world.

Back she fell, deeper into the silvery earth.

Where was Sade? Her eyes were blinded by the brightness of the silver, by the heaving weight of the liquid earth. She no longer felt his touch. She floated and sank, unaware of up and down or sideways.

With a hard slap she hit a paved floor.

Chapter Twenty-nine

Sade rolled the boulder back across the tunnel's entrance. One woman would not be disturbing his pleasures anymore. He smiled and brushed the earth from his clothes.

"Monsieur Sade."

"Ah, Mel. I didn't expect you to be walking about this late."

"That girl . . ."

"She left, Mel. She won't hurt any of us."

Mel looked at Sade and then at the boulder.

"She was one of them? One of the carriers of the plague?" Mel asked.

"See to it, Mel, that no one comes around to this area of the grounds. She has friends who might seek her."

"They too have the plague?" Mel's body slouched into an old man's pose. His eyes were round and watery, reflecting his fear.

"All these years we have shared a peace. Not a soul will break the spell of that. I will see to it."

"The woman who services the cathedral has been with the young man. He has visited the girl many times," Mel said.

"Has he?"

"Yes, and he has been inside the cathedral with the old woman. I have never followed. I don't know what they do inside the cathedral, but could it be demonic? She brings flowers to the altar and sees that some candles are kept lit, and the priest has fresh wine and hosts. She metes out the holy water, not only to the fount in the cathedral but also to the locals, who take it home to bless their houses. Yet she still brings that foul son into the cathedral."

"Mel, neither of them have power over what is sealed inside these walls."

"She speaks to them."

"Only to quiet them. And the young man will be leaving soon."

Mel looked again at the boulder.

"He will not be remaining with us. He is not in very good health. Neither is the woman who travels with him. You should say a prayer for them."

"The old woman who takes care of the cathedral— will she be going?"

"I see a spark of lust in your eyes, Mel. Have you spoken to the old woman as yet?"

Mel looked back at Sade and shuffled his feet in the grass.

"She is too busy to speak with me. She has only one interest, and that is the cathedral."

"Must I play cupid for you, Mel?"

"Oh, no, Monsieur Sade. I am beneath your attentions and . . ." He mumbled the rest of the sentence.

Sade walked over to Mel and placed an arm around his shoulders.

"I'm afraid that, like you, I am getting on in years and could not hear the last part of your sentence."

Mel looked down at the ground, and Sade embraced the man tightly. "You should look at me when you speak to me. Your words should ring out clearly, as the bells do on a Sunday morning."

Mel looked into Sade's eyes, fear replacing the wonder that had been there a short while ago.

"I only meant that I would be embarrassed to have someone else speak for me."

"Of course. I will not intrude upon the pace your love has set." Sade freed Mel.

"Thank you, Monsieur Sade. In return I'll see to it that this area is not disturbed."

Sade smiled, and with a light-stepped walk he started on his way back to the estate.

The trees along the path were full and wild. No one ever came to cut back nature here, to mold it into a specific shape. The grass was a deep, dark green, rich in the minerals that the earth offered. Weeds and flowers scattered themselves about the forest, releasing their seed to the winds. Freedom surrounding him, Sade stumbled slightly in the dust of the path. Up ahead he could see the opening that would reveal his own estate.

Should he quickly do away with Marie or play her for a time? Should he allow Justin to run scared from this land or disembowel the youth? Once again he felt that he was gaining control over the situation. He could afford to play games as time permitted.

He broke out of the forest and immediately saw at the border of his estate a vision from a prior century. A tall pike had been driven into the ground, and propped atop it was a human head. The mouth gaped open, aghast at its final demise. The eyes stared into death. Blood rolled down the pike, evidence of a fresh kill.

As he moved closer to the pike, he saw a mound not far away. The mound had at one time been a female form, familiar to him on promiscuous nights when he feasted on his own servants. The chest and abdomen had been ripped open and the innards were missing.

But this body had not been left just for him to see. It was meant to attract the villagers, call up old wives' tales and legends in their impressionable minds. The bitch meant to discredit him.

Sade swung around and knocked the head off the pike, causing it to roll several feet away from its own body. He pulled the pike from the ground and broke it in half. He'd have to bury the debris before the nosy gossips in the village came poking around on his land.

He never expected Marie could be guilty of cowardice, but obviously she meant for him to die at the hands of mortals. Or could this be her way of torturing him? Driving him from one place to another, until, breathless, he rested unwisely, and she could finish the task she had set for herself?

In Darknesse Let Mee Dwell

In darknesse let mee dwell,
the ground shall sorrow be,
The roofe Dispaire to barre
all cheerful light from mee,
The walls of marble blacke
that moistned still shall weepe,
My musicke hellish jarring sounds
To banish friendly sleepe.
Thus wedded to my woes,
and bedded to my Tombe,
O let me living die,
til death doe come.
In darkness let mee dwell.

—ANONYMOUS, ELIZABETHAN

Chapter Thirty

Cecelia curved her body into a fetal position. Her fingers scratched at the hard floor. Her eyes she kept shut tight.

Did a breeze flow through this hidden world, or had someone just moved past her shivering body? If she called out, would a hand touch her gently on the shoulder, or would she be ripped to shreds? Worse still, would she never find another being?

"Damn you, Sade!" Her voice echoed around her. "Damn the pain you've caused me in so many ways. How many lives will you steal from me? You stole my youth, my baby, and now I'm to be locked away forever, living and dead."

Her eyes squinted open to see darkness, a darkness to which her eyes quickly became accustomed.

A smooth, barren floor lay under her body. Her hands pushed against the floor until she sat. Immediately she searched the walls on either side of her. The silvery earth was gone; only red brick was left.

She stood. There was a draft, a minor draft that seemed to be coming from the venting in the ceiling. On closer examination she saw that the venting was made of several layers, none of them penetrable even with her supernatural strength.

"Justin!" she called, hoping that her voice would carry into the church. "Sade!" she desperately screamed.

She waited in the silence, her ears alert for any noise that could indicate a means of escape. She waited an hour, her voice becoming more hoarse as the time passed and she continued her screams for Justin or Sade. Giving up, she decided to move farther down the corridor. As she walked, she noticed shapes cut into the walls, which had turned from brick to stone. Gryphons poised for attacks, slyly made so that they appeared to be in motion, the eagle heads alert, the lion bodies tense. Nests of golden gilt haloed each design. Harpies frowned down upon the gryphons from niches cut into the ceiling, their wings spread wide, as if in flight.

Inside a church Cecelia would have expected to see cherubs and angels offering solace. But this wasn't part of the main body of the church. No one saw these corridors except the lost.

A sigh repeated itself in a monotonous song. She followed the sound until she reached a large painting of the centaur Nessus; an arrow deep in his chest, he offered the onlooker his bloody shirt. Kneeling on the floor before the painting was a beautiful young vampire. Her hair was plaited with multicolored strips of cloth. Her sighs kept a rhythm for the swaying of her body. Occasionally she would reach out for the bloody shirt. Her hands would try to dig into the walls to remove the bloody cloth.

"Excuse me," Cecelia said, but her words didn't interrupt the sighing rhythm that remained stable in pitch. She looked again at the vision of the shirt dripping blood. She understood how a vampire could become fixated on something that was a depiction of the food it so badly needed. "Are you alone?" she asked. Again there was no answer.

"You shouldn't disturb her."

Cecelia turned around to see a vampire with paper-thin skin. His veins had collapsed within his body and shone through the flesh as flatworms winding up and down. High cheekbones almost broke free of the flesh. His mouth was almost covered with tiny gnats. His nose ended in a sharp point, and the weary eyes had left behind fear and aggression years ago.

"She still has hope." He chuckled. "Although it is a very empty hope."

"She must realize the painting isn't real," Cecelia said.

146

"Nothing is real and nothing is unreal." He walked up to the painting and ran his tongue across the bloodied shirt. "A superb taste," he said, looking again at Cecelia.

The vampire kneeling on the floor grabbed the male's ragged pant leg, pleading for a taste.

"You must earn it, princess," he said, and the female buried her face in her hands.

"Do you enjoy torturing her?" Cecelia asked.

"I don't torture the princess, I give her hope. If I can be satisfied with a single lick, can you image what delight the entire shirt will give? At one time the princess had to fight for her position kneeling before the painting. She brutally mauled a mindless woman who withered into an invisible dust. Or at least she seemed to dissolve before our eyes. And now the princess has adopted the mindless hope."

"What happened to the woman she defeated?"

"I told you: The woman turned to dust. The two had a brutal battle, their long nails digging clumps of flesh from each other. Meat and blood were eaten up by the nearby vampires who stopped only to replenish themselves. The battle ended with the older vampire limping away."

"Haven't you seen her since?"

"Never. The white dandruff of her flesh lay scattered on the floor. No one followed the trail she had left behind. We all believe she ended up dust."

"You must have looked for an escape."

"Our only escape is a woman the villagers call Lottie. We hear the villagers call her that name

147

when she comes to clean our home. But Lottie has given us strict instructions not to reveal her promises."

"Does she promise you wholeness?" Cecelia asked.

"Each of us wants something different to make our days more fulfilling. Me, I asked for a young woman to keep me company, to lick my wounds and cut her wrists when I ask. Is that why you're here?"

"I was forced here by Sade, not by an old woman."

"Most of us are invited guests of Sade. He lured us into primitive pleasures and then condemned those pleasures."

"How many vampires have died here?" Cecelia asked.

"We had already died before we were sealed into this church. Like the woman from whom the princess stole this painting, we turn to dust just as all good dead appropriately do." He took several steps in Cecelia's direction. "I can give you wise advice."

"Do."

He beckoned her closer with dried-out fingers that stretched too tightly over his bones.

"I can hear you from here," Cecelia said.

"That was my first advice: Never allow any vampire to come too close to you. I was going to demonstrate in a very elaborate style. You are fresh. You still contain the juices of the mortals." He took a deep breath. "It smells so much better than the stone-cold blood depicted on the wall. A small bit of your blood would truly warm me."

"I'll need every drop," Cecelia said.

"That would have been my second piece of advice after you had shared with me."

"I can't afford your advice." Cecelia backed away from the two vampires.

"Thirdly, stay away from our ancestors. They can still suck sustenance from the air."

"How will I know them?"

"They aren't to be seen. No, they're locked away inside coffins. Nailed and bolted coffins weighted down with their sins so that they can't escape. But they will call to you with voices so charming and urgent that you will get too close. Most of us have. Even those who have been warned. The sirens at sea couldn't compare to the throbbing resonance of our ancestors' voices."

"Basically I should trust no one."

"If you stayed with me and shared just a tiny bit of your blood, I could keep you safe."

"And could you contain the urge to suck me dry?" Cecelia asked.

"You are so much stronger than I. I could be defeated by a very young child vampire. An infant, perhaps." His eyes looked down at the ground.

"I don't have any pity for you. I'm not even sure I can believe anything you've told me."

The male looked back at Cecelia. "Don't pity me, for I would never have pity on you. I do not want to lose any more strength, so I do not attack. But when time has passed and you've weakened even more than I have, I will shred that smug face of yours with these nails." He raised his fragile fingers to show the blackened nails curling inward toward his palms.

"I should destroy you now," Cecelia said.

"If you did that, I would haunt you as a spirit. As for myself, I no longer fear spirits. Oftentimes I depend on them to keep me company. They whisper stories and fables into my ears. They abuse my mind and flesh at times, but even that I can tolerate as long as they give me company. You're not far along enough to take on spirits. They would crush your mind and leave you to fight the princess for the right to kneel before a dream."

"There's a vent not far down the corridor. Do you know of it?"

"Of course; we all do. That's the first thing we find. Not even the strongest vampire has been able to break through. It is said that the vent is strongly blessed in the name of God. Personally, I believe the demon resides inside that vent and watches our agony. Hour after hour he seeks his pleasure in our pain. He must have leapt for joy when you joined us."

"I'm sure he'll cry when I leave."

The woman on her knees had only stopped sighing briefly when she had grabbed onto the male's pant leg. Now she was back to sighing and rocking, a backdrop that Cecelia could have done without. Cecelia moved away from the two vampires. The male watched her until she was about to turn a corner. With an incredible fury for one who looked so weak, he lashed out at the woman at his feet, biting into her neck and face to drain her dry.

Chapter Thirty-one

"He will be angry when he finds the pike with the head," Andre predicted.

"And when he finds these beauties savaged in his bed he will roar," said Marie.

"I'm not sure that making Sade angry is a wise choice. Shouldn't you find some sly trick to do away with him?"

"I want his household servants to find these concubines first." She looked down at the bloodied sheets that were wrapped around bare legs and broken arms. Thick chains were wrapped around throats and acid disfigured faces that had once been so classic. "And these two you say were his favorites?"

"They visited often," he answered.

"I'm so glad he had used you as a liaison once in a while to invite these precious girls. They instantly followed your direction."

"I don't think we should have done this."

"But you had such fun, Andre."

"They were ripe and well-trained to accept the torment. When they became aware of the permanency of our work, their fear almost caused me to hesitate. I have never been with one who suffers so much that near the end the person is eager to die."

"Breathe in the scent of fear. Taste the coppery blood. Dream of this tonight, Andre. Upon rising you will be stronger."

"Never as powerful as Sade."

"He will break, my little Andre. Look at the blood that mars your chin."

Andre quickly dipped a handkerchief into the glass of wine beside the bed and scrubbed hard at his chin.

"Sleep with me this coming day, Andre. He has no idea where I lay for my rest."

"Does Justin know?"

"Justin wouldn't take Sade's side. Justin is too disgustingly faithful."

"He will be mine, right?"

"Do you think perhaps your smell has been left on the bodies, Andre? Sade may search for you."

"And you were part of this too. He will smell your scent."

"Ah, but the overpowering odor comes from your seed, Andre. That pungent odor will be the first he'll notice."

"We must get the bodies out of here, then. Let them be found floating in the river."

"Nonsense. The murders wouldn't be connected to Sade. Certainly it will be hard for him to explain two dead bodies lying on his bed in his own bedroom. Even if he suspects you, he will have to find you."

"I can no longer come back here?"

"A vampire without a home and mistress. Sad, very sad."

"You promised me Justin!" Andre yelled.

"That was before you got yourself into deep shit."

"Where do I go?"

"Far away from Albi, my little Andre. Pull the bell for the servants. If you're lucky, they'll find the bodies first, and all hell will break loose."

Chapter Thirty-two

Lottie scrubbed the cathedral floor with a horsehair brush that lifted the manure the farmers had brought in on the soles of their boots. She worked violently in order to avoid Justin. Her hands were calloused, and the soapy water must have stung.

Justin wondered whether he should pull her away from her task. Demand that she introduce him again to the spirits who lived within the cathedral's walls.

He was at odds, since he had been unable to find Cecelia, and the caretaker had been vague about her whereabouts. The caretaker had been brusque in his dismissal of Justin. He had refused to answer questions and simply muttered that he had no idea where she had gone.

Justin knew she wouldn't leave without obtaining her revenge on Sade. Justin had visited her coffin, hidden in the hills, and hadn't found her there. He had carefully pressed some grass around the bottom edge of the coffin's lid. If she opened the coffin, the grass would fall out. If the grass was still there when he returned the next day, he would notify Marie and ask her assistance in finding Cecelia. It was probably fruitless to ask for Marie's help, but he had to try.

He watched Lottie stagger to her feet while holding the back of a pew. When she lifted her water bucket, Justin called her name. Instantly she froze but didn't turn to him.

"Lottie, I still need your help," Justin said.

"They don't like you, half-breed." Her voice barely carried from the front of the cathedral to the middle, where Justin stood.

"I have only your word on that. I want them to tell me themselves. I think you may be jealously keeping me from them."

Lottie turned with a broad grin on her face.

"You think I want to be the only one burdened with their sufferings? Stupid. The oppressiveness of their pain has turned me into this wizened old woman. Years of listening to their tears and confessions. You look surprised. Yes, just like the priest I hear confessions, but I never grant forgiveness."

"Why not?"

Lottie gently put the water bucket on the floor.

"Because their sins are so malevolent that I would volunteer to torture them myself." Slowly Lottie walked the center aisle toward Justin. "They've killed. They've maimed. And worst of all, they have reproduced. Not just a thing like yourself, but they have made other vampires to carry on their blood thirst."

"But you allowed your daughter to be taken into Sade's fold."

"I told you before, I couldn't face losing my daughter."

"So when it suits you, Sade's gift is a perfect answer."

At this point Lottie stood only inches from Justin.

"Look at my hands, stupid, then look at your own. Besides the calluses and wrinkles and sun damage," Lottie said with a smirk, "do you see any differences?"

"I don't understand."

"Place your hands on the walls and let your mind run free with the spirits trapped within the walls. They will guide you. Guide you into horrors you never wanted to see. Eventually their words will make sense, after you've witnessed what they have seen. Beware losing your soul to them. Or do you have a soul, half-breed?"

"We all have souls, including those trapped inside this cathedral."

"Black souls they have. Heavy with sin and devoid of hope."

Lottie looked to her right at a statue of the infant Christ, crown upon His head, holding a scepter in His hands and covered in a long blood-red robe.

"They don't even fear Him. They talk behind his back within the walls and plot to topple Him in this world. That statue was closer to the wall, practically touching it. One day it swayed back and forth while Sunday mass was being said. Those seated closest to the statue noticed the movement first, of course. Elbows nudged ribs and hands clasped other hands. Gradually the whole church sat in awe, waiting for the statue to fall."

"But obviously it didn't."

"The priest and the altar boys left the altar to attend to the statue. The priest wrapped his arms about Christ's robe, steadying the movement until the statue came to a stop. The mass was disrupted, and some parishioners never returned to the cathedral after that day. Some of the congregation took up pagan ways; some knelt for services on the outside steps of the cathedral but would never enter."

"An earthquake, perhaps."

"My guess is that one is the thinnest wall, and the spirits can reach out their energy to attempt damage. Go over to the statue and tell me what you feel."

Justin crossed between pews to touch Christ's image. He pulled away his hand immediately.

"The statue is like ice, and there are cold waves of air pelting the marble."

"It's their anger. Their hate," Lottie said.

Justin set his palm against the back wall. Ravings that might come from an insane asylum bombarded his ears.

"How do you get them to stop?" he asked.

"They never do."

"Why doesn't the priest move the statue away from this spot?"

"Because he doesn't want to give in to the spirits. Doesn't want to relinquish any portion of his cathedral to the devil."

"They were human beings once," said Justin. "Not devils. They are still God's children."

"They don't want to be. They feel abandoned by Him. The longer they stay within these walls, the more energy is leeched from them. The weaker they become, the more futile their lives."

"That is not God's fault. It was Sade who locked them up."

"Sade was merely one of many. Initially the religious walled them up because they wouldn't stay in the ground. Hands forced their way up through the dirt to leverage themselves out of their graves. The religious used babies, small children to entice the fiends into the cathedral."

"What happened to the children?"

"No doubt they died. Sucked dry out of hunger or anger."

"You mean they walled the children up too?"

"Couldn't reach the children without putting their own lives in danger. The children served as human sacrifices, just like in the pagan religions."

"Didn't the parents protest?"

"The parents weren't asked. Trusting those in religious garb, the children wandered off with the priests and nuns, fearing no danger. For a long time the parents blamed the gypsies. Gypsies were hanged and beaten to death whenever they were seen, and their orphans were taken in by the religious but never seen again."

"There could be vampiric children inside these walls."

"I doubt they would have survived. I doubt that the fiends caressed the young any closer to their hearts than the religious did."

A rush of cold air caused Justin's hair to fly up off his shoulders. He pressed both his palms against the wall and bowed his head.

Lottie shrugged and went back to throwing away the bucket of cold water.

Chapter Thirty-three

As Cecelia walked, her face passed through a large web wrapping her features in invisible silk. She brushed her hands across her face and through her hair. Her right hand came away carrying a large, black, flat spider. Its legs were stubby. The tiny hairs tickled her palm.

"How did you get in here?" she asked the spider. "What crevice did you mistakenly enter?"

The spider stood still for a moment before biting into her flesh. Still Cecelia didn't rid herself of the spider.

"My blood won't feed you, it will poison you. Drink up and die soon, before you're crushed or eaten."

One would think the spider understood her

words, for instantly it ran to the edge of her palm and leaped into the dark.

She heard the shuffle of feet slide across the cement floor. Whatever was coming would be upon her in a few minutes. She wondered whether she should wait and face the source of the sound, or if she should move forward and try to avoid it. Certainly she could walk faster than the tired gait coming up behind her.

"Ah, there you are. I've heard whispers of your arrival. They say Sade himself tossed you into our midst. Did he tire of you all that quickly? Or did you do something absolutely repugnant to him? I hope it's the latter." A rasping voice came out of the darkness. "He and I had been courting the same woman, you know. But you don't know, because you've just gotten here."

Cecelia turned and faced the shade coming out of the darkness. A horse blanket was slipped over his shoulders, and he clutched it tightly around himself. The hands were blackened stubs of flesh. His face was raw and half-peeled, as if burned. The swollen features were difficult to make out.

"Not a pretty sight, am I? And you can barely see a third of me. My legs are bone and ashen flesh, my feet blistered and deformed. But my trunk is beautiful; it is a whirl of white scars and tattoos. I'd show you, but I find it much too chilly in here."

"I don't need to see your body," Cecelia said.

"Sad; I was hoping I'd kindle some sort of pity in you. I don't like standing, 'cause it makes my toes feel like they're about to fall off. If we move down a few paces, there'll be a bench on which we can sit."

She allowed him to take a few steps but didn't follow.

"Come on. Don't you want to know how to escape?"

"If you knew, you wouldn't be here."

"Do you believe I'd want to return to the outside world the way I look? Nonsense." He continued on, and she followed.

"We may sit here. Okay, it's not really a bench. It's an old rack that isn't used anymore, but think of the excitement of sitting on the ghosts that cling to their deathtrap. Sometimes I smell them. Never see them, mind you. Although, strangely, I sometimes find small rivulets of water as if there had been a group cry." He sat down and gave Cecelia a lopsided smile.

"You smell funny."

"How unkind of you," he said. "I used to constantly be aware of the smell of burned meat, but not anymore. I guess I've grown used to how I smell."

"No, it's not your flesh. You don't have the blood-hungry odor that vampires carry."

"That's simple. I'm not a vampire."

"How do you survive in here?"

"The vampires turn away from me. Even in their desperation they don't find my blood to be palatable. Funny, isn't it, because I'm easy prey. Perhaps too easy, not enough of a challenge for the rogues who wander these labyrinthine corridors."

"You can't have been here too long. How do you survive?"

"Rats. Sometimes cats even find their way inside these walls. Insects. Fried, they can be quite good. Vampires who have given up."

"You eat vampires?" Cecelia's face crinkled into an unpleasant grimace.

"They're not very good. And it is distracting when the paralyzed body can speak and beg you for mercy. I'm not sure what kind of mercy they want. They've given up on life the way they live it. I believe they want me to somehow darken their minds so that they have no idea what is happening to them."

"You make me want to gag."

"And what about vampires who drain blood from a living mortal? Digging their teeth into flesh and causing enough pressure at the wound to drain the mortal dry."

"Did Sade maim you?"

"Maim? It seems like such a mild word when I think about what he did to me. But the greatest torture is knowing that the woman I love ... loved ... proved herself a fool and chose him over me. I suppose the main problem was that she was more girl than woman. Innocent in so many ways, yet easily attracted into sinful lust. Madeline is delicate. Her skin the purest white you've ever seen, except for those spots of freckles that crop up now and then. I think about how she would look against this flesh of mine. The black, blistering peeling would glide onto her flesh, dotting it with my pain. I imagine her under me and gain strength from seeing such ugliness lying atop such beauty. It is far more erotic to think of my despoiling her with my filth than when I was handsome and whole, because then we were a match. Now I am the oppressor forcing myself on her. A twisted mind dreams so many indelicate fantasies."

"You never loved Madeline if you can find pleasure in debasing her," Cecelia said.

"Did I touch upon a sore spot with you? Do you feel betrayed by a lover? Let me guess: Sade? I am right. I can tell by your face. If you were mortal, you would be sobbing right now."

"I'm not that weak," she replied. "But I'm speaking to you not for your life story but for information about how to get out of here."

"Do you expect me to tell you to hang a left at the next crossroads and follow the yellow brick road home?"

"You told me you knew of an escape route."

"No one has been able to break through it, but you could try. Everyone seems to try. There is a flaw in the walls. A spot that wavers and almost gives."

"That's where I came in, but I couldn't see a way back to the other side," Cecelia said.

He leaned closer to her. "What would you do if you escaped? Would you kill Sade? Certainly not become his lover again, I would hope."

165

"He is no longer interested in me as a lover. No, he sees me as an enemy."

The man reached inside his blanket and pulled out a wooden stake. "If I were to give you this, would you promise to use it on Sade?"

She noticed that the stake had been carefully carved to a sharp point.

"Did you have the stake with you when you tried to destroy Sade?"

"No, else it would have gone up in flames."

"Save the stake for your own use. At some time you'll need it for your own protection."

"I made this stake from a cross I found in here. I whittled and scraped until it was perfect. A blessed stake. Sprinkled with holy water, it would be impossible to defeat."

"Have you used holy water on it?"

"Haven't found any within these corridors. But you could dip it in a fount after you escape." His lips creased and decomposed as he kissed the stake. He offered it once again to her.

She shook her head.

"But I want the stake to be fashioned by my hands. I want him to think of me while he's dying. With this stake stuck deep into his heart, he will feel my hate."

"I'll take it if you show me how to escape," she said.

"I can't show you how. I can only tell you of the weakened wall."

"It seems to be a one-way wall. But there is a vent nearby."

"On Sundays, if you rest your ear against the vent, you can hear hymns being sung. I hear Madeline's voice above all others. Do you think she prays for me? She must think me dead, or such a coward that I ran away." Tears spilled from under his downcast eyelids.

"Have you ever tried to call out to anyone while standing at the vent?"

"I whisper Madeline's name. Prayerful. And her voice seems to rise higher above all the others."

"Has anyone tried calling for help through the vent?"

"Who would want to help us?" he asked.

"Don't you want to let Madeline know that you're still alive?"

The man stood and dropped the blanket from around his shoulders.

Cecelia flinched but did not move away from him.

"Would you take me to bed?" he asked. "Would you wrap me in your arms to soothe the hurt? I am unrecognizable to those who knew me. They would destroy me as fast as they would destroy anyone else imprisoned here."

Cecelia reached down to the floor and picked up his blanket. She circled him so that she could lay the cloth back over his shoulders.

"You tease me with your kindness," he said.

"I think you're hideous and refuse to look at you naked."

The man's shoulders slouched, and he wrapped the blanket tightly around his body.

"If I break free from this place, I swear I'll destroy Sade, but not for you. For myself. I don't need your stake. Fire is the way he'll die. His coffin and he will rise into black smoke and pollute this town."

"Won't you at least mention my name to him?" he pleaded with outstretched stubs where his hands ought to be.

"I'll do better than that. I'll take you with me. What is your name?"

"I no longer have a name. Call me crispy man, singe or soot if you like."

"Rover it is, then." She waited for a reaction, but none appeared. He seemed willing to tolerate any form of shame. "Still no name?" she asked.

"Call me lover and I will prove my worth." He reached out a stub to touch her face.

She felt the rough rounded flesh against her cheek. She didn't shy away from him. She allowed him to move slowly across her face, stopping briefly in his amazement.

"You said I was hideous."

"Those stubs are purer than most of the hands that have touched me." She grabbed hold of the stub and kissed it. "And your name?"

"Michael. Michael La Crosse."

"Michael 'leader of God's host.' Angel of repentance, righteousness, mercy, and sanctification. My Michael will be righteous and have no mercy."

168

Chapter Thirty-four

As Sade set a foot on the staircase he heard hysterical screams. His room. He could sense it. He ran up the steps and at the doorway to his bedroom he ran into the kitchen maid. She was a short, middle-aged woman who normally never wandered from her domain. Her hands shook, and the gray in her hair seemed to stand on end. She was far more pallid than usual, and her round eyes never blinked as she stared into Sade's face.

"What are you doing here, madam?" he asked.

Her lips moved, but her tongue was frozen.

He grabbed her plump arms and pushed her back into the room, slamming the door behind him. She screamed so loud that it deafened him. She doubled up, and he let her drop to the floor. He looked to

169

the bed and saw the massacre that had taken place while he had been gone.

When he turned back to the maid, he saw her crawling across the Persian rug, heading for the door. He lifted her by the scruff of her neck until her feet dangled in the air. Her arms flailed out for purchase, but there was nothing to grab. He flung her body onto the bloodied bed.

"Tell me what happened here!" he shouted.

She used her hands to lift herself up and then looked down on the viscera that clung to her flesh and clothes.

"Tell me now, *femme de chambre.*"

Panting and holding her hand to her heart, she finally found the breath to speak. "I work in the kitchen, Monsieur Sade. I should not be here, but I was asked to cover. I must go back to the kitchen." She moved to rise from the bed. Sade grabbed the front of her throat.

"You are here this minute. Tell me what you know."

"There was a ring from this room. I tried to find the regular maid but couldn't. I thought I did right in answering the call."

"Besides the bodies on the bed, was there anyone else in the room, or walking away from the room?"

He could feel the pulse in her neck, and his blood hunger ignited.

"No one."

Without letting go of the maid, Sade took in the complete scene that lay before him.

"Marie," he muttered. "Marie and Justin."

"Please, Monsieur Sade, I never leave the kitchen. Only this one time."

"How unwise of you," he said.

"I thought . . ."

"That I would be grateful. A special bonus for the kitchen maid who answered the call would be due." He placed his face against hers. "Do you have a family?"

"A husband. Two little boys and a girl."

He smelled her stale breath and clutched his hand tighter around her neck. "What will they do without you?"

"No, Monsieur Sade." Her voice choked off.

"You want me to let you go back to the kitchen?" Her head nodded frantically.

The blood she spilled would lack flavor. Her flesh was clammy in his hands. She had already been tainted by the vinegary scent of the dead bodies.

She had folded her hands in prayer, but she wasn't praying to God. No, she pled for her life.

"Soon I'll be leaving this estate and will have no need for a kitchen maid." He sank his fangs into her neck and felt the gush of boiling blood rush into his mouth. Hot blood that tasted of smoke and poverty. It would be enough, though, to soothe the mad hunger his anger had started.

Chapter Thirty-five

Justin sweated in his eagerness to climb the hill. Beneath the trees up ahead two coffins were hidden. One belonged to Cecelia. He hoped the grass had fallen from between the crevice of the lid and the coffin. It would mean that she still walked this town, although he would never understand why she would hide from him.

Clouds filled the night sky so that very little light passed through the trees' branches. The forest itself was filled with the scampering sounds of small animals fleeing his path. The night was chilly, and he had worn a thick woolen turtleneck sweater to keep him warm. As he neared the coffins, he could smell the hint of decay that always seemed to linger in the vicinity of a vampire's casket. The odor was stronger than he had remembered it on his previous visit.

First he saw the boulder next to which he had left the coffins. Next he saw the pile of forest debris he had used in his attempt to camouflage them.

Quickly he pulled the deadened branches and leaves from the coffins until Cecelia's was bare and he could see that the grass still remained untouched. His hand slammed down on the lid, sending a muffled echo through the forest. He opened the coffin and saw only the pale satin and lace-edged pillow she had so carefully chosen. He lifted the pillow and brought it to his nose, and then rubbed it against his cheek when he caught the singular scent of Cecelia. Carefully he placed the pillow back in the coffin, spreading the lace evenly around it.

Marie's coffin was still partially covered with debris, but it took very little time for him to clear it away. When he opened the coffin the odor of death was fresh. Marie had recently risen; however, it seemed mingled with another odor of the undead. Not Cecelia's scent, but something newly ripened into a vampire.

She's reproducing. The idea angered him. They had agreed before the trip not to make any more vampires, not to cull one's own cult from the town's people. But here was proof that Marie had. There could be no other reason for her to share the coffin with another vampire. Frequently vampires would bed with their own children the first few nights, to comfort the new undead. He believed that the closeness also cemented the fledgling closer to his or her maker.

173

"It is night. Why would you find anyone inside the coffins, Justin?"

Standing atop the boulder was Andre, his clothes stiffened and stained with blood, his dirty hair falling into his eyes, which peered out in an insane fashion.

"I'm looking for someone."

"Will I do?" Andre leaped down onto the ground in front of Justin.

Justin smelled the blood hunger on the man and knew instantly that Marie had made herself a cohort.

"But I've never been able to entice you before, have I? At the party you preferred the dainty morsel, Madeline, to my company. She belongs to Sade, you know, and anyone who belongs to Sade is in danger."

"From Sade?"

"He is only a minor threat compared with the greater hatred Marie carries."

"What has she done?"

"You're mine now. She promised to give you to me."

"Marie can't fulfill a promise like that. I am not under her control."

Andre drew the back of his left hand across his lips.

"She has to pay me somehow for what I did, or he will destroy me."

"What did you do?"

"Marie wants to destroy all Sade's playthings and hopes Sade will be blamed. She'll take Madeline when she gets a chance." Andre sat on the ground

174

and cried dry tears. In between his sobs he attempted to speak, but he kept covering his face and muffling his voice.

Justin left Andre and stood over Marie's coffin, opening the lid. He spat down onto the creamy satin that lined the coffin.

"How many people has she killed so far, Andre?" He heard no answer, no sobs. Turning, he saw Andre scrambling back up the boulder as if he were a four-legged insect.

Marie tapped Justin on a shoulder. He knew her touch, knew the smell of her body since babyhood.

"Are you here looking for me?" she asked.

"He's mine. He's mine. You promised!" Andre shouted from atop the boulder.

Marie shook her head. "He is so gullible."

"You were here to destroy Sade, no one else," Justin reminded her.

"And you're just as gullible." She laughed, a horrible laugh that turned his mother's soft voice into that of a rasping harridan.

"Where is Cecelia?"

Marie's laughter quieted.

"At the church. At the cemetery. Perhaps having a fling with the caretaker. I don't care."

He faced her and grabbed the lower part of her arms.

"Have you hurt her?"

Marie pulled away from his hold and swung her fist into Justin's face, forcing him to fall back onto the ground.

"Not his face! Please, not his face. He's too pretty to damage," Andre cried out.

"You like missing teeth, Andre. How about my taking out several of Justin's?" She kicked Justin hard in the mouth.

Andre jumped up and down in frustration. "I want him whole," he kept crying.

Justin attempted to stand, but she kicked him off balance.

"I brought us here, Justin. Without me, you and Cecelia would still be wandering around looking for Sade. That's what you would have liked. You and Cecelia roaming the countryside. You hoping that Sade would never cross paths with you both. Cecelia and you as lovers. Isn't that what you dreamt about?"

"Who's Cecelia?" asked Andre.

"Your competition, my little boy. Competition for Justin's heart. You need to destroy her before you can ever touch Justin."

"Cecelia never comes to the estate. I have met no one by that name."

"No, Andre, she lingers on the periphery. Waiting for her chance at Sade like the rest of us. And this wimp . . ." She kicked Justin in the head just as he was halfway to his feet.

"Not the face," Andre screamed again.

"This trash desires Cecelia. He follows behind her. But you've lost your mistress, Justin. Maybe she's in bed with Sade, fulfilling all his fantasies, and at the final moment of climax she'll cut his head from his shoulders and toss it to the floor." Marie lifted Cecelia's coffin into her arms and crashed it down on Justin.

"He's mine," whimpered Andre.

The wood split around Justin. The satin clinging to his face interfered with his breathing and disoriented him. He could hear wood being split apart. By the time he was free of the satin, Marie stood over him, a large pointy wood slice in her hands. She raised it over his chest.

Chapter Thirty-six

Sade locked the door to his bedroom. He had to find Marie and Justin. Since Justin was half-human, he would be no problem in a fight. Marie, however, might have gained strength. She knew he would truly destroy her, and that knowledge made her more treacherous. Her coffin had to be kept someplace nearby. He thought of the hills surrounding the estate, and of the caves and cubbyholes spread throughout them.

Andre would know the land better than he. Quickly he made his way down the stairs and out the back door. Andre's cabin was only a half mile from the main house. Sade would drag the man out of bed, and if necessary force him naked to lead the way through the hills.

He was almost to the cabin when the cathedral's caretaker, Mel, called out to him.

"The young male; he has been looking for Cecelia. I fear that he may rescue her," Mel shouted.

Sade stopped in midstep and waited for the slow-moving caretaker to catch up.

"The young one. The one visiting from America. He wants Cecelia back. He has been listening inside the cathedral. What if he hears her voice among the others?"

"Where did he go? To the cathedral?"

The caretaker shrugged. "He has been walking the aisles of the cathedral with Lottie. She has been tense around the young man. She doesn't seem to trust him, but she refuses to banish him from the cathedral."

"Some voices get lost, Mel. There is a voice that Lottie should have heard but hasn't. The more wicked, the stronger the call. Cecelia is neither old enough nor wicked enough to bray her voice over the chorus. And even if she does, let him rescue her. Let him find his own way into the labyrinthine corridors. Show him the way, Mel. Lead him into the tunnel and up to the silver wall."

"I can't."

"I did not hear you, Mel."

"What if he drags me with him?"

Sade reached out and pulled the old man close.

"What if I crush you right here and leave you for the hawks?"

"Please. I do not have much time left, Monsieur Sade. I don't want to add any new sins to my soul."

"One more isn't going to send you to hell. One less isn't going to bring you into the kingdom of God. Understand, my humble man, that your life is worth as much as the dirt beneath your feet." Sade saw the frightened look in Mel's eyes turn into rage, an old man's rage that must always remain contained inside his mind. For Mel could not vanquish a vampire in his physical state. And truly the rage changed into self-pity. "You will seek out the young man. Ask others where he may be. Find him and lead him to his beloved."

The old man nodded his head, and Sade loosened his grip.

"Your clothes are old and stale. Come up to the main house sometime and I will give you my hand-me-downs."

Chapter Thirty-seven

Andre jumped from the boulder and rolled onto Justin's prone body.

"No, no. You promised him to me. You can't destroy him. He is too beautiful to be wasted in death."

Justin could see Marie's rage explode in her eyes, on her twisted lips and frozen face. A moment of stillness, then she jammed the stake into Andre's heart. She pulled out the wood and stabbed him again. He tried to twist away from her, forgetting his heroic attempt to save Justin in the blinding pain that looped his body.

Justin once again heard the wet sucking sound of the stake being pulled from Andre's body. Almost immediately it was driven back in with a terrifying strength. Blood splattered his clothes and even

touched his lips. He spat and wiped the blood away
with his hand.

Soon Justin was on his feet, watching Marie lost
in her rage. Even after Andre stopped pleading and
moving she continued her rampage of his body.

Cecelia would never stand a chance before this
woman, he thought. Again he tried to consider
where she could be. He must go back to the caretaker and cajole or beat her whereabouts out of him.

"You'll never again wrack my body with your tortures," Marie shouted. "Or destroy my baby girls'
lives with your carousing. I allowed you to live when
I should have let the people take you to the guillo-
tine before you knew of your own strength."

Justin realized that in her mind she was destroying
Sade. The mangled flesh on the ground before her
was not her helpmate Andre but her nemesis.

She threw the stake aside and reached inside the
bloody body to rip out the heart. A hole had been
driven through the center and it barely held together.

Justin backed away, closer to the forest of trees.
The night animals had stopped their prowling. He
meshed with the trees when he saw her bring the
wet, non-beating organ up to her mouth.

Relieved to be surrounded by silence, Justin ran
deeper into the forest. Once he tripped over a
downed branch but caught himself before he fell. He
continued to travel for many miles until he arrived
at the river. There he took off all his clothes and
dove into the water.

The icy cold thrilled his body with wave upon wave of chills, chasing away the visions he had just witnessed. The water swept away the blood that slipped easily from his flesh. Blood from a vampire he would never have to rescue.

He had never seen such anger, such hatred. His mother's features had been twisted into those of an unrecognizable monster. The limbs had performed deeds that they'd never before considered. His mother was truly gone. She would never return to him. She had kept him alive when he should have died and he had responded by doing the same for her. Only his failure was far more wicked. He had left her vulnerable for a beast to claim.

The chills had passed and he floated, weary and numb.

Chapter Thirty-eight

"The elders are down this way," Michael said, leading Cecelia through a narrow corridor. "But why do you seek them?"

"I've heard that they can draw strength from those around them without laying fangs on flesh. I have to experience this. Maybe I can learn something from them."

"The elders are very wicked. They don't know what mercy is. They'll steal from you as quickly as from a mortal."

"Have you been inside the room, Michael?"

"No. Like you, I was curious, but not stupid enough to step within their circle."

"Are you calling me stupid because I want to learn more about what I am?"

"You're a fresh vampire compared to them. You won't be able to communicate with them or learn anything."

The corridor became just wide enough to bring a coffin through. Up ahead was a wooden door, to which a huge crucifix was affixed. The model of Christ seemed so real that she halted for a few moments, waiting for a groan or a slight movement. Then, realizing the statue was only plaster, she moved forward.

"The coffins are stored behind the crucifix?"

"Yes. I don't know why. Crucifixes can't stop vampires; that's only an old tale."

"But the people who built this place believed in the power of the cross."

As she drew closer to the crucifix, she could see layers of dust building in the crevices of the statue. Several large webs stretched from the Lord's chin to his shoulders.

"The blood looks wet," she said.

"Only an illusion." Michael wiped a stub across the painted bloodstain covering Christ's wrists. His stub came away dry. "Another form of torture, I would guess."

She put her hand out to touch the knob of the door but hesitated.

"The door's knob seems very clean, as if people have recently come and gone from this room."

"Some peek in from the hall. Crossing the threshold takes immense stupidity."

Cecelia grasped the doorknob and slowly turned to open the door. It didn't stick; instead it immediately fell back, allowing her to peer inside the room.

"There are candles near the entrance," Michael said.

"I don't need them. I can see fine in the dark."

"Perhaps you could light one for me, since my eyes aren't as sharp as yours."

"Will you come in with me?"

Michael shook his head.

"You won't need any additional light if you stay out here."

"I can make out rows of coffins. Shadows low and long. Some seem to gleam of jewels or locks."

He was right. Several of the coffins had figures encrusted in jewels on the lids. Whether they were crests or something to prevent the vampire from arising, she did not know. Many were wrapped in chains, with old rusted padlocks drooping off the sides.

"I don't feel any presence, Michael. Do you?" She turned to face him as he stood immediately behind her.

"It smells like a sewer with damp bodies rotting away."

"But there's no presence."

"They are here, but they are wary. They don't want to frighten you away."

"Have you ever felt a presence, Michael?"

He was quiet and drew the blanket tighter around his body.

186

"Have you?" she demanded.

"I saw evidence of a presence."

"Explain."

"Once I almost crossed the threshold. My feet were halfway into the room. I stood there for a very long time, deciding whether I should cross over completely. One or two of them became tired of waiting for me. Suddenly I heard banging coming from the inside of at least one coffin. I don't know which one. There must not have been any satin lining inside the coffin, because the sound wasn't muffled. Chains began to rattle. A deep sigh crossed from the room to my ears. I swear they must have sighed in unison, because the impact against my eardrums drove me backward. I slammed the door closed and, since I'm a coward, I haven't thought of crossing over into the room again."

"Did you come back after that episode?"

"Yes, but just to stare into the darkness like a small child intrigued but fearful of a ghost house."

"Do you want me to hold your hand, Michael?" She smiled at him, knowing that she would have to go alone.

"I have no hands, Cecelia. And I don't wish to lose any more parts of my body."

She turned back to the room and looked down at the floor. It was different inside the room, a combination of earth and gravel. Of course, she thought, they need the earth to give them existence. Some moss had started to build up, making her first step feel soft and spongy. This hushed any sound that her shoes could have made.

Once entirely inside, Cecelia's mind swept the room, seeking another intellect with which to connect.

"Nothing, Michael. Absolutely nothing inhabits this room."

"Don't allow yourself to think that. They'll draw you farther in and prevent you from leaving."

"I see no skeletons on the floor, Michael."

"You wouldn't; the vampires that stayed would soon turn into ash."

She walked deeper into the room, seeking out the center. She felt dizzy and laid a hand on a coffin. Her palm stuck to the walnut wood, which acted as a magnet for her flesh.

"If there is life here, I need your help. I want to learn from you." Her hand began to feel warm. A slight smoke drifted up from the spot where the hand touched. She ripped her hand away and saw the crust of her palm baking atop the coffin, as if it was the crust of a pie. Turning her hand over, she could see that several layers of skin had been shed.

"Why are they so hot, Michael?"

"Because this is hell," he answered calmly.

"Hell," she repeated, looking around for the flames and pitchforks that should be crowding the room.

Again a dizziness overcame her, but she refused to prevent her fall by grabbing hold of a coffin. She fell to the floor. The moss felt sticky against her hands. But was it moss she had touched? A closer look showed that it was a thick, syrupy goo that had been leaking from the coffin on her right. Channels of the ooze dripped from the slender openings in the decaying wood.

She used several fingers of her unhurt hand to wipe at the ooze. Her fingers tingled, and when she looked closely she saw tiny maggots swarming in the goo.

"They're decaying in their coffins. At least this one is," she said.

"But I'll bet the vampire is still alive," Michael said.

"I could try to open the coffin and find out." She wiped the maggots onto the moss and reached for the chain circling the coffin. "The chain is rusted. Shouldn't be a problem to break it."

"Damn! Are you really going to open the lid?"

"I must see what's inside. After centuries this could be me," she said.

She found the padlock and tried to undo it. The hinge gave slightly but held. She searched for the most rusted portion of the chain and tugged at that link. Nothing. She looked around her and saw a large jewel attached to the lid of the coffin just beyond the one she wanted to open. She retrieved the jewel, ripping it free from its crest, and returned to the rusted loop.

A heavy sigh was heaved within the room.

"I think you've pissed them off," Michael said.

Cecelia slammed the jewel down on the link several times until she could see a crack forming.

"It's coming," she said. "A few more raps should do it."

She heard Michael move a little closer. His curiosity was overcoming his fear.

When the link did break, the entire chain fell away, as if a spell had been broken. She let her hand drop the jewel to the floor.

"How many centuries do you think this vampire has been locked up for? Two? Three? Maybe more?"

Michael crossed over into the room and grabbed at a fat candle that stood near the door. Fumbling badly with what remained of his hands, he finally managed to light the candle with a cigarette lighter he had on his person.

"Shit!"

"What's the matter?" he asked.

"The damn lid is nailed onto the casket. The wood's badly decayed. Maybe we can force the wood apart."

Cracking sounds of the wood echoed in the room. She worked quickly, and sensed that Michael was almost by her side. Several of the panels in the lid gave way, and she ripped them apart and flung the pieces across the room.

The smell was horrid, but she wouldn't stop. Finally she was able to rip off a large slab of the lid. Michael vomited onto the floor, his candle throwing eerie waves of light as his body shook. Large portions of what looked like adipose fat shimmered in the light, glinting with its swarm of maggots seeking darkness, burying themselves deeper into the flesh.

"This is what you've been so afraid of, Michael?"

Catching his breath, Michael turned to peer into the coffin.

"It's alive," he said.

She looked down at a face that was gaunt and almost featureless in its decay. The eyes opened, and she saw tiny insects fleeing the light. The eyes took in the invaders' presence. What should have been a mouth opened and revealed a number of sharp, oversized teeth. The nose had flattened and the nostrils flared open, doubling its normal size. A hand dripping flesh reached for Cecelia. Instinctively she pulled back.

"Should we set it afire?" Michael asked.

Fire, the greatest fear of the vampires. No, she couldn't do that. Besides, she doubted the vampire had very much mobility.

The vampire must have understood the words because it blew a wad of spit and flesh at the candle. Incredibly the clump hit its mark and the candle was snuffed out.

She turned to see the suddenly blinded Michael, riffling for his lighter.

"Don't," she said. "It will only blow it out again. Wait until your eyes become more accustomed to the darkness. You may not be able to see as well as I can, but you will begin to see shadows. Concentrate on the shadows, Michael. Watch where they

191

go. Use your senses to be aware of anything coming closer to you."

Michael heeded and slowly regained control over his anxious body.

The heavy sigh swept the room again, enveloping Cecelia and Michael in a filth-infested breeze.

The thing lying before them gurgled. Whether it tried to speak or simply laughed at them, Cecelia couldn't tell. She watched maggots drop inside its open maw.

Gradually the sludge of flesh moved in unison, creeping up the side of the coffin closest to Cecelia and Michael. Eventually the vampire rested its arm on the edge of the coffin.

"We can't let it get out!" Michael shrieked.

Cecelia felt pulled toward the rising vampire. An awkward sympathy built up inside her head. She wanted to reach out and assist the vampire in its escape from the coffin.

"We are one," she heard it whisper inside her head. "We are the same. Your blood and flesh will meld with mine, as if we were born of one woman and conceived at the same moment."

She found herself staring down at the palms of both her hands, one palm smudged with dirt but still whole, the other raw, the fresh wound already starting to heal. Her flesh didn't look anything like the vampire's in front of her. The muscles in her arms and legs weren't atrophied. Her mind was still hers.

"No," she answered the vampire out loud, even though she knew that it could read her mind.

Muffled thumps began to fill the room as other vampires encouraged the one before her.

"Come away," Michael shouted, his right stump touching her elbow.

"Will this be me?" she asked. Michael answered in the negative, but she wasn't asking him.

The vampire tilted its head. "This can be you now."

"Why the hell would I want that?"

Confused, Michael again attempted to answer but finally understood that the vampire was taking control of her mind.

"Don't let him in," Michael said. "He will capture all that you are and leave a shell behind."

Cecelia was mesmerized by the vampire's face. The flesh undulated in slow, haphazard waves from the life within it. The maggots had managed to bury themselves deep enough not to be visible, but alive enough to mobilize the flesh.

"Cecelia," Michael called. "Stop." He pulled her back.

Finally she realized that she had been moving closer to the vampire, inching her way to oblivion. She heard the vampire speaking inside her head.

"See the beauty. My flesh isn't dead and sagging. My limbs bristle with life. My eyes see into the future. Our future together. A strong and beneficial union. The door is open. Let us leave together, meshing our powers into one being. Give me balance and strength to walk. I'll give you the knowledge of all my centuries."

"Knowledge to destroy Sade?" she asked.

"I knew him well. I touched his flesh. I ate and drank at his table. I was privy to his secrets, and in me he confided his weaknesses."

Chapter Thirty-nine

"Lottie!" yelled Sade from the back of the cathedral.

She immediately stopped her dusting of the statues and turned to face him.

"You shouldn't be here," she whispered, as if God might not have noticed Sade's presence as yet.

"I want to talk to you. Come here."

She neatly placed her rag behind a statue, out of sight, and almost ran down the center aisle. After curtsying to Sade she stood looking down at the marble floor.

"Why?" was his simple question.

She looked at him with curiosity.

"Why did you allow that boy Justin inside this cathedral?"

"He can hear them like me. The words are sometimes jumbled for him, but he has visions. Cleo entered his mind with promises."

"Wonderful; and I suppose now he is eager to meet this woman."

"He is eager to save their souls. I told him it was futile, but he feels that he has a quest."

"A quest?"

"To free them from this cathedral, and most of all to free them of the vampire life."

"Where is Justin now?"

"I don't know. Seems he's been looking for the accursed girl that he arrived with. She is bad. I saw her desecrate the cemetery, tumbling down one of the stone angels."

"She has done worse but will not disturb us anymore."

"Has she been destroyed?"

Sade wavered in answering Lottie. If he told her, she might well tell Justin, or worse, try to communicate with the brat.

"She is not your business, Lottie."

He watched her eyes search the walls of the cathedral. She knew. She had seen him dispense with a number of his enemies.

"I forbid you to speak with Justin. Promise me on your daughter's existence you will not."

"I promise," she said without hesitation. "Is she still angry with me? Will she not once come to see her mother? When she stopped visiting I worried and felt so guilty. Giving you my daughter was a difficult decision, but I couldn't lose her so young."

"Her time is taken up with a full life, Lottie."

"And you will give her back to me when I die?"

"I hope that you live way beyond your life expectancy. You have been a good servant. Except for your error in allowing Justin to speak to the boarders."

"But it is natural for him. He doesn't need me to communicate with them. They find some sort of affinity with him."

"He is half vampire; why not?"

"It is difficult for me to keep them quiet when he is here. You come and there is nothing but silence from within these walls."

"They fear me," Sade said, bringing his body to its full height.

"They hate you. If . . ."

"If what, Lottie?"

"If they could touch your body, your flesh would instantly go up in flames from the hatred they feel for you. Some you have put here. Others resent that you make no effort to set them free."

"Free to suck the world dry? No, madam, I will never set them free to rampage through the world and end all our existences."

A wail rose into the rafters of the cathedral. A pitiful wail that spoke of eternal pain.

"They hear us, Monsieur Sade. We shouldn't stand here and talk of them. If we must speak, it should be far away from this place."

"Fine, we'll speak of Andre, then. Have you seen him?"

She shook her head.

"He was not at home, and I need his assistance in taming the beasts that have surrounded me."

"Justin and that woman Marie?"

"Yes. Don't look so worried. Marie will never join the clutter of souls imprisoned in this cathedral. No, she will be completely destroyed, and next time her ashes will flow in the Tarn River."

Chapter Forty

Wet and naked, Justin traveled the town's alleyways, seeking any kind of rags to wear. He couldn't put the clothes he had worn back on his body. They reeked of Andre's blood and the smell of Marie.

When he reached a main street he waited and ducked his head out of the alley to make sure no one else was out walking at this hour of the night. But there was another, and Justin was so stunned to see her that he hadn't pulled back soon enough to miss her gaze.

"Justin," Madeline cried out, crossing the street to approach him. "Justin, what?"

He stood before her, untroubled by his nakedness. Instead of turning away she stared.

"What are you doing out at this hour?" he asked.

"I am heading to the estate. I had a sort of quarrel with Monsieur Sade and wanted to right it." She looked down at the ground.

He knew she wasn't shy of his flesh. No, she was embarrassed to admit that she was unable to break her ties to a man who could take her away from the town in which she had been born.

"I need clothes, Madeline. Do you know of someplace where I can find clothes that will fit?"

"You're of similar height and weight to my father. I can go back home and return with clothes for you."

"Do that. Obviously I have no choice but to wait here. Who knows what fragile waifs I may frighten looking like this?"

"You don't frighten me, but then, I guess I'm beyond being a fragile waif. Monsieur Sade has seen to that."

He waited no more than fifteen minutes before he saw Madeline running down the street, a bundle held tightly in her arms.

"I picked his Sunday best for you," she said, offering the clothing to Justin.

"You could have brought his old work clothes. Wouldn't he be less likely to miss them?"

"No. Even to church he wears his work clothes, causing weekly arguments between him and Mother."

Justin chuckled as he stepped into the slacks she had brought. Madeline moved toward him with a shirt in her hands, ready to assist him.

"Thank you, Madeline. Now you should return home and sleep."

"Where are you going?" she asked.

"I can't think of anywhere else to go except to the caretaker's house. I need to find someone, and he and Lottie are probably the only two people who can help me."

"A woman?"

"Yes. A woman I've been traveling with."

"Not the older woman at Sade's estate?"

"No. Madeline, if you want to leave this town, then go. By yourself. Don't seek anyone else's help. Not Sade's. And not mine. Like Sade, I can only bring danger into your life."

"And the woman you're looking for—don't you bring danger into her life?"

Justin laughed. "She apparently brings more danger to me than I could ever bring to her."

"Then why search for her? Why not escape this town with me?"

"I cannot leave Cecelia behind." Justin finished buttoning the shirt and tucked the ends of it inside the pants.

"Do you love her?"

"I can never love, Madeline. My love brings death. I only know how to take away pain. I wouldn't know how to give joy to another."

"I feel joy when I see you," she said, reaching her right hand out to him.

"Go home, Madeline. Don't waste time with me and don't visit Sade. Go home." He began backing away from her.

"I'll come with you. I've known old Mel a long time. Maybe he'll tell me what you want to know." She took a step forward, and he immediately pushed her away.

"Don't you understand? If I find Cecelia, I will try to get her to return to the States with me. I'll stay with her."

"Why?"

"Cecelia needs my help."

"I have need of you too. Justin, I might even love you. Doesn't that matter?"

He shook his head. "I never should have approached you. I belong with Cecelia. We are both lost and can do no further damage to each other."

"How do you know she wants to be with you? She hasn't tried to contact you. You've visited her, but she has never gone to the estate to see you."

"Sade knows her and would destroy her. That's why I must find her. Perhaps he has already harmed her. She was once his lover, Madeline. Now she is the same kind of monster he is."

"I won't go back to the estate if you let me come with you."

"He'll see us all dead. Sade will destroy anyone who takes our side. If I find proof that he has destroyed Cecelia, I'll do away with him."

"Kill Sade?" Madeline's eyes were wide, her lips seeming to tremble. "You couldn't kill anyone, Justin."

"I drove a stake into my mother's heart."

"We all hurt our parents."

"No, Madeline. I literally drove a stake into my mother's heart and allowed a foul entity to use her body."

There was no shock in Madeline's eyes, only a searching stare to uncover the meaning of his words.

"All this is confusing, Justin."

"Stay away from Sade and me. He will rob you of a peaceful death."

"And you?"

"I will complete his destruction of you." Justin turned away from her and quickly walked back down the alley from which he had come.

Chapter Forty-one

"Cecelia, don't touch him," Michael said. "Listen to me, not to the horror inside the casket. He wants freedom."

"And I want revenge on Sade," she said.

"Sade is weak in many ways," the vampire whispered in secret breaths inside her head. "His destruction is inevitable. He cowers in dark corners and is weakening day by day."

"He never appeared that way to me," she replied.

"He shielded your eyes so you would not see. He plays tricks. Sade is a scavenger upon this earth. He robs the sight from such as yourself. He steals life without giving anything back."

"But you can give me something?"

"Eons of knowledge. Strength to last eternally. And the body of Sade in ashes."

"All I want is to know that Sade no longer walks the earth."

"Specks of his dust will wheel in the winds, scatter so far apart that he would never be able to return."

"But you want my life for his?" she asked.

"I want only to strengthen both of us. You have the freedom to move about, but I have the knowledge you are seeking."

"I let you crawl into my head and make a new home. And what happens to the body you leave behind?"

"It lives on like a rag doll. Pushed and pulled by the insects that crawl through my flesh."

"But they can't help you walk?"

Its maw widened as if in a grin. "They are mindless and wouldn't know how to guide me. They bring no nourishment to me; they simply feed."

"And you want my body to feed yourself."

"I want your intellect, your emotions, and your strength. I do not need to destroy the physical body."

"But the mind?"

"Mindless you would be useless to me. Just as I am now worthless to you without a usable body."

"No, not worthless. You could share what you know without living inside me. Why should I take you with me?"

"Because I will tell you nothing as long as I am bound to this coffin." It again reached its hand out to touch her arm, and she didn't shy away.

Its touch was wet. Its flesh spread across her skin like spilled liquid. However, it was not cold as she had expected; instead it felt like tiny sparks licking the hair from her forearm.

"Cecelia!" Michael yelled. He attempted to pull her away from the ancient vampire, and as he did strands of flesh stretched from the coffin to Cecelia's body. From the coffin the vampire spat again, this time hitting Michael just below his right eye. It burned like acid, causing Michael's already burnt flesh to float free as flakes of soot. Michael pulled away from Cecelia and saw the thing smirk at him in all its hideous splendor.

"Tell him to wait outside, my dear," it said.

"Why can't he stay?"

"Because he is a distraction. We cannot bind ourselves in love and hate with his crass manipulations."

"Love and hate," she repeated. "Where does love find a part in this?"

"In the gratefulness I feel toward you. But all the hate will be directed toward Sade."

"I don't yet know how to get out of this place. If I never do, the hate will go to waste."

"Hate and love can never be wasted, my dear. Our love will keep us alive eternally, and our hate will never abate until we destroy Sade. Both emotions will motivate us on our quest."

She looked at Michael and saw that he had backed away to the door. He stood on the threshold, his stump resting on the spot where the saliva had burned his face.

"Michael, you will help me."

"If you combine with that monster, I will not."

"You will, Michael. I will take you with me, but first promise that you'll destroy my body if this thing takes me over completely." She turned back to the ancient vampire in the coffin. "Did you hear what I just said?"

"He will see no difference, because we will meld as one. What and who you are I will be."

"And your own spirit? Will you be a silent partner?"

"Never silent, but forever respectful." The thing bowed its head for the first time, humbling its petition.

"I can't walk these corridors eternally, Michael. Neither can I walk the same earth on which Sade rests his feet. This may be a mistake, but promise to avenge me if it is."

"By turning your flesh to ash?"

She nodded.

Chapter Forty-two

Marie ran her hand across the dead vampire's features. Not the one she imagined seeing just moments before. No, these were peasant features. Andre's.

She had wanted so much for the dismemberment to leave her with Sade's head resting in her hands. Instead she had lost an ally. A treasonous ally who would put his lust before her demands. She flung the head far from her and turned to where Justin had stood. Gone. The half-breed who should be dead had escaped. However, he wasn't important to her, only a thorn to be plucked when she had the time.

Marie stood. Her head ached. The pain almost blinded her eyes. Her body was unsteady but still whole and strong.

The coffin to which she had finally become accustomed sat a few feet away from her. She could rest and leave the debris to the animals. Or she could go to the river and wash the blood from her clothes.

She sank down onto her knees and knew her strength wasn't as great as she had supposed. Fearing that she would pass into her dark sleep here, just beyond her coffin, she forced herself to stand and move in the direction of the coffin.

The portrait on the coffin was once again stained. Droppings from trees dusted the lid. She saw that the coffin was encircled by ants. Curious, hungry, and vigilant, the ants sensed death.

"Wrong place, fellows. There's a whole body over there, and somewhere in the bushes you'll find Andre's empty head." She swept her shoe across the line of ants, sending them into disarray. "Stupid fools," she muttered.

She used some spit to wipe the portrait clean and took time to admire herself before opening the coffin.

"I become more attractive in each new life," she said as she stepped onto the yellowed satin. She would be glad when she could return to her life as a harlot. The choice suited her disposition and beauty.

She lay down to rest, carrying the lid down with her. In the dark her body relaxed into the old woman she knew she truly was. In the dark no one could catch her in her lies. In the dark her poisonous, maniacal smile frightened no one.

Chapter Forty-three

Cecelia watched the flow of putrid flesh climb her arm, spreading in amoebic motion, covering the tiny hairs and shading her skin. The ooze felt neither hot nor cold; instead she barely sensed the foreign matter on her flesh. Fingerlike projections wrapped around her forearm. She felt a yank pulling her closer to the coffin.

"We must join completely for this to take," the old vampire's voice whispered inside her head. "I must seep into you and you must allow me entrance. Don't block a single molecule that will pass into your flesh. Let me seep deep into your core."

A slight movement at the threshold forced her to turn her head in that direction. Michael had taken a step forward and stood with his charred mouth agape. His eyes were wide and reflective with forming tears.

"Are you crying for me, Michael?"

"Yes. And I cry for all of us who will have to bear the burden of your mistake."

"No mistake, child," the vampire whispered. "Fate has united us. Fate and Sade."

She returned her attention to the coffin.

"Sade may have changed since you last met him," she said. "He may be stronger than you remember. This won't be easy."

"Are you afraid of him, child? He never had power over me."

"Who locked you in this musty room inside that coffin?"

"I did. I lapsed but once. My attentions were stolen by a woman. A woman who lies with me in this room. She brought me here. Sade only took advantage of a single moment. She stole my desires, my love, and my hate. They all lie at rest with her now. But your body, blood, mind, and spirit will return all those emotions to me. And I will be stronger because I've learned what true treason is."

Cecelia's skin began to tingle. Prickles of pain dabbed at her pores. The old vampire was forcing entry. She looked into the thing's eyes and saw the small insects floundering about. They were losing their host and knew it. The insects scattered, crawling out of the eye sockets and down the vampire's molten cheeks.

She pulled back from the coffin, but the vampire kept hold of her.

"No!" the vampire shrieked inside her head. "No! Do not desert me. My time has melted into an eternity lying here. My thoughts skim the past, not believing in a future."

"Those dreadful insects that infect your body, will you also be passing those to me?"

"They will stay with my rotted flesh, for my body is now their home."

"They seem to be swarming to the surface of your body," she said, seeing insects crawl from every visible opening on the vampire's flowing flesh. So many that they crawled over each other in their panic.

"Back away from him slowly." Michael spoke in a calm voice.

"He has my forearm, Michael. I can't break away from him now. His grasp is too powerful." Her arm had become numb where it was covered with the ancient vampire's flesh.

"Give me your free hand," Michael said.

"You'll join us?"

"No. I'll help you escape."

She looked down at her hand, the smooth, creamy skin that belonged to her. She turned the palm up and studied the lines and wrinkles, and remembered the damaged flesh of her other hand.

She heard Michael move behind her. He reached around and placed one of his stubs in the center of her palm.

"Grip it tightly," he whispered.

She stood between two mutilated bodies and was asked to which she would give herself.

"You're not strong enough, Michael."

Michael's charred lips touched her ear.

"He isn't as strong as he says. Grab hold of my stump and he will lose some of his power."

"What force will you give me, Michael?"

"None. But you will break the spell he has over you by showing him that you don't want this horrible thing to take place."

Her hand closed around the stump and her fingers stroked the charred flesh.

"He will take you into human weakness, child." The vampire seemed to almost speak out loud. His lips seemed to move with the words, or was it an illusion caused by the fleeing maggots? "You know the powers we vampires have. Think of the knowledge I will bring to you."

The flowing flesh moved up to her elbow. The bone seemed to collapse.

"What the hell is happening?" she asked.

"He's destroying your body bit by bit. Clasp my stump hard and I'll help you move away from him."

She did. Michael moved slowly toward the door. She followed as far as she could.

"He won't let me go, Michael. He's holding fast."

"You must pull away even if it means losing the arm."

The arm was no longer hers to use. With a loud scream she pulled back and watched the molten flesh separate. Her arm was still covered, but the flesh was no longer connected to the body leaning against the side of the coffin.

"Foolish child," the old vampire called. "If you leave me here with the others you will be lost."

"Come, let's get out of this room before the others take up his battle."

She knew Michael was right and found herself leaning against the blanket that rested over his shoulders. By the time they reached the threshold, the thing in the coffin was thrashing about, limbless itself since she now wore his arm's flesh.

Chapter Forty-four

Madeline sat on the stone step of the caretaker's house. Justin saw her plush red lips smile broadly when he appeared.

"I know a shortcut," she said.

"And couldn't tell me?"

"If you had let me come with you, I would have." The wrinkled linen dress she wore hid her legs.

"You chased Mel away?"

"Why don't you trust me?" she asked, her smile sagging into a pout.

"Where is he, Madeline?"

"He wasn't here when I arrived."

"Do you have any idea where he might've gone?"

She shook her head, and her red locks flew in all directions.

"He should be in bed, but he's an old man, and perhaps he couldn't sleep."

Justin looked around at the trees and the path leading to the cathedral.

"He might even be inside the church praying," she suggested.

Justin chuckled. "You think he is a holy man."

"Age brings one closer to God and faith."

Justin started down the path leading to the cathedral. He sensed Madeline trailing behind him.

The massive brick building looked weaker somehow. The statuary stood vulnerable. The stained-glass windows were dim in the moonlight. The heavy front doors offered no opposition to his shove.

"It feels different," she said.

"The cathedral is losing the battle."

"What battle?"

He walked down the center aisle of the cathedral and tried to make out the hush voices that floated in the air. Even the vampires feared whatever had happened or was happening; he didn't know which. He remembered the flirtatious vampire, Cleo, her body naked above him in his daydream. He called out to her with his mind.

"I smell decay, Justin. An animal must have died in here."

He felt Madeline pull closer to him for protection.

He heard a woman crying. Could that be Cleo? He called out to her again with his mind.

"The smell is so bad that they'll have to cancel services until they find the animal." Madeline reached her arms around Justin's waist.

The crying woman attempted to speak, but the words came out garbled with her sobs.

Justin shouted Cecelia's name, frightening Madeline into springing away from him.

"Vampires can't cry. They don't feel sorrow the way humans do. Unless . . ."

"Vampires? You're speaking of the plague," Madeline said.

Justin turned to look at her.

"It's an old tale about the plague of vampires that attempted to suck Albi dry. Only a tale. How did you know of it?"

"I have to free the vampires, Madeline. Even they are suffering such sorrow that they cry again as if human."

"There are no vampires, Justin. It's only a tale."

"Has Sade ever tasted your blood?"

Madeline drew farther away from Justin.

"Sometimes he behaves strangely."

"He likes it when you bleed. Doesn't he, Madeline? He savors every drop you shed."

"Because he's cruel and needs to imitate his ancestor."

"No, Madeline. He really *is* Sade. He has survived all these years on blood."

"Blood and fear." Sade stood at the back of the cathedral. "I like to watch the victims' eyes darken with terror. Their hands tremble and fall away from my chest as they succumb. They lose all sense of the use of language and remain silent as I approach."

217

Sade began walking down the center aisle toward Justin and Madeline.

Justin pushed Madeline to the side and told her to run. She tripped on the leg of a pew and fell to her knees.

"Do you want to join them, Justin?" Sade pointed to the walls of the cathedral.

"Then it's true," Madeline whispered.

"You've put Cecelia inside these walls," Justin said.

"And many more. They didn't know how to act in public. This is a common practice, to shut away the deviants." Sade paused and took a seat to Justin's right.

"You drive them mad," Justin said.

"Not directly. They drive themselves crazy with their hopes for escape and their ill will toward me.

"Stand, Madeline. You look so pitiful on the floor."

Madeline obeyed.

"Allow her to leave," Justin demanded.

"Am I forcing her to stay? Perhaps it is simply my charisma that holds her." Sade smiled at Madeline and gestured that she should take a seat.

Justin reached out and grabbed her arm.

"Leave."

"She doesn't want to leave, Justin. And I surmise that I am not the cause of her desire to stay. The silly girl has become your lapdog. You don't even know what he is."

"He's kinder and gentler than you."

218

"Only because he is confused. He's unsure of what world he should be living in. Isn't that right, Justin?"

"I live to rid the world of the pain you and all your kind feel."

"That is good. You should put a positive twist on what you do. Makes it easier to live with, I bet. He kills, Madeline. He wants to kill everyone locked inside this cathedral except for one."

"I'm going to find a way to release them."

"And they will scatter before you have the chance to do away with a quarter of them. But let's not forget that you'll also be distracted, looking for one in particular."

"Do you love her?" Madeline asked Justin.

"Jealousy; that's a weakness you should never reveal to your men, Madeline. No, Justin would cringe from such an emotion."

"Where is the entrance that will take me inside these walls?" Justin let go of Madeline and moved closer to Sade.

"I could take you there and lock you in. But I fear that just being with Cecelia may make the situation easier. Maybe even for Cecelia." Sade shrugged. "Hmmm. But I might give you Cecelia for Marie. Tell me where she hides her coffin, Justin, and I will consider taking you to Cecelia."

"I hate Marie, but I don't trust you, Sade. You won't keep your end of any bargain."

"I am far more trusting than you. I am willing to lead you to the entrance; at that point you can reveal Marie's whereabouts to me."

"He won't take you directly to Cecelia, Justin. You won't know whether he has taken you to where she is."

"Madeline! I'm surprised that you'd put such a hideous idea in Justin's head."

"I've been in your bed. I've watched you lie to so many, including me. I've never seen Paris—only the lust that causes you to be so cruel."

"The child has always wanted to go to Paris. Like a misguided parent, I have encouraged her dream."

"Give Cecelia back to me."

"Do you own her, Justin? If so, you should take better care of your possessions, or choose them more wisely. Tell me where Marie is, and take the chance that I'll give you back your Cecelia."

"He'll never do it," Madeline said, clinging to Justin's left arm.

"It is Marie I want, Justin."

"And what will you do to her when you find her?" Justin asked.

"Why should you care?"

"She's my mother."

Sade laughed.

"She stole your mother's body. Marie is far more powerful than I thought, or your mother was terribly frail."

"My mother was staked."

"You killed your mother?" Madeline's voice quivered with her doubt.

"You realize that Marie can do more harm to your mother than I could? You talk of release, Justin. Allow me to free your mother from this pervert. Your mother will finally be at peace, and Marie will be forced to take her energy in search of another form that will bring her to me."

"She would be a fool to seek you out again," Justin said.

"She is."

"What will you do with my mother's body?"

"Ash."

"I'll never see her again."

"Oh, please. Can you stand looking at her now, under the spell of that wicked woman? Marie will never give up your mother's body willingly. Where is Marie's coffin, Justin? Tell me, and I will perform two favors for you. I will take you to the entrance into which I sent Cecelia. Secondly, I will free your mother from Marie's influence."

Chapter Forty-five

"Get it off me," Cecelia screamed as the molten flesh began to harden.

Michael had slammed the door to the vampire vault. The crucifix affixed to the door seemed to tremble with the force.

With her free hand Cecelia reached over to rip the vampire's flesh from her arm but was stopped by Michael.

"No. What if it spreads to your other hand?"

"Cut off my arm!" Her voice rose in panic. "Do something to stop this thing!"

The elderly vampire's flesh weighed down her arm. Ribbons of live flesh percolated amid the flesh that was hardening.

"We need a tool to pry it off," Michael said, looking around the empty corridor. "Come on; we must move away from this place. There is nothing we can use here."

Cecelia ran toward the crucifix. She raised her arm to the symbol of Christ and let the old vampire's flesh touch the feet of the statue. She tried to rub off the flesh using the pedestal on which the figure's feet rested. A cry rose from inside the vault, as if someone had been set afire. Her free hand reached out to touch the figure's painted-on blood. When her fingers touched the surface they felt wet. She took her hand away and saw a damp red stain covering her fingertips.

"Michael," she said.

He moved closer to her.

"The paint must be coming off," he said.

She brought her fingertips to her lips and tasted blood.

"No. This is my punishment," she said, indicating her arm, where the old vampire's flesh still clung.

Michael attempted to pull her away from the door.

"They're whispering, Michael. Can't you hear them? They're whispering about us."

"I don't hear anything, Cecelia. Please, Cecelia, flee with me. I don't want to leave you here alone."

Cecelia rested her ear against the door.

"They want us to come back. They'll make amends for what they've done if we return to them."

"That's only what they think you want to hear, Cecelia." Michael reached out a stump and almost touched the elderly vampire's flesh. "I can't stay here

223

with you. If you insist on remaining with them, I can do nothing else for you."

She raised her hand and touched his face. Ash now coated the bloodstain on her fingertips.

"I'll be taking a part of him with me into the outside world."

"That's if we ever get outside. This flesh need not have any power over you, Cecelia. It doesn't have a brain of its own. It mates with your flesh for survival only."

"I would rather meld with your charred flesh, Michael. But all your flesh does is come off in my hand in black specks, and when I rub my fingertips together . . ." She demonstrated. "It falls to the floor."

Michael spread his blanket wide and wrapped it around Cecelia, drawing her into his arms and against his chest. As he took a step, she moved with him. Only once did she turn to face the vault, and that was in answer to a cry of Sade's name.

With me a vampire, you a witch,
Bite and suck at me till I cry;
I'll suck and bite you till you die,
If need be, my opponent: bitch!
                    —PAUL VERLAINE, *"Sadism"*

Chapter Forty-six

Terror dragged Marie up from her sleep. Was it the sun? Was it fire? She felt vulnerable to some wickedness. But she was so tired and needed rest to recuperate from the frenzy that had caused her to kill her own minion.

She opened her eyes and saw that Sade sat on the edge of her coffin, backlighted by the sun. He had managed to drag her coffin out of the shadow of the trees into open space and had opened the lid.

His head was covered by a broad-brimmed hat, the type commonly used by the local farmers. His hands he kept shielded by his own fully clothed shadow.

" 'Morning, dear Mother-in-law." He smiled and reached out a hand to help her up. She spat into his hand.

"A lady such as you should always carry a handkerchief. Do you have one that I can borrow?" Upon receiving no answer, Sade brushed the palm of his hand against the coffin's satin.

"Get back," she demanded, feeling the limits set by the coffin in which she lay.

"I offer assistance and you rail at me. Perhaps I am here to make amends."

"Never. I will not move until you back away."

"It would have been so easy to kill you while you slept. It took a lot of energy on my part to rouse you. I could have cut off your head and staked your heart in less time."

"You didn't because you want to torture me."

"True. I could have set fire to the coffin and hoped that you would awake to the roaring flames. Hope isn't good enough. I want to be sure you experience every moment of your demise. I'm sure you recall the last time I destroyed you. I bet you can even feel the pain as if it were happening again. Have you dreamt of that destruction, Marie? Ah, I have. And it has given me much pleasure." Sade rose to his feet and ripped the lid from the coffin. "Inferior. American-made, but not mass-produced, at least."

He shredded the wood in several swipes.

"By the way, it's a shame what you did to Andre. He was never a favorite, but he did my bidding. Most of the time."

Marie sat up in the coffin. Her body still ached from the strenuous night she had had. Andre's blood clung to her flesh in remembrance of the event. Her hands shook slightly from fatigue or fear; she couldn't decide which.

"Come out, Marie, and view the evening's chaos."

Marie stepped out of the coffin and saw first the mangled body of Andre lying beneath one of the trees. Last night she had seen him as Sade and vented all the rage that had been building inside her over the centuries. Did she have the capacity to expend such energy now, when she really had Sade standing near her?

"This is a far better body than the old one," Sade said, rubbing the back of his hand against her right cheek. She pulled away and turned her back on him. "A body that easily seduced me. I am grateful to you, Marie, for being so set in your ways. I almost took you to bed, except there was something so familiar in your speech, in your actions, in the way you fed. Hungry, gluttonous. That is what you are, Marie.

"Did you know Liliana tried to come back into this world?" He leaned closer to her to whisper. "Only briefly did she survive. I saw to that."

"Liliana, your favorite. Difficult for me to believe you would prevent her return."

He walked around and stood in front of her.

"No one will ever endanger me and survive, Marie."

Should she fight him or flee? She was too weak to succeed at either.

"You want me to make the first move," she said. "You want me to cling to this body. Go mad with the knowledge that I will lose again. What if I peacefully accept your verdict? Will the pleasure you take be lessened? I think so. The struggle is what makes your life worthwhile. Defeating those who would be independent of you. Destroy me now, Sade. You taught me that there is no end. You've made it easier for me to face destruction. Thank you."

She watched his eyes darken, his lips form an involuntary sneer, his hands ball up into fists, his inability to verbalize all the anger he felt.

After several seconds his body relaxed and his lips jerked into a smile.

"You are a saint, Marie. You toss yourself to the lions for your own godlike pride."

"And you blanch at the thought, Sade. Even under the protection of that hat I can see the frustration show in the whiteness of your flesh." Feeling far better, Marie stood taller and looked down at the clothing she wore. "At least you won't be ruining a good dress. I already did that last night."

"There is no one to miss you, Marie. No one to cry. Justin gave you up to me."

"Not a surprise, since I almost killed him last night. You can say nothing to weaken me. I gain strength the more you try."

Sade reached out and took hold of Marie's arms.

"Woman, I cannot think of any torture that would be sufficient to make you suffer for what you have done. And yes, you are right, I wanted you to fight. I wanted to defeat you and have you know it." He wheeled her around, flung her to the ground, and dragged her to Andre's body. He grabbed a piece of Andre's flesh and forced it inside Marie's mouth.

"What does it taste like, Marie?"

She choked and spat it into his face.

Sade's right arm held her in place while his left hand forced the top of her body back. She heard the crunch of her spine.

"Perhaps I should keep you as a plaything that I can mangle every night. Just when you begin to heal, I can inflict the same injury over again. I can take handfuls of your flesh and feed it every day to the carnivores that live in the woods. I can make you understand what weakness is. What humility is, my dear Marie." He dropped her body to the ground. "Do I want you out of my control?" He shook his head. "I want you wounded and helpless."

Chapter Forty-seven

"He may have lied to you, Justin. She may not be here."

Justin looked down at Madeline.

"He was right. Jealousy doesn't suit a companion of mine. You heard from Sade what I am, and still you persist in shadowing me. I can never be a true man for you. Would you want me to father misshapen children? That is, if you survived the mating."

"I don't want to go back to Sade."

"You need not decide between me and Sade. There are human men who would love you who have never seen what Sade and I have experienced."

Madeline bent down and picked up a stone. She threw it at the silvery wall, where it vanished into the convolutions that shimmered brightly.

"The wall eats what is fed to it. It will eat you just the way it has eaten others."

"The wall is an entrance, Madeline. Perhaps it doesn't allow egress, but it does not eat one up."

"You don't know that." She pouted and rubbed her nose with the back of her hand.

The childlike gesture softened Justin's resolve.

"You would be better off if it did eat me." From somewhere she had touched he found the ability to chuckle. Her scream caused him to stop.

Looking to his right he saw Mel, the caretaker, running as fast as his old man's legs could carry him. He was obviously aiming to send Justin through the wall, but Justin easily took a step back out of the old man's path. Madeline panicked and reached out to shove Mel away from Justin and into the wall.

The old man didn't vanish as quickly as the stone. He lingered, glued to the wall, slipping into the sparkling, silvery tremble of earth. His face was buried deep in the soil while the back of his head lolled from side to side, attempting to dislodge itself.

Too stunned to react, Justin and Madeline watched Mel slowly sink deeper, until only the worn-down heel of his boot was visible; then even that disappeared.

"I didn't . . ." Madeline raised her hands to her lips. "I thought he would hurt you. I wanted to stop him."

"You did." Justin couldn't find forgiveness for someone who would banish him to a lifetime in prison. "Tell me, do you believe the wall ate him?

Or is it possible he now exists in a world hidden from us?"

"Don't follow him," Madeline said, wary of the way he hovered near the wall.

"What do you think he will find, Madeline? Certainly not peace, but most certainly death."

Chapter Forty-eight

"Come along, Cecelia. Don't look back."

"But Michael, they want revenge, and so do I. Revenge on our common enemy, Sade. If I stay—"

"If you stay you'll lose yourself completely." He dragged her down one corridor after another until they were in sight of the entrance wall. On the floor lay a bundle of clothes, almost lifeless except that a sleeve seemed to jerk and a shoe seemed to tumble to its side.

"I think Sade has added to the number of his guests," Michael said.

"It's the old man, Michael. The caretaker of the cemetery. Remember him?"

"He's a strange old goat. Keeps to himself. His best friends are the dead."

"That includes me, Michael." Cecelia pushed herself out of the cocoon in which Michael had enveloped her. "Mel, were you sent by Sade? Did he send a message?"

The body on the floor rolled over, hiding his face, as if he could protect himself from the vampire's cruelty.

"If not to bring a message, then why would Sade send you?" she asked.

She knelt next to Mel, and without thinking reached out the hand that was covered with the elder's flesh. She touched his white hair and noted how clumps of it became attached to her hand. Mel screamed as she pulled her hand away to show Michael the intertwining. A bald patch was left on the top of Mel's head.

"It combines with anyone, Michael. I wasn't specially chosen." She flexed her fingers in awe of the power of the elderly vampire. "Do you think his flesh would have covered me? I would grow into a giant monster with flesh swelling up on all parts of my body. How strong I would have become! How powerful. I could have joined with Sade and known what he thinks and how his flesh can delight in torture."

She looked back at Mel and saw that he was sitting up now, facing her, one of his hands resting on the bald patch.

"Get away, you evil thing. The Lord will protect me." He searched through his pockets until he found a black set of rosary beads.

She noted that the beads were plastic, cheap. No fancy golden cross dangling from them. Instead a plain, figureless cross had been reattached to the set of beads with sewing thread.

"Let him be, Cecelia. If he was sent by Sade, it must mean he has earned disfavor."

"Or perhaps he is here to show us the way out, Michael. Where do we go, Mel? Is it up through the vent somehow? Or are there magic words that will turn this brick wall into the silvery wall it is on the other side?"

"He'll never let any of you out." Mel's voice spoke with more spirit than he had reason to have.

"Then why send you?" she asked.

"He isn't the cause for my being here. It is that stupid girl, Madeline."

"She is nearby. If I touch the wall, will I feel her presence?" Michael rushed to the wall and rested a stump against it.

"What power protected you from the fire?" Mel asked Michael.

"He's not a vampire, Mel. He's human like you. Only not as appetizing as you appear to be." She smiled at him.

Mel shoved himself farther back, away from Cecelia.

"Don't be afraid, Mel. Not of me. You took me into your cottage and offered me food and a place to stay. The wrong kind, granted, but still you made an attempt to befriend me."

"I don't sense Madeline. I can't hear her voice or hear her moving about." Michael turned and faced Mel. "Are you sure you aren't lying? She isn't there, is she? You want me to believe. You want me to regain hope."

"I don't know who you are, but she is with the half-breed. She has taken to protecting him."

"Justin is nearby," Cecelia said. "She was protecting Justin; that's why she forced you through the wall."

Cecelia stood and joined Michael at the wall.

"How do we push through this, Mel?"

Silence answered her question until she heard the old man stumble as he tried to run from them. Cecelia took after him, her weighted arm hampering her speed only slightly. She reached out with her good hand and pulled him down on the floor. They toppled together, over and over, with Mel trying to free himself.

In order to keep him still Cecelia reached out with her other arm and circled his neck. She could feel his pulse, could hear his heartbeat, could smell his fear. The flesh on her arm stuck to the flesh on his neck like taffy. His pulling from her did nothing to disconnect them.

"You've been Sade's minion, Mel. I see it in your mind. I see you fawn on him, as if he was a great man. As if he could return your past to you. He can't do that, Mel. I can. I can give you the eternal life that Sade would refuse you."

"No, I don't want to be a vampire. I would rather die."

Cecelia looked deeply into Mel's eyes and saw he had spoken the truth. She leaned over and bit into his carotid, sucking away the life he had freely offered.

Finished, she lifted her head to Michael and smiled.

"I am reborn," she said.

"You've killed him." Michael stared down at her. "He was only here by mistake, Cecelia. Sade didn't send him for your salvation. Madeline . . ." Why had Madeline so cruelly sent Mel to his end?

"He's nothing, Michael. Only a bag of flesh. Putty flesh," she said as she saw the rubbery display of his face.

She had managed to touch his face with the weighted hand and softened Mel's flesh.

"I don't recognize him, Michael. Who is he again? Remind me."

"The cemetery caretaker," Michael said in a flat voice.

She played with Mel's features as if she were sculpting.

"I can make him look like Sade."

"But he never will be."

"So sad. We could have played at defeating Sade. The bones in his cheeks have broken. The cartilage in his nose has flattened. His lips have disappeared. He's worthless!" She lunged backward, separating herself from Mel's dead body.

She looked above her head and saw the vent. Rising to her feet, she tried to hear words spoken in the church. All she heard was Michael breathing. His breath shallow, she caught a rasping sound deep in his lungs. Pneumonia, she thought.

Both sets of her fingers slipped between the narrow slits of the vent, one set of fingers looking pudgy and fat from the other's flesh. But the flesh slid back on bone to accommodate the size of the opening. She pulled hard. The vent shivered but didn't budge.

"This is the way out, Michael."

"Even if you could rip away that vent, you would never fit through the channel."

"I could make myself very small. I could dislocate my joints. Spread out my weight so that I was elongated into a stream of flesh. A river of revenge. See me climb, Michael. See me reach the marble floor of the church. Oooh! So cold. And Lottie is there, waiting for me. She's pointing the way to Justin. I only have to follow her lead. Justin will make it better. He will clear my mind of memories I never lived."

"You have some of the remembrances of the elderly vampire and the caretaker."

"Is that why I don't recognize faces? The names are peculiar. But the screams are familiar. They all die the same."

"The victims?"

"Some are volunteers. They only fear when the end draws near. Then their doubts surface. They hold to the warmth of life for as long as they can."

239

She lowered her arms and looked at Michael. "I'm very cold. I can never be warm again. Even fire chills me. The delicate lapping of each flame darkening my flesh just makes me shiver. Hold me, Michael."

He took a step back from her.

"Hold me like before. Wrap me in your blanket. My misshapen hand and arm I'll keep under the cloth. I won't infect you, Michael." She took a few steps in his direction.

She saw him look down at her swollen arm.

"It smells bad. It smells of age, of disease, and of . . ." She halted, trying to put words to the additional scent in the air.

"What do you think, Michael?" she said, offering her arm for him to smell.

"You smell of Satan's touch."

Chapter Forty-nine

"And this is the storeroom. Fairly empty. Centuries ago it would have been full of provisions for a full-size family and its servants. But I have little use for it. My servants don't like to stay in residence. They prefer commuting to their cottages."

"But they don't know what you are." Marie's voice was weak.

"I'm a wealthy eccentric who pays good salaries." Sade ran a finger across a dusty ledge.

"What food there is can all be kept in the kitchen. They buy fresh every day. You remember how particular I was about food."

Marie wished he would stop moving about the room. Her nausea was becoming worse.

"I shall confine you here. I doubt any rats bother to visit, since nothing but a few canned foods are left here. If they do come, it will give you something to suck on until I decide to bring you some token blood."

"I cannot sleep without my coffin."

"But I made such a mess of it, didn't I? Ripping apart that lid so inconsiderately. I don't apologize, Marie, but I do regret that it will probably shorten your existence. The healing process will be difficult. I'll have to parse out my punishment more carefully than I would have wanted."

"At least bring me fresh clothes."

"There'll come a time when you will be glad to have these bloody rags to suck on."

"The servants will find the bodies."

"One already has. What will her family think? Ah, well, I do not plan on staying long."

"So there is an end to my torment."

"Maybe I'll pack you in a trunk and send you by boat to my next destination."

"Which is?"

Sade shrugged.

"You've spoiled my comfortable stay in Albi, Marie. I do thank you, though, for ensuring that I did not find myself in a fanciful love. Madeline would have destroyed me if you hadn't tried."

"Love will be your downfall, Louis. You long too much for someone dear. The flesh you take is no substitute."

He laughed.

"I will leave you here to crawl around the room."

"I heal as we speak."

"Yes, you do, but slower than you would like. That is why you wanted your coffin, isn't it, Marie? You could lay yourself in the folds of the satin and sleep would blank out the pain of healing vertebrae."

"It will never end. I will seek you out and you will pray I do not catch you. If you can pray at all."

Sade squatted down to her level.

"Neither of us pray, Marie. We fight to exist because God would wish to destroy us."

Chapter Fifty

"Do you think they're still on the other side of the wall?"

"Who?" Cecelia asked, still holding out her arm toward Michael.

"Madeline and your friend Justin." Michael turned away from her and faced the wall. "Do you think one of us could reach them? Tell them we're here?"

"What good will that do? I can barely remember Justin now anyway. There are all these dead bodies being dumped in the ground. Some of them are still alive. I see a hand move, a finger twitch. I swear, a chest is heaving. And they're dressed in rags. But I don't know them, Michael."

Michael looked at Cecelia and saw her glassy eyes looking into the past—the vampire's past.

"We must see if we can break through this wall," he said.

"Why? You said you never wanted to return to the outside world. Madeline will think you're ugly."

Michael banged his stump against the brick wall. The healing flesh broke open and blood trickled down his arm. Cecelia slipped under his arm and smiled up at him.

"You should be sated by now," he said.

"I am." Cecelia's voice was airy and light. Her eyes had lost the glitter of recollection, and she seemed wizened.

"I thought you wanted to communicate with Justin."

"I do." She began to rub a finger across her bloodied lips. "Most of all I want Sade. You bleed a lot. How can that be? In battle you must have lost so much blood. Yet you continue to bleed."

Michael pulled back from the wall and Cecelia.

"I hear them coming, Michael." Her eyes were wide and stared straight into Michael's face.

"Who?"

"The others. All the others who want to taste you. They can smell you now. Even in your ugliness your blood will appeal to their hunger. Let me make you my own, and then no one else can have you."

"Part of the ancient vampire is talking through you, Cecelia."

Her good hand reached down to her misshapen arm, and she gouged out a piece of flesh. She went deep enough to draw her own blood.

"Taste me and I will drink from you, Michael."

"You need to keep me separate from you. You need my guidance against this freakish vampire who has penetrated your flesh."

"Only a small part of him stays with me. Most of his spirit writhes in his casket, cursing me."

Her eyes caught sight of a wraith with matted hair tied in ribbons of various colors.

"The woman at the foot of the centaur painting."

The wraith was wrapped in torn rags that barely covered her body.

"Mama sent me here to live," the wraith said.

"You must have been a very bad girl," Cecelia said.

Michael slowly turned around to face the intruder.

"Mama doesn't miss me. *He* told me so." The wraith's eyes looked down at Michael's bleeding stump.

"Did you smell lunch, my dear?" said Cecelia.

"Who is she?" Michael asked.

"I thought a papier-mâché vampire had destroyed her. I met her kneeling before a bloodied centaur and left her to turn to dust as she had done to another like herself."

"Mama was so beautiful when she was young." Slowly the wraith moved toward Michael.

"Stop!" he shouted.

The wraith cowered before him.

Cecelia giggled at the sight.

"Such a domineering man, Michael. I never thought to see anyone frightened by your voice. But perhaps you have opened her eyes to your ugliness, and she shivers from the sight of you."

"Mama," the wraith said. "Mama will never come for me now. She talks to many of the others but never calls my name."

"What is your name?" asked Cecelia.

"Anna. Little Anna. Mama brushed my hair, telling me how pretty I was. The prettiest little girl. Her only child. Her only sin."

"Lottie," Cecelia said.

"They call her Lottie now."

"What was she called before?" Cecelia's voice lowered to a whisper.

"Mama."

Chapter Fifty-one

"Justin, if you go through this wall of earth and survive, how will you help your Cecelia? You too will be Sade's prisoner. That is what he wants."

He looked at Madeline and knew she spoke the truth. Somehow he had to tear down a wall, any wall, to get inside the corridors. He guessed the wall in front of him was the hardest to destroy. The silvery, wavering earth could adjust to any kind of onslaught.

"We must break down the walls from the inside of the church."

"That is desecration, Justin. You would be struck down by the Lord."

"He entertains far worse mockery within his home. Why doesn't He strike down the vampires imprisoned here? Why doesn't He strike down Sade when he dares to come near the holy walls that are supposed to protect His church?"

"Don't bait the Lord, Justin."

"He has left the job up to me."

"What job?"

"Destroying the mutants He has created."

"Maybe they have a purpose in this world."

"To bleed the masses? No, Madeline, there can be no sacred reason for the vampires. They give nothing back to man. They suck bodies into hulks and never even bury the dead."

"All this is so new to me. I mean, I had heard of it only as a legend. I associated no truth to the concept of vampires. As children we ran through the graveyard chasing each other down, challenging each other to be the last to leave, not stopping to close the rickety gates behind us."

"The cemetery is safe," Justin reminded Madeline. "It is the church itself that is the source of pain."

"The cathedral protects us by containing the horror."

"No, it merely limits the vampires' movements until they can be released in an angry rage."

"What do you think happened to the caretaker?" Madeline's gaze shifted from the wall to Justin.

"If he is still alive, he trembles with terror. If he was lucky and died, then he is at peace."

Madeline drew close to Justin, almost touching him.

"Do you want to die?"

"It isn't my time yet. I have much to accomplish."

"Are you afraid of your own death?"

"I am half-vampire. I destroy God's creatures. I have partaken in sordid acts and deprived escape for others. What do you think, Madeline?"

"You're terrified. Is that why you kill?" Her right hand softly stroked his cheek.

"I need a reason to exist."

"And all this hunting down of mutants and vampires is the only reason why you exist?"

Justin took her hand in his.

"What other reason would I have to be here?"

Madeline stood on tiptoe and was barely able to kiss Justin's cheek where she had been caressing him.

"Making love is another reason to live, Justin. Make love to me."

His hand tightened around hers. He almost stopped breathing when she spoke the words.

"And when I am done, what do I do with your body? Dig a grave for you just outside this cave? Carry you to your parents' doorstep and beg their mercy? Or simply be the coward and cast you into the Tarn?"

"At least you didn't suggest feeding me to this wall." She smiled at him. "What makes you think I'll die from your love?"

"Other women have."

"Am I just another woman to you, Justin? Am I not someone you wish to keep with you forever?" She leaned her body against his.

He felt her breasts softly touch his chest. She used her free hand to find his erection.

"I care about you too much, Madeline, to make love to you."

"Is that because you lust after me so much that you would lose control of your senses?"

Her hand was warm and expert. Of course she would know how to bring a man to gratification; Sade had taught her well.

He pulled away from her and let go of her hand.

"I am here to find Cecelia and bring her home with me. She and I are meant to be together. You follow me at your own peril."

Justin turned and walked toward the cave's opening.

Chapter Fifty-two

Sade paced the front hall of his mansion. He noted the scuff marks on the floor, the cracked first step of the marble staircase, the dust covering the portraits on the walls, and especially the blotch of sunlight that he had detoured around too many times. Rather like slow dancing with Marie, he thought. It would be so easy to draw the curtain blocking the sun for the rest of the daylight hours. Why did he insist upon keeping Marie as a floodlight in his life?

Slowly wearing her down into a helpless creature would only set his own life in turmoil. Move on and forget the woman, he told himself. Destroy her in such a way that there won't be a speck of her to regenerate.

He wondered whether Justin and Cecelia had been reunited, and how Justin would like the claustrophobic corridors of the cathedral. How would a half-breed fare among insane vampires who knew nothing but hunger? Sade smiled to himself.

And Madeline . . . How would he deal with Madeline? She would come back to him begging for mercy. Tears flooding her eyes as she wondered at Justin's poor taste in selecting a vampire over herself. But he would leave her behind in this town. The closest she would ever come to Paris was when she lay in Sade's bed with the assortment of visitors. The woman was a peasant and belonged tied to the bogs and spongy earth of Albi.

Mel and Lottie could watch over the cathedral's guests. When she was ready to die, Lottie would ache for her daughter. Ache for the years they spent apart, and most of all for sacrificing her daughter's soul.

"Henri," Sade shouted.

He watched the man enter the room and admired the leather ensemble clinging to his body.

"Do you remember Marie from Paris?"

"Yes, sir." Henri's eyes were hooded.

"I'm going to throw a party in her honor. She seemed taken with you ever since the first day she arrived here and you slacked her thirst."

"She was with a young man."

"Yes, Henri. He will not be joining the party."

"There are rumors that they both left the mansion."

"Marie is back, and if her young friend does return, he'll be invited to the party. I want you to call some friends down from Paris. Don't invite any of the locals except for one: Madeline. Be sure she comes. Of course, if her family tells you she is missing, then we both can breathe a sigh of relief."

"Will this be a blood orgy?"

"Many may die, Henri, but you and I shall be leaving immediately after the festivities."

"It will be difficult for us to return if we leave the mansion in disarray."

"Marie has managed to sour my taste for this town. It will be a long time before I return."

"If at all?"

"I have reasons to come back. I have responsibilities to see to nearby."

"The cathedral?"

"And what do you know of the cathedral, Henri?" Sade saw the other man's body stiffen.

"Come, Henri, tell me what you have heard."

Sweat broke out across Henri's forehead.

"Only that you've been giving protection to this town through the cathedral."

"Have you ever known me to be a holy man?"

"No, Monsieur Sade. Only . . . There is a rumor that an evil from this town's past is contained within the walls of the cathedral."

"And what would I have to do with that?" Sade moved closer to Henri. He could smell the man's fear. "You stink, Henri. Haven't you bathed today?"

"I've been working out."

"No. That kind of sweat is different. This is a kind of skunk odor. Poor Henri, you are such a coward.

Often I wonder how you bear the pain that I mete out to you. Do you swallow your screams like gobs of phlegm? Does it ever sicken you? Are you ever angry with me, Henri? Answer freely in whatever order you choose."

Sade waited patiently, enjoying the building tension.

"Nothing that you will ever do will sicken me, Monsieur Sade."

"Delightful! Henri, you are baiting me to even greater heights of torture. And your screams, Henri. I've never heard your screams."

"I was taught not to fuss as a child."

"Not to fuss." Sade broke into laughter. "And are you ever angry at me?"

"You are the master."

"Ah, that means I can do anything and you will accept the bruising and cutting of the flesh, the bones broken, the degradation." Sade shook his head. "I don't believe that, Henri. I've seen the hatred in your eyes when I've permitted guests to use you as they like. You resent the punishment and love it. I will have a special surprise for you at the party."

Chapter Fifty-three

Michael kept banging his stump against the brick wall. Cecelia and Anna watched, seated together on the cement floor. Blood dripped from Michael's stump. Saliva dribbled down Anna's chin.

"He's human, Anna." The girl didn't react to Cecelia's comment. "He is quite vulnerable."

There were puddles of blood on the floor—fresh blood from Michael's veins and coagulated blood left over from Cecelia's feast. Anna got down on all fours and crawled toward the blood directly next to Michael's foot. He allowed his bloody stump to hang by his side while he attempted to overcome a bout of coughing. Anna reached out to place her upturned face directly under the dripping blood. A drop fell gently onto her lips, which opened wide to allow her tongue access to the salty taste. A few more drops fell directly into her mouth and she gargled with delight.

Cecelia noted how disconnected yet symbiotic the two figures were. Each caught in his own pain. One finding sustenance and the other motivated by the fear of such people as Anna. Motivated even though exhausted and ready to give in to death.

Anna became more bold and raised her head so that her lips could encircle the wound. Michael had stopped coughing and attempted to catch his breath, still oblivious to what Anna was doing. The soft sucking noise went unheard by Michael.

Cecelia wondered whether she should halt the exhibition or have mercy on Anna. Michael's death was only a short time away. In the meantime he could serve a purpose.

"What the hell!" Michael had come to his senses and pulled away from Anna.

Anna screeched and arched her back, as if ready to leap at him. He turned to run but stumbled over Mel's body. Anna flew through the air, driven by an energy that had not been apparent before. She landed on Michael and bared her teeth.

"Anna!" Cecelia called. "Mama would not approve."

Anna's mouth closed around the word *mama*. Michael reached out, threw Anna aside, and immediately stood.

"You bitch! You watched this happening and made no attempt to stop her until it was almost too late."

"We vampires must stick together, Michael. The ancient one taught me that."

"Was it so fascinating that you would have watched me die?"

"You were going to be too easy a kill for the girl. She needs practice. She needs to relearn her vampire skills. Perhaps we can try it again later."

"I saved you from the old vampire. I put myself in danger to free you from his spell."

"You've admitted that you don't have much to live for, Michael."

"I have yet to see Sade's destruction."

"Mama," a soft voice appealed.

Cecelia ran over to the vent and yelled, "Lottie. Lottie, your brat is inside here. Come and get her, Lottie."

"You're hoping that woman knows a way out. Why would she save you if she *did* come for her daughter?"

"Because I'm more powerful than that old lady. Get up, Anna."

Anna lay sprawled on top of Mel's body, her head cocked to the side, her eyes attempting to recognize the deformed face that lay before her.

"For heaven's sake. That's not Mama." Cecelia pulled Anna to her feet. "Mama is up through the vent. You must call to her. Tell her you're sorry and want to go home. Come on." Cecelia pulled the girl over to the vent. "Now yell 'Mama.'"

Anna's hands reached up and her fingers caressed the slopes of the vents. "Mama," she whispered.

"She's never going to hear you that way. Scream out her name. Demand her attention. Don't let her ignore you. Scream."

Anna's voice didn't seem to be able to rise above a soft pitch.

"Lottie! Your retarded daughter is here waiting for you. Yell, Anna, yell."

Frightened by Cecelia's passion, Anna pulled away and refused to speak.

"Damn, I bet if anyone besides Sade knows how to get us out it would be your mama."

Cecelia heard Michael fall against the brick wall and turned to see him slip down to the floor.

"Useless," she murmured. "A useless pair of misfits."

Chapter Fifty-four

"The voice. Sounds like Cecelia." Justin stopped in front of the statue of Christ as a child.

"I don't hear it," Madeline said.

"She's here. But she's calling for Lottie. Why would she do that?"

Justin placed both his palms against the wall, hoping to hear more clearly. Madeline ducked under one of his arms.

"Don't do this, Justin. She doesn't want you. She wants Sade's forgiveness. That has to be why she's yelling for that old woman."

"Cecelia!" Justin's voice echoed throughout the cathedral. The statue of the Christ Child seemed to throb from the resonance of Justin's voice.

Madeline pushed against his chest, attempting to win back his attention, but he ignored her.

"Don't let her destroy you, Justin. Forget her. You have me now. I need you more. Besides, I'm human, and you're more like me than like her."

Justin looked down at Madeline's face and saw the weariness of a missed night's sleep in the shadings under her eyes, her love in the sadness of the pupils of her eyes, her beauty being spoiled by his callousness.

"How many times must I try to drive you away? You think you can defeat me by always being present. I can't forget what I am, Madeline, especially when I look at you. You strengthen my resolve to banish all this horror before it can touch you."

"Sade has already laid hands on my body. What worse evil could follow that?"

"My making love to you." Justin stepped back, dropping his arms to his sides. "You and I aren't even of the same species."

"Ridiculous. You admitted to being half human and told me that Sade is a vampire. He made . . ." Madeline faltered. "He fucked me and didn't kill me."

Too weak to stand, Justin sat down in the pew behind him and covered his face with his hands.

"The vampire hunger possesses me when I make love. I can hear the woman's blood speed through her body as she becomes more excited." He placed his hands on the ledge before him. "I don't know how to take blood. I rip the woman's flesh and can't even feed after I've killed her." He looked up at Madeline. "Yes, I've only made love to a handful of women, but they're all dead." Tears rolled down his cheeks.

Madeline kneeled beside him and coaxed his hands into her own.

"It's because no one understood your powers or your needs. Had you told any of these women that you were half vampire?"

Justin shook his head. "I should have, because then they would have had a chance to save themselves."

"I know what you are and can help you control the passion." For the first time Justin saw her blush. "I have been trained in the ways of . . ." She hesitated. "I guess I've been trained to be a first-class prostitute."

Justin immediately freed his hands from hers and touched her lips, preventing her from continuing.

"An evil man took advantage of an innocent child. He filled your head with dreams and promised to fulfill every one. But he lied, Madeline. He lied about what your dreams should be and about the ways to attain them. I won't lie to you, Madeline. I can't give you anything like a normal life."

She pulled his hands away from her lips.

"I don't want to live and die the wife of the local postmaster. I want to learn new things, experience situations the people of this town could never dream of. Most of all, I want to be with a gentle, honest man who makes me feel the gamut of my emotions."

Justin smiled down at Madeline.

"Yes, I'm honest, but certainly not gentle. The humans and vampires I have destroyed would never nominate me a saint. Perhaps Cecelia is right."

"About . . . ?"

"My carrying out the devil's work."

Chapter Fifty-five

Marie was pissed. She had been lying on the cold marble floor for at least a day and a half and no one had bothered to see to her needs. Not even a rat had scurried into view to give her some hope of sustenance.

The outside shutters were closed on the one small window in the room, which was either stuck or locked somehow. The empty shelves had been covered with thin layers of newspapers as part of the closing up of the room. She had managed to pull some of the newspapers down and read about the Paris of eight years ago.

Her body ached and she needed her death sleep to repair it, but she didn't dare nod off without having her native soil nearby.

The sound of the lock turning and the squeak of the door opening made her come to attention. She recognized Sade's servant, Henri. He looked around the room, then entered to tidy the newspapers she had managed to scatter across the floor. He neither spoke to her nor gave her more than a glance. When he finished, he walked back outside to the hall and disappeared for a few minutes.

Could he be helping her to escape? she wondered. But what would it matter? She wouldn't get very far due to the damage Sade had done to her body. Still, she might as well try, since the final result was probably going to be the same either way.

As she gathered her energy, she was disappointed to hear Henri returning, and he seemed to be wheeling something down the hall. Seconds later he rolled a coffin into the room. A peasant's coffin, she thought. The wood was cheap and water-damaged; the craftsmanship was that of a novice.

Henri stopped in front of her and flipped open the lid. The coffin shook in its flimsiness.

"Monsieur Sade ordered that this be brought to you, madam."

"What for? Does he expect me to climb in without my home soil?"

"The soil you need has been added."

"American soil, idiot. My body now needs American soil."

"Yes, Monsieur Sade required that I go to the part of the forest where you had been keeping your coffin

265

and retrieve the soil from the old casket."

"How do I know you've collected American soil? This could be a way of destroying me."

"Sade said that I should tell you that he wouldn't give you such an easy way out."

Marie laughed.

"He wants to build me up so he can break my spine again, or perhaps find another way to maim me."

"He didn't share his intentions with me, madam. However, there is one more command that I must follow."

Marie's body stiffened. Had he sent this slave to finish her off? But no, he needed the pleasure of watching her be destroyed. She looked around the room, suspecting that she would find some indication of a hidden camera.

Henri kneeled down before her on the hard marble floor.

"Will you require me to lie down? I notice your injury has limited your ability to move about." He removed his leather vest, revealing the damp sweat that covered his chest, making his chest hair appear matted.

"Are you again offering yourself to me, as you did on the first day I arrived at this cursed mansion?"

"Yes, madam. Monsieur Sade said that you would heal faster with some nourishment."

"Is there a limit to how much blood I can drink?"

Henri looked into her face. She saw his shoulders and chest expand in defiance of her words, but he dared not give her an answer.

"Louis wouldn't care if you returned to him, would he, Henri? I bet he gave you a list of instructions, and you were to follow them in the order they were given to you. And this is the last on the list, Henri." Worry furrowed his brow. "Didn't you think of that? You must know how expendable everyone is. Louis wouldn't trust me to contain my hunger. Hell, he would think me a fool if I did." Henri began to rise from his knees. "Ah, but you can't leave without completing your assignment; otherwise Louis would have your blood."

Henri stood. He took several steps away from Marie.

"Why warn me of this?" he asked.

"Because fear in the blood adds spice."

Marie altered her position so that the wall better supported her body.

"Close the door, Henri. Then come lie before me. Right here would be good," she said, indicating the empty space next to her. "Head closest to me, of course. Don't hesitate. As I said, this is a gamble for you. If you return to Louis and I have taken no blood, he will drain you dry. However, I might choose to be lenient and just take enough to assist me in making my climb into that horrid casket."

"I can lift you into the coffin."

Marie wagged a finger at him.

"That will never satisfy Louis, and you can't lie to him. He will see the lie on your face and hear the lie in your voice. He will see an unblemished body where he knows there should be open wounds. I am

Louis's mother-in-law. Have been for centuries. He knows my tastes and practices well. I'm sure that's how he found me out. I allowed myself free rein with you the first time. I held nothing back. I gave you the full range of my attention without intelligent consideration of the fact that Louis would watch every move I made. But I was hungry, Henri, and you were lusciously sexy. No, you *are* lusciously sexy. Still, you have a better chance that I will allow you to live than if you returned to Louis with the job only partially done."

"You are advising me not to return to Monsieur Sade?"

"Henri, Louis will never allow you to escape. He'll find you and be especially angry. Angrier than you've ever seen him. Visualize the worst you've seen Louis do. Multiply that ten, no, a hundred times. I know, because he destroyed my original body in a hideous fashion, and he made sure I was aware of every sting, every depravity, every taste and smell of my own body.

"Henri, you will fare much better with me. I simply seek to heal my body with blood and sleep. I needn't take all your blood. Only enough to make my sleep worth the time I take away from this world."

He walked to the door, placed his hand on the outer knob, and meditated on her lecture. Finally he moved his hand to the inner knob and closed the door.

"Here, my sweetie," she said, patting the floor on which she sat.

"I don't want to die."

"I don't want you dead. Much better to keep you for munching on." She smiled. "Come, give me some munchies, sweetie."

"Do you want me to undress?" he asked.

"Offering me something else to encourage me to keep you alive? Now I bet that's a treat. Those tight leather pants can't slip off easily," she said, rubbing two of her fingers across her lips.

He slipped the zipper down and snapped open the button before slowly, teasingly, removing the pants.

"Always ready, Henri. Certainly that gives me cause to pause when I hear your breath becoming shallow from the loss of blood."

Chapter Fifty-six

Cecelia turned to shake Anna's shoulders, but she was no longer next to her. She looked behind her and saw Anna moving slowly toward Michael.

"Cecelia, please," he begged.

Cecelia walked over to him and squatted down.

"You're dying, Michael. No one can save you. You must feel the sickness that has ravished your body."

"I must have revenge on Sade." His voice cracked toward the end of the sentence.

"And Anna needs to feed. It's more likely that she will survive. Your lungs are infested with disease, Michael. You can no longer recognize your own body."

Michael reached inside his blanket and pulled out the stake he had personally carved.

"Take this, Cecelia."

She didn't reach out.

"Please, Cecelia, have some mercy on me. If I cannot destroy him, then do it in my name at least."

"Anna, how do you feel about Sade?" She didn't turn to face the girl, but waited several seconds for an answer.

"Mama said he would help me."

"Did he?"

"He gave me life before I could die."

"Are you grateful for that?"

Again there was a long pause.

"Mama was."

"But you, Anna—would you have preferred to die?"

Anna sank down onto the cement floor.

"I am too much of a coward to wish for death," Anna answered.

"If Michael gave you his stake, would you be willing to destroy Sade?" Cecelia turned her head toward Anna. "Or would you prefer being the first to spill your own blood on the stake?"

"Let him keep his stake. I won't ask to be freed, but I would bless the moment my body was released from this passion for blood." As her strength slowly returned, so did her ability to speak.

"Does that mean you'll not take Michael's life?"

"I killed only once in a frenzy. All the others I permitted to survive."

"So a taste of Michael's blood is all that you need."

"Cecelia, you know Anna is famished. She wouldn't have control over the hunger."

"You're a selfish man, Michael."

"Because I don't want to commit suicide?"

Pain gripped Cecelia's body, and her mind turned to battles she had never fought. Horses and men covered in bloodied mud, caked in layers upon their flesh. The whimpers of men dying. The snorts of horses attempting to pick themselves up.

"He's with me again, Michael. He's showing me things I never wanted to see." She gripped Michael and held tight. "Why does he do this? Why must I relive his life?"

"These are memories that haunt him in his coffin. He can't stop the thoughts from coming, and you can't block them."

"I associate smells with sights that turn my stomach."

"And you always will, Cecelia."

She pulled away from him.

"The three of us should invite true death to take our souls."

"Mama," Anna whispered.

Cecelia lightly slapped Anna on the side of her head.

"You'll see your mama again. And I'll carry Michael's stake with me in case he doesn't live long enough to use it himself."

"Thank you," Michael said.

"I'm going to win over this ancient vampire. I know now he lied to me. He knows nothing about

Sade's weaknesses. He wanted to survive like the rest of us. I was his only way out of the coffin. Thank you, Michael, for helping me retain some of my sanity. If the ancient one had stolen my body and mind, I would never be able to continue this quest. Instead I would be causing havoc down every corridor until I could find my way out. And probably then he would have complete control and run in the opposite direction from Sade."

"Remember the holy water, Cecelia. Before leaving the cathedral, dip the stake in holy water."

Chapter Fifty-seven

Lottie watched Justin and a young red-haired girl leave the cathedral. The girl looked familiar. She came to pray on Sunday, but she had also seen the girl admitted to the mansion. Maybe she would know Anna. Maybe she could help her to win back the daughter she had given away. She was about to call out to Justin when she heard a voice she hadn't heard in years. Another voice drowned out the first. Lottie wanted to scream at it to shut up. *Let me hear the gentler voice*, she wanted to cry out.

Lottie watched Justin and the red-haired girl cross the cemetery. He held the girl's hand, but he looked so pained and the girl looked hopeful.

Again Lottie thought she heard her small tiny daughter calling out for her mama. She slowly climbed the cathedral stairs. Her hand shook as she reached out to take hold of the door. Perhaps Anna had come to pray, or better yet was inside the cathedral waiting for her mother.

Only a small boy and his grandmother knelt at the front railing inside the cathedral. The little boy was agitated; the old woman managed to ignore his movements.

Lottie searched all the alcoves of the cathedral. The small chapels were hidden off to the sides, some in darkness, some brightly lit with candles and reeking of the odor of flowers. The darker chapels were poorly kept, even though she had tried to give them all equal attention. No one donated money to the shadowy chapels. No one sent flowers to adorn the saints worshiped there. Few of the candles had ever been lit. Sometimes Lottie hid in the darkness of these chapels, not to pray but to make the world outside go away.

The child gave a loud sneeze that almost frightened Lottie. The echo seemed to ring from all sides.

"Mama."

The other voices were all silent now, as if in respect for this frail wraith of a voice.

She wanted to scream out her daughter's name but knew it wouldn't be necessary if she could calm herself and try to connect mentally.

"Anna, my love, where are you? I can't find you. Are you playing games with me the way you did as a child? Are you hidden within a pew? Can you see me? Anna, I mean to find you."

Again she began to wander the aisles and cubbyholes of the cathedral. Frequently she checked over her shoulder in case her little girl was running to a new hiding place. Anna always loved to tease. Her games sometimes drove Lottie to chastise her. And always Lottie regretted sitting her daughter in a corner or sending her off to bed. She regretted the time they spent apart. Eventually Lottie would peek in at her daughter and, as a magnet, she would be drawn to her daughter's side.

"Mama."

Lottie looked up toward the altar. The little boy had taken to watching her travels. He no longer kneeled; instead he sat on the bench and gaped at her.

Quickly she moved to the altar. Would her daughter dare to step beyond the communion rail and hide up near the steps to the altar?

"Anna," she whispered, hoping to draw her daughter into the open.

The old woman looked up toward Lottie.

"I'm sorry. I didn't mean to disturb you, but have you seen any young girls in here?"

The old woman looked at her grandson, who in turn whispered in her ear. The old woman shook her head with a guilty pout, annoyed because she had been disturbed and embarrassed about being so engrossed in her prayer that she hadn't noticed anyone.

The boy pulled on his grandmother's arm, telling her that it was time to go. The old woman grabbed the railing and pushed her body up to a standing position. The curvature of her spine made it difficult for her to look straight ahead, but her grandson did a good job of guiding her to the front doors of the cathedral.

"Mama."

"Anna, baby, what are you doing here? Why hide from me?"

"Mama, please forgive me."

"You've done nothing wrong, child. At least nothing that I'm aware of. Are you here to do penance for some sin you've committed?"

"Lottie!"

A harsh voice broke Lottie's concentration.

"Go away. I'm trying to speak to my daughter."

Lottie spun around and climbed to the top of the altar stairs. She looked out over the huge cathedral and saw no one, but still she heard the weak voice cry out to her.

"She's with the rest of us, old woman."

"Who are you? You're trying to trick me."

Lottie rushed to her right and laid her hands against the wall of the cathedral.

"You're in there haunting me. There's no little girl in there with you."

"She's not a little girl anymore, Lottie. Evidently she's been a bad girl, and Sade has abandoned her within these walls."

"Lying bitch!" Lottie screamed. Her fists hit the wall, causing loose paint to flake onto the floor.

"Your daughter stands next to me, her hair plaited with multicolored strips of cloth. Her eyes resemble yours. She's a vampire, Lottie. Sade has made her into a vampire and deserted her."

"He said he wouldn't do that. He said he would keep her with him until I died, and then he would release her and bury her with me. It was an exchange. I carried out his tasks and he prevented my daughter's death."

"She'll never die, Lottie. Never will you unite with her because she's now bound to the earth, not God's Kingdom, not even hell."

"Anna. Anna!"

"Mama, please forgive me."

"But you never did anything wrong, child. You were perfect, a blessing."

"Mama, take me back. Please don't leave me here."

"Anna, this is a game. You're not held prisoner within these walls. I'll turn around and you'll be standing there, smiling at your heartless joke." Lottie turned and looked out toward the pews. No one stood there. No implike smile won her heart over instantly to forgiveness.

Chapter Fifty-eight

Sade heard the heavy pounding of the door knocker. Most of the servants were preparing for the party he had planned. He looked out the window and saw a ragamuffin shape huddling on the front steps. He recognized the rags as belonging to Lottie.

Why had she come? he wondered. Could it be that troublesome Justin ruining his plans?

He opened the door and invited Lottie in. Lottie didn't look into Sade's face; instead she held her head down and almost slithered into his house.

The serpent knows something is brewing, or else she has uncovered one of my loose ends.

"I don't remember giving you permission to pay me a visit, especially not through the front entrance."

She appeared to be hiding in the bushel of rags that she wore. Her thin body shrank among the folds of her mismatched garments.

"Did I give you permission, Lottie?" He walked closer to her and caught the odor of unwashed wool and old age.

"No, Monsieur Sade, you did not ask that I come. However, you have never told me that I couldn't come if there was an emergency."

"Emergency! Does this have to do with Justin?" He walked past her into the salon. She followed, keeping her head down the whole time.

"No, Monsieur Sade."

Sade plopped himself into the leather wingback chair and threw one leg over an armrest.

"Not Justin. Can't be Cecelia . . ."

"She spoke to me."

"When?"

"Less than an hour ago."

"From inside the cathedral walls?"

"Yes."

"She's harmless inside those walls, Lottie. She can't touch any of us from there." Sade leaned over the side table to smell a vase full of fresh red roses.

"She told me she was with Anna, though she didn't have to, since I recognized my daughter's voice."

Sade pulled a single rose from the vase and stood.

"Anna," he whispered.

Lottie's head moved upward, and she stared into Sade's eyes.

"She is truly locked away inside the cathedral?"

Sade presented the rose to Lottie, but she didn't accept it.

"Your child still exists. Is that not what our bargain was? I was to keep her alive for as long as you lived."

"At your side."

"I don't remember saying that she would always be by my side, Lottie. Few women keep me entertained for a long time. And if I make the mistake of allowing them close to me, they usually are cause for great pain."

"You used her and tossed her away. She didn't refuse to see me. She was forced to stop seeing me when you locked her inside the cathedral walls."

"I wish you'd take the rose, Lottie. My arm is getting tired of being in this position."

"As you tired of my Anna."

Sade poked the rose inside Lottie's rags. When he let go the flower drooped.

"I didn't exactly tire of her. She became irksome. She began to talk about sin. It quite ruined many of our orgies.

"Ah, I see shock on your face, Lottie. Come now, your daughter was naive when she came to me but certainly you are not. A woman like you, who gave birth to a bastard, can understand . . ."

Lottie dropped the shawl that kept her rags together and the rose fell on the floor. She moved closer to him.

"My child is not a bastard."

"Does your child have a father, and do you know the father's name?"

Lottie made a feeble attempt to strike Sade. He easily caught her by the wrist.

"Your child is a bastard and you're a whore, madam. An old, used-up one, but still a whore."

"My child. I want Anna back."

"Then you will have to join her inside the walls of the cathedral. There is only one way in, Lottie, and I can show you the doorway. I cannot take anyone out. The cathedral would have to be destroyed in order to free any of my tiresome acquaintances or enemies. The walls would have to come tumbling down, Lottie."

"Tear down the walls if you must, but give her back to me."

"I'll never give her back to you, Lottie. If you wish to see your daughter again or be buried with her, then come with me to the cathedral and I will show you the secret passage willingly."

"You need me to keep the monsters quiet."

Sade disliked seeing a snarl on the face of an elderly woman. It was rude enough for this woman to enter his house, but to turn her face into a mask was disgusting.

"I am leaving Albi. I will throw one final party, and then I will be gone. Those devils can roar all they want, because I won't hear them."

"The townspeople . . ."

"Did you hear me? I will be gone. The townspeople can take their torches to this mansion and I won't care."

Lottie spat into Sade's face.

Sade heard one of her wrist bones break.

"Monsieur Sade."

Chapter Fifty-nine

Lottie allowed the pain to escape with her cry. Sade let go of her wrist, staring at someone beyond her. She turned and saw one of Sade's servants in the doorway. His body seemed to be propped up by will-power alone. He had a white pallor, and as he moved toward them she could see how unsteady his gait was.

"Henri," Sade said. He sounded surprised.

The servant noticed Lottie.

"I'm sorry, Monsieur Sade. I didn't mean to interrupt."

"Lottie appreciates the interruption, I'm sure." Sade grinned down at her as only the devil could.

"I wanted to report that everything you requested has been done."

She looked again at Henri and saw his glassy eyes. His face was tattooed with a number of scratches, some deep. His mouth was colored with caked blood. Henri was determined to press on with life, even though his body was ready to surrender to the grave.

"Have you met Lottie, Henri?"

"No, Monsieur Sade."

"She's in need of a guide."

Lottie immediately pulled back from the two men.

"She has great interest in the cathedral and wants to learn about all its secrets. Henri can take you to your daughter, Lottie. At least he can deliver you to her world and toss you in if you should hesitate."

Henri took a step in her direction but swayed too badly to continue. Sade raised his right hand and gently touched Henri's shoulder.

She realized Sade could nudge his servant into a fall from which Henri would never again rise to his feet. She saw how Sade contemplated that same idea. Sade hesitated, smiled, and decided Henri's condition was humorous; he laughed out loud at his servant, his derision another form of torture.

Confused and weakened, Henri seated himself without Sade's permission.

"Henri appears to be unable to assist you right now, Lottie. And my time is too precious to waste on you. You'll have to find your own way inside those walls."

"Monsieur Sade, I am sorry." Henri attempted to stand but couldn't.

"This is just another cruelty of my mother-in-law. I can see that, Henri. No fault of yours. You're her warning to me."

"Pawn. He is only a pawn to you and whatever beast did this to him." Lottie clenched her fists, wincing in pain from the broken bone.

"I must admit it would have been kinder of her to put Henri's soul to rest. It's what I would have done in my mercy."

Lottie's wrist stung as he spoke.

"Monsieur Sade . . ."

"Do not speak, Henri. You have nothing of interest to say."

Lottie saw the poor man's head flop back against the leather chair. His eyes rolled in his head and he panted for air.

"Do something, Monsieur Sade. He is near death." Lottie took a single step toward Henri.

"Closer than he or Marie could imagine."

Sade walked over to a spindly antique chair and ripped one of the legs free. He brushed against Lottie as he walked over to Henri. Her rags passed his chill into her bones.

She turned away quickly, knowing that Sade was about to plunge the wooden leg into Henri's heart.

Chapter Sixty

Justin and Madeline heard her name being called long before they saw her home. Madeline recognized the anxiety in her mother's voice and worried that Sade had taken some revenge upon her family. She broke into a run and only stopped when she saw her mother pacing in front of their farmhouse.

Justin caught up with her and placed his arm around her shoulders.

"Perhaps I should come with you?" he said.

"The panic in my mother's voice may be a false alarm. She may only miss me." She looked up at Justin's emerald eyes, which were turning a muddy color. "I'll talk to my mother alone. If everything is well, I'll wave to you to leave."

"Sade is deceitful. He may—"

"My mother is hysterical enough without meeting my new beau." She kissed him on the lips, tasting the saltiness of his human flesh.

"Mother, I'm here," she said, walking directly toward the house.

Her mother met her partway and threw her arms about Madeline. She smelled slightly of wine, a sure sign that her anxiety level had peaked.

"What is wrong? Has something happened to Father or Nathan?"

"No, no. I was afraid that I might not be able to pass the message on in time."

"Did someone come from the mansion?"

"Yes. It's wonderful. You have been formally invited to a party. The servant—I think his name was Henri—even brought a gown for you to wear. It's beautiful, covered with lace and pearls. It's a blush pink that I have never seen before. And the pumps match, except that they have a slight sparkle to them. A fairy princess, my daughter. He must have great interest in you."

Madeline looked back at Justin. He stood alert, ready to run to her, even though it meant danger to himself. He loved her. She waved good-bye to him and walked with her mother to the house.

"Who is he? I've never seen him before."

"He is new to the town, Mother. He is an art student down from Paris to see the wonders of the cathedral."

Her mother nodded.

"And you took him on a tour, didn't you?"

"In a way."

"I'm so proud of you. Beautiful, bright, and someday the wife of a wealthy man. You will never have
to see your hands turn into the cracked, bruised tools
mine have become. He's very wealthy, you know.
His family is old."

And so is he, Madeline thought, knowing that her
mother was talking about Sade.

"We know very little about Monsieur Sade,
Mother. This generous offer could only mean—"

"Hush! We all know what it means. He has a special interest in you and is willing to make it public."

"There are stories about him."

"Jealousy. People make up all sorts of stories
about wealthy, celebrated people. You can't let those
stories drive you away from your future."

"My future is not with Monsieur Sade, Mother."
She looked over her shoulder and saw that Justin had
gone.

"That young man is merely traveling around seeking fun before he returns to class. Monsieur Sade is
mature and settled. What can a young fool offer in
comparison?"

"Youth and passion?" Madeline said.

"Both age, Madeline. You will attend the party."

Madeline noted that her mother hadn't asked but
demanded.

What if her mother knew about the debauchery
she had been forced to engage in with Sade and the
other stupid chattel? Madeline wondered. Certainly
her mother would reject Sade as a suitor for her

daughter. Would she still admit to having a daughter after hearing what Madeline had been doing?

"See, here's the dress, child." Her mother moved quickly into the family room, where she had the dress laid out on the sofa. "I'm sure it will fit perfectly. I don't know how he could have guessed your size so accurately."

The dress wasn't new. She had seen it hanging in Sade's closet. He had promised that one day she would wear the dress when she was laid away in her coffin. He had laughed and said that she might, of course, be an old lady, but she'd be the very best-dressed corpse in the cemetery.

Chapter Sixty-one

Lottie ran from Sade's mansion when she heard the thrust break open Henri's chest. There had been no cry from Henri. No plea for mercy. He had been so close to death that he might not even have been aware of Sade's actions.

She stopped under an oak tree and leaned her body against the massive trunk, fighting off the instinct to vomit. She looked back toward the mansion to make sure Sade hadn't followed her. Instead she saw the gardener heading for the maintenance building. His scruffy clothes were spotted with dirt, and he wore Wellington boots even though it hadn't rained for several days. He was a middle-aged man with an old man's gait. He swayed a bit to his left when he walked and had a slight limp.

She followed him at a distance. When he reached the maintenance building he pulled a ring of keys from his denim overalls and unlocked the front door. He went inside and didn't bother to close the door. She quietly approached the doorway. Inside she caught sight of him digging under some oil-stained tarps. Finally he pulled free a bottle of red wine that had obviously been opened earlier. He yanked the cork free and drank directly from the bottle. He took several swigs before falling down on the tarps himself. She watched him yawn and spit out his false teeth, which he slipped into a pocket of the overalls. Within another five minutes the man was snoring.

Lottie dared to cross the threshold, and when she did she could smell a combination of cheap wine and gasoline. The fumes were quite strong, and she worried about safety. What if the gasoline suddenly . . .

She gave another look at the gardener and drifted farther into the room. The gasoline had to be nearby because the smell was so intense. She hoped it too wasn't buried under the tarps, because there was no way she could move the gardener without waking him.

Bags of earth, hoes, rakes, and a big box of small pebbles were visible instantly. A wheelbarrow stood at the far wall and appeared to be propped up against something. As she moved closer the smell of gasoline intensified, and she saw the can near the front wheel of the wheelbarrow.

At the door a cat meowed, making Lottie's breath stop for an instant. She watched the gardener mechanically take off a boot and throw it at the cat without bothering to open his eyes. The cat gave one last screech before disappearing. The gardener cradled the bottle of wine in his arms and rolled to his left side. The still-open bottle trickled what little wine was left onto the tarps, where the wine beaded into small drops.

She had no excuse for being here and knew the gardener only by sight. He most probably would choose to drag her back to the mansion. She measured the distance she still needed to travel to grab the gasoline can. Because of her injured wrist she couldn't be certain she could lift the can without knocking it against the wheelbarrow. The doorway was near enough that it seemed like the safest route to take. Safe, but the situation would be hopeless without the gasoline.

Facing the gardener, Lottie backed up several steps. She waved her hand behind her to see how close she was to the wheelbarrow. *Damn!* She wasn't close enough yet. She spaced her steps wider and felt her right calf hit against something. Looking over her shoulder, she saw the wheelbarrow.

She squatted and heard her joints cry out for relief. One leg shook, and she wasn't sure how long she would be able to keep the position. Lottie made a quick grab for the gasoline can, sliding it closer to her in order to be balanced enough to lift it. The wheelbarrow crashed forward, and several large rocks rolled out.

"Barney, what the hell are you doing?" cried the gardener, who this time threw his wine bottle in the air, where it crashed just shy of Lottie. He grumbled some more, then buried his face in the tarps, using his right hand to free a single airhole.

The pain in Lottie's knees was unbearable, but her fear of Sade's retribution kept her quiet.

As the gardener's snores picked up a regular rhythm, Lottie slid the can against her breasts. The smell of gasoline numbed her senses enough that she was able to stand. Her head felt light, her legs tired. Her precious booty was heavy. She stumbled toward the doorway, constantly taking side glances at the gardener.

The cat waited outside and maneuvered in and out of her feet, brushing its fur against her legs. She felt sure she would miss a step and fall, but the cat took off after a squirrel that rooted around an acorn tree.

Her pace barely increased as she moved across the field with her burden, determined to free her daughter.

Chapter Sixty-two

Marie lay in her pauper's coffin, which smelled of manure, the wood having been stored in some old barn. She rested on dark soil that she hoped was American. The sides of the coffin were bare; no satin to run her hand over, no smell of antique lace, no cushion to cradle her head. *The bastard!*

She had left Henri near death and would have completed the task except that her body ached too much. Her soul wanted to rest and repair itself from the hideous damage done to its body.

If Henri was wise he would not return to Sade. She had given him a taste of her own blood and hoped he would be waiting for her when she arose. She had had very little success with the minions she tried to make. Most were too dull to comprehend the vastness of her plans. They tended to anger her, and she had a very short, uncontrollable temper.

A hand passed over her coffin. She couldn't see it but sensed it.

"Marie, are you comfortable?"

Sade's voice disheartened her. If Henri had stayed in the room to wait for her, he most certainly had been found by Sade by now and disposed of.

"Your mother's milk failed poor Henri."

He had done away with the only minion she could have depended upon.

"It was painless and quick." This time his voice seemed to be within the coffin.

She imagined Sade with his lips almost touching the lid of her coffin, his whisper easily penetrating the wood. Yet the smell of him was faint, overcome by manure.

"You tricked me, Marie. I expected an aged slut, not the beauty you managed to capture. Another reason for me not to trust any woman.

"I know you bleed for me, Marie. Your silent sobs are appreciated but can never turn my heart."

She heard Sade chuckle.

"I do hope your son/lover joins us for my last party in Albi. I enjoyed this town. But now you have forced me to move on. By the way, I met Cecelia on the path to the cemetery and disposed of her. Justin won't follow me, as you hags have done. However, I do hope he has chosen to join Cecelia. I think they are a perfect pair."

Marie scraped her nails against the sides of the coffin.

"Keep those claws sharp, my beautiful feline. They will be your last defense against what I have waiting for you. You may actually enjoy the blood-bath until you smell your own blood and feel the drip running down your flesh."

Chapter Sixty-three

With a great deal of difficulty, Lottie carried the gasoline can up the steps of the cathedral. Her arms ached and her legs were unsteady. She had to place the can on the top step in order to open the cathedral doors. Tired, she dragged the can inside the building. The can tumbled over onto its side as it passed over the sill of the door, rolling several feet before being stopped by a pew.

She looked around the cathedral, wondering whether anyone had noticed her. The cathedral was empty. Not even the town's homeless drunk was there. As quickly as she could, she lifted the can and carried it to the center of the aisle. She had thought to use the wooden pews, but she feared they wouldn't flare the way she wanted.

On either side of the cathedral were several confessionals; a burgundy polyester velvet curtain hung from each door. Inside each was a prayer book, the paper old and crisp, browning from the number of years the books had served sinners.

She looked up at the altar and saw the massive tome used by the priest for the various rituals. Lottie remembered that a pile of newspapers waited for collection inside the vestry.

If Sade wouldn't free Anna, she would burn the cathedral to the ground.

Lottie moved from confessional to confessional, tearing the burgundy curtains down into piles, wetting them down with gasoline. She ripped each prayer book into shreds and tossed them atop the curtains. In one confessional the crucifix fell into the pile when Lottie brushed against it.

"Wood. It should burn well with the globs of oily paints laid upon it."

Christ had fallen face down into the folds of the curtain. All she could see of Him was the flesh-painted feet that were nailed to the cross. She would forsake Him just as His father had. She moved on to the next confessional.

Finished with them, she climbed the steps and lifted the tome that lay upon the altar. Her body almost sagged down with the weight. Slowly she carried the tome down to the bottom of the marble steps and passed through the gate of the communion rail.

She knew a beautifully carved wooden chapel was to her left and gingerly carried the tome in that direction. At the wooden gate of the chapel she dropped the book to the floor and watched as a number of holy pictures scattered out from it.

She pulled on the wooden gate, but it didn't open easily. Her breath was coming in harsh puffs. Her heart beat fast, and she felt a twinge of pain in the center of her chest.

There was much to be done, but she had to sit for a few moments or she feared her life would be taken before she could rescue her child.

While sitting on a nearby pew, she became aware of the crosscurrent odors that were filling the church. Incense, candle wax, wood oil, and gasoline fought for dominance. A faint smell barely clung to the air. She looked down at the plastic-covered kneeler. She could rip each open and use the stuffing to help start the fire.

"Mama."

The voice surrounded her in echoes.

"Mama."

"Anna, I'm coming for you. I'll get you out. I promise."

Lottie decided she could waste no more time at rest.

Chapter Sixty-four

"I told you, Michael. When she comes for her daughter we'll slip out with them." Cecelia rested her head against Michael's chest and listened to the rhythmic rales in his lungs. He'd never be able to walk on his own, and she wondered if she should waste time in playing his crutch.

"Mama heard me. She said my name." A smile curved Anna's lips, then passed into a frown. "Do you think she's only teasing? Can she hate me so much that she would add to Sade's torture?"

Cecelia touched one of Michael's stumps with her good hand.

"Did he burn you piecemeal?"

"This curiosity comes from the ancient vampire."

"No, Michael. I want to think of your pain when I'm destroying Sade. I want to remember for you.

The ancient one doesn't care about your pain. He's inflicted far greater on others and never turned away."

"Do you still see his visions?"

"Sometimes, though it's becoming easier to ride the memories."

"Almost pleasurable?" Michael asked.

"You insist that I am taking on his beliefs. No, Michael. I'm learning to separate myself. All his memories run like a movie." She laughed. "I've even gotten used to the smell of your charred body."

"Why is he so badly burned?" Anna asked.

"Because Sade thought Michael had been a bad boy. A boy who coveted Sade's property."

Anna looked confused.

"A woman, Anna. A woman brought about this ugliness we see."

"Most women he throws away freely," Anna said.

"Yes, he does. Marie insists that he longs for love, but he never reveals the need to the women who service him."

"Anna." Lottie's voice was frail

Cecelia raised her head to listen.

"She's dying, Michael. I hear a dead person's voice."

Michael stirred, also attempting to raise his head.

"Who's dying?" Anna asked.

"Anna." Spoken so softly, the word sounded more like a summer breeze.

"Mama?" Anna stood and turned in a circle, obviously hoping to see her mother. "I hear you,

Mama." She turned toward Cecelia. "Her voice is weak. Will I never see Mama again?" she asked.

Cecelia got to her feet, allowing the stake Michael had so carefully designed to fall to the floor.

"We've been abandoned," Michael said. "Our lives have been stolen from us again. Anna will never die and see her mother. You, Cecelia, will never fulfill our dream of revenge." His voice caught in a fit of coughing.

"If she has the slightest bit of strength, she'll come for her daughter." The crude mounds of flesh on Cecelia's arm pulsated. "The ancient vampire senses that we're close to freedom. He whispers for me to return for him. I won't carry you with me as an anchor. He wants a kill, Michael. He needs the sight of blood. There have been too few victims all these centuries. And he recalls the slaughter, the tortures, the innards wrapped around poles and pulled free from living bodies. He remembers, and I cringe." Cecelia looked down at Michael.

"You promised to save me from him, Michael."

"I would have to drive the stake through your heart right now in order to keep him from you."

"Look, Michael." Cecelia held out her arm, enabling Michael to follow the trail the ancient vampire's flesh was making on her skin.

The cells multiplied and reached up her arm, dissolving clothes, weakening bone.

Before she could be prevented from it, Anna laid a hand on the gliding flesh. Her fingers were immersed into the folds of the flesh.

303

"I would gladly give him to you, Anna, if I could," said Cecelia.

When Anna pulled away her hand, the bones of her fingers were shining with a sparkling liquid. The flesh was gone. Childishly she showed the damage to both Cecelia and Michael.

"Anna, don't touch Cecelia anymore," Michael advised.

"But she's taken my flesh."

"*He* has," Cecelia responded.

"No, no. Michael has done nothing."

"That's our problem. Michael does nothing except complain and peel. He drops ashes of himself on the floor. He rubs against us and we find white ash clinging to our clothes."

Anna touched the bones of her fingers.

"Why?" Anna asked. "Why take a part of me? I touched you because I was curious, but I meant no harm."

Cecelia swung around with her burdened arm and knocked Anna to the ground. She lay stunned, looking back and forth between Michael and Cecelia. A part of her ring finger bone had snapped off during the fall.

"Your damn mother had better come through for us, Anna, or I'll go mad with this blood hunger.

"He moves inside me, Michael. I feel the tendrils of his intellect spreading throughout my body. Can he still reach me from his coffin?"

"It is said the ancient vampires can pass though air into a person's soul."

Cecelia picked up the wooden stake.

"I could have you drive this through my heart." She looked at the stake with longing.

"I no longer have the strength, Cecelia. Anna would have to be the one to do it."

"I can't!" Anna shouted.

"What if I said I would use the stake on *you* if you didn't destroy me?" Cecelia asked.

Anna scuttled across the cement floor, adding several more feet to the distance already between herself and Cecelia.

Cecelia stooped forward. Her disarrayed hair fell into her face, but she didn't bother pushing it back.

"Imagine your blood dripping off this stake. Imagine the sudden pain and the brief chill death would deliver. But we aren't afraid of death, are we, Anna? The two of us have already died." She swung around and faced Michael. "No, it's Michael's turn to die."

Chapter Sixty-five

Justin hated leaving Madeline behind but knew she would be safer with her family than roaming the forest with him. Instinctively he headed back to the cathedral. The caretaker's shack was dark. It was the first time he had ever seen the shack dark. Dark and deserted, he thought. There were bundles of flowers on several tombstones in the cemetery. Colorful flowers that looked out of place in the cemetery's grayness.

The massive cathedral backgrounded the cemetery, its red bricks dirty and its windows soiled by nesting birds. He took each step one at a time, counting them until he reached the number thirteen and faced the doors.

He remembered the prayers he had overheard in cemeteries when a body was laid to rest. He would stand in the shadow of the trees and hear the mumbled responses of the mourners. At times there were as few as two mourners, while at other times a huge crowd would gather around the plot. Justin often blended in with large crowds, acting like a mourner himself. Sometimes the mourners' sobs were a distraction from what the priest was saying. Justin would lose track of the service and find himself alone in the middle of a dispersing crowd. He would peer down at the ground and hope that no one would approach him.

Once at a funeral a small girl of not more than five touched his hand and looked up at him. She had a runny nose, and streaks of dirt marred her face where her tears had flowed. He wanted to wrap her in his arms and cry with her. Without thinking, he found himself kneeling in front of the child. She reached out both her arms and pulled him gently close to her. His own arms hung down by his sides. And the child patted his back as if she knew. He heard someone call, "Belinda!" and the little girl took her arms from his shoulders and ran away without a word.

Justin shook his head to drive away the memory. He reached out a hand and pulled open one of the wooden doors. Immediately he smelled gasoline and hurried inside to see what had happened. The confessionals had been vandalized; heaps of cloth and paper lay at the door to each confessional.

Quickly he walked down the center aisle until he saw a chapel with its wooden door splintered. As he drew closer he could see mounds of newspapers piled around wooden statues. He thought of the historical witch burnings. Lying near one of the piles was another bundle of cloth. One that moved. He kicked up the kneelers on the pew in front of him and carefully worked his way to the chapel.

"Who are you?" he asked, but no one answered, though the bundle seemed more aroused than before. Perhaps an old drunk, but that wouldn't account for the odor in the air.

He touched the clumsily broken wooden door and pushed it back to make his entrance easier.

"You do all this?" he asked.

He heard a feminine groan.

As he reached the bundle he recognized the colors and the shape.

"Lottie, what happened to you? Who did all this damage?"

Justin knelt next to Lottie. He turned her from her side onto her back so that he could see her face.

"Lottie, are you badly hurt?"

Her eyes squinted, trying to recognize her savior. Spittle ran down the left side of her mouth.

"Can you stand?"

She shook her head and reached for his shirt so that she could pull him closer.

"Save my daughter," she whispered.

"Where is she?"

"Inside these walls." She grimaced.

"Sade."

"Save her from his torture and save her from my selfishness. Destroy her, Justin. Don't make her live for centuries within these walls." Her voice caught, and she had a short coughing spasm.

He wanted to berate her for what she had set into motion. He wanted to spit in her face and tell her that she had gotten what she deserved. She must have seen all this on his face because tears ran freely from her eyes.

"You were trying to burn down the church." He looked around the small chapel and didn't see a single lighted candle. "With what, your hatred?"

Her hand let go of him and pointed toward the main body of the cathedral.

"There are lots of lit candles to the right of the communion rail. Hurry before someone stops you." Her hand dropped down by her side and her shallow breaths came less frequently.

Justin stood and looked around the chapel until he found a metal window pole leaning against the far wall.

He stood and started to walk away from Lottie, away from the exit into the main part of the cathedral. Lottie's voice softly whispered, "No."

He grabbed the window pole and swung around to face Lottie. She covered her heart, as if she believed somehow she had become a vampire that he would destroy.

"We need more fuel," he said and began splintering the wooden statues with the sharp end of the pole. The aged wood fell apart quickly; it scattered at his feet.

When he was finished he looked back at Lottie, who was smiling. He dropped the pole to the floor and approached her. He reached down to pick her up, but she shook her head.

"Leave me. Set the fire now."

"I must get you out of here first or you may be caught in the fire. You want to see your daughter again, don't you?"

"I will see her again in hell, and it will be all my fault."

He backed away from the old woman and headed for the main portion of the cathedral.

Chapter Sixty-six

Fawning Parisian perverts milled around the enormous front hall of Sade's mansion, waiting for the massive doors, decorated with gold leaf, to open. Most were dressed in outrageous fashions. Few wore enough clothes to cover their enhanced sexual characteristics. Some sported long black capes and held their heads aloof, imagining the wonderful shock and awe that would spread through the crowd when the doors opened and they unlatched their capes, allowing them to fall to the floor.

The air inside the front hall was spiked with perfumes, colognes, alcohol, tobacco, and sweat. People couldn't avoid bumping into each other as the crowd grew larger and the appointed hour approached.

"A very short-notice party."

"I wonder if that means the champagne will be inferior."

"No, I'm sure Louis keeps a well-stocked cellar," said an invitee who dared to call his host by his given name. He had never actually met Sade, but he wanted everyone else to think he had.

One woman fanned herself with the invitation, hoping the body heat in the room wouldn't mar her makeup. Another kept holding her long, sheer skirt off the ground and away from the soiled shoes of her fellow debauchees.

"A grand idea, don't you think?"

"Sorry, I wasn't paying attention. See that woman over there with the chartreuse hair? Damn, that old man just stepped in front of her. If we could maneuver over a bit, perhaps we would have a better view."

Some of the guests decided to wait outside in the cool evening air. Those less inhibited sat on the red brick porch, while others barely managed to keep the evening dust from speckling their garments and makeup.

Most of the guests were despised by Sade because of wrongs or slights done him in the past. He looked down from his window, watching the horde multiply by the minute. His hunger for blood both literally and figuratively would be sated tonight. He had as yet to see Madeline. Perhaps the foolish girl had followed Justin into the corridors of the cathedral. Terrible waste, he thought, recalling the sweetness of her blood. Henri never had a chance to tell Sade whether he had found her at home or only left the message with her family. Sometimes Sade regretted his temper tantrums.

He could be sure Marie would be there, though, and that was most satisfying to his damaged ego. He had left an old woman's dress in the room with her. A dress that would reflect her true number of years. How insulted she would be, he thought with relish. Of course, knowing Marie, she might dispense with wearing clothes entirely, though she would know that even in this crowd it would be considered vulgar.

He laughed, and because the window was open, one of his guests looked up at him. A frail, pretty girl of not more than eighteen, with doll-like features undoubtably paid for by doting parents. She wore a sheer blouse that stretched temptingly around her breasts.

He could do with an appetizer before the party, he thought. Sade waved her around to a side door and strode confidently out of the room.

Chapter Sixty-seven

With a dark, unfamiliar glee, Cecelia, stake in hand, advanced toward the defenseless Michael.

"Ticktock. Can you hear the sound of your final minutes, final seconds . . ."

"Something is leaking through the vent," Anna cried.

Cecelia turned to see Anna's hands shine with a clear liquid that dripped from the overhead vent.

"It smells like gasoline," Anna said.

"Gasoline? Is your mother trying to rescue us or destroy us?" Cecelia raised Anna's hands up to her nose and immediately recognized the odor. "Why would she be setting fire to the place?"

"Perhaps she doesn't know the way in after all," said Michael. "She may be desperate to reach her daughter."

"But we all could burn inside these walls before we found our way out," Cecelia said, forgetting the blood lust of just a few moments ago.

"Are you frightened, Cecelia?" he asked.

"We should all be frightened," she said, turning once again to Michael. "Especially you. You've already felt the pain that flames can cause. There's still enough of you to catch fire, you know."

"But not enough of me to care." Michael eased his back against the brick wall.

"Mama is still angry with me?" Anna looked sad, and without thinking rubbed the gasoline onto the folds of her dress.

"No, she's stupid," Cecelia cried.

"It was your idea to let Lottie know about her daughter. Now do you regret what you have begun?"

"There were wooden walls down that corridor that led to the ancient vampires. That might be the weakest point into the corridors of the cathedral."

"And into the flames," Michael reminded her.

"I'll find a way around the flames. The smoke means nothing to me." As Cecelia spoke she smelled the waves of debris burning. "Anna, come with me."

"What about Michael?"

"He'll die from lack of oxygen whether he stays here or goes with us. He would only slow us down, and we need to be out of here before the flames can lick our souls clean."

"Maybe the fire is a blessing then, Cecelia. The only way to expunge your sins from your soul." Michael grimaced and brought one of his stumps to his chest.

"Do you want Sade dead?" she asked.

"Go with her, Anna, and see that she doesn't stop at the room where the ancient vampires are kept."

"Why would she do that?"

"Because one of those vampires breathes through Cecelia now. He travels wherever she goes but hasn't been able to gain complete control. He'll make another attempt when he senses her near."

Anna looked down at Cecelia's arm. "Is that why you're deformed?"

"Do you have the strength, Cecelia, to ignore his call?" Michael leaned forward. "Think of the blood, the deaths, the tortures, and the pain you have witnessed only in your mind and tell me honestly that you don't need assistance in passing the ancient vampire by."

"I've seen worse with Sade." Cecelia tossed her head in the midst of her lie.

Anna walked over to Michael and knelt down.

"Leave him!" Cecelia shouted.

"But his blood would make me stronger."

Chapter Sixty-eight

Madeline's dress was purposefully tight around her bosom to force her breasts to rise high above the material. She looked at herself in the mirror and was ashamed of all she had done.

"You are beautiful, child. Come show your father."

Madeline followed her mother into the family room, where both her brother and father were sitting, meditating over a game of chess, a game that seemed to have lasted for several days, with neither contestant able to move faster than a snail.

Her mother announced "Princess Madeline" in the doorway and reverently bowed out of the way for her daughter's entrance.

"Too much," her father said.

"Our daughter certainly deserves beautiful clothes and—"

"No, no. Too much revealed upstairs," he said, using hand gestures on himself to show the area of the body he meant.

"She looks slutty, Mom."

"Slutty! How can you speak of your sister in such a term? Especially you, who hides filthy magazines under your mattress. What, you didn't think I would find them? I'm everyone's personal servant, and as such the one who knows the most about what goes on in this house."

Madeline had never seen her brother blush before. She smiled at him to ease the tension.

"I leave them there because your father believes they'll teach you something. See what it teaches him? He compares his sister to the sluts in the magazines."

Her father sighed and leaned back in his straight-backed chair.

"Your sister is gorgeous in this dress. You've never seen her look so wonderful."

"She'd look better with a shawl around her shoulders," her father said.

"And do we own a shawl that would match the beauty of this expensive dress? My shawls all come from my mother's knitting needles and are meant to last and keep me warm while I do my chores. Madeline doesn't even own a shawl. She has nothing to wrap around her on cold nights."

"Come on, she has several jackets and sweaters. The girl has never even asked for a shawl. She'd probably think it old-fashioned, anyway." Her father was becoming irritable, and her brother had started to look out the window, hoping to be rescued by a friend or visiting neighbor.

"I can use a scarf," Madeline offered.

"Yeah, you could stuff it in across the top of the dress." Her father perked up at this idea.

"A scarf? First of all, there isn't a scarf in this house that would match that dress, and secondly, there is no elegant way of wearing a scarf with the dress.

"And you," shouted her mother in the direction of her father, "you can stuff it!"

"I'm going to be late," Madeline said. She couldn't believe she had said that when she didn't even want to go at all.

"Cab money." Her mother put out her hand in front of her father.

"It's not that much of a walk."

"You expect our daughter to walk through the town with everyone staring at her?"

"If you think she's so beautiful in that dress, what's wrong with that?"

Her mother rolled her eyes. "Then we'll be using the food money, Madeline. Come with me to the kitchen."

"Does that mean we'll be doing without supper?" her brother asked.

"You, young man, will be lucky if I cook you breakfast in the morning." The indignant mother turned away from the chess players and led Madeline out of the room.

Chapter Sixty-nine

"I've never been here before. I've been warned off," Anna said, following Cecelia down the corridor toward a huge crucifix.

Cecelia tried to listen to Anna's words, but as she drew closer to the room at the end of the corridor she could hear the ancient vampire call.

"Only the fools and the cruelest come here," Anna said.

Fools. Cruelest. Anna's words were rumbling inside Cecelia's head. Fools. Cruelest.

"Welcome back, child."

He was there inside her mind. She could see him now, even though the door wasn't open.

"I can lead you out of the fire, child." His voice sounded concerned, but not for her life, she knew.

"I need to rest, Cecelia." Anna tugged on Cecelia's clothes.

"You've just fed, Anna."

"He wasn't full of nourishment. Instead he had disease sweeping through his body."

"You wanted him, Anna."

"Only because I was hungry."

"I, too, am hungry, child. Hungry for blood. Hungry for freedom. Hungry for the strength of your body," said the ancient vampire.

"And you won't get any more of me."

"But I haven't—"

"Not you, Anna. Michael was right; the ancient vampire is calling to me."

"And what will you do, Cecelia?"

"Ignore him."

"You can't ignore me, child. I am always with you. Always guiding you. Always revealing the lust and violence I have been robbed of."

"Do you smell smoke, Anna?"

"It's coming from under the door."

"Damn!"

"I will show you the way, child," the ancient vampire said.

"This is a trick."

"No, child. The weakest walls are those that guard us. It has been built that way, so that we ancients could smell and hear but never touch the outside world. It is hell with the flames soon to be added."

"Anna, we have to go in there."

"Are you strong enough to fight the ancient ones?"

"Of course. I did it once before."

"I don't think I'm that strong," Anna said.

Cecelia reached out and grabbed Anna by the hair.

"We're going in and you're going to stay close to me. You will refuse to acknowledge any of the voices."

"But I hear nothing."

"You will once we're inside the room. You'll hear the envy in their sighs. Their hunger in the rapping sounds they make. Don't let them break you down. They can do nothing for you. Remember that, no matter what they promise."

Cecelia reached out and touched the painted crucifix.

"Are you praying, Cecelia?"

"No, Anna. Praying would be useless. God no longer hears my prayers."

"He has never heard mine," Anna said. "I had no father. No last name. Mama didn't lie. She was too proud. Sometimes I wish she had concocted a story about a young man, and how he loved her, and how his life was suddenly snatched away."

"I had a mother and a father, Anna. And I disappointed them both with my pride, and caused my mother's death."

"Did you . . . ?"

"No, I never laid a violent hand on my mother, but I did put her in harm's way. I was going to do wonderful things with an elegant man who had a sugary tongue."

Cecelia pulled open the door, and the smoke rushed out into the corridor.

"Back again," the ancient vampire whispered.

"But not for you."

Cecelia pushed Anna into the room ahead of her, so that the girl couldn't retreat.

"It smells of moss and putrefied bodies," Anna said.

"We won't be here long."

"Long enough to fetch me," the ancient vampire said.

Anna walked deeper into the room until she came face-to-face with sagging flesh that had two spots of squirming vermin where the eyes should have been. Cecelia jerked Anna back and away from the ancient vampire. As Anna took a step back, the form sitting upright in the coffin reached out to her.

"Don't go near him, Anna."

"He's the one who did that to you?" Anna asked, pointing at Cecelia's ruined arm.

Cecelia and Anna were startled by the sudden noises they heard. Each coffin echoed of fingernails scratching against wood. Cecelia moved around the room, her hands skimming the walls.

"Child, you would not leave without me."

"I hear him, Cecelia."

"Shut him out of your mind!" Cecelia screamed.

"How?"

"Carry me to safety and I will give you my strength."

"If you have so much strength, why don't you take yourself out of the coffin and help me find the easiest way out?" Cecelia stopped at a wall and felt for the differences in temperature.

"I think I've found where the fire is, Anna."

"Then we should stay away from there."

"Help tear this wall down. Grab anything you see that might weaken the wall."

"But we would be letting in the fire."

"Child, she means to run through the flames."

"You don't, Cecelia."

"Shut up," Cecelia raged at the ancient vampire. She walked over to his coffin and found the jewel she had used to break it open. "Don't stand there dumbfounded, Anna. Look around for something sharp and heavy."

Cecelia watched Anna obey.

"I have something in my coffin that could help, child."

Anna looked up at the ancient vampire and took several steps in his direction.

"He has nothing, Anna. He's lying."

The ancient vampire's flesh dripped over the lid of the coffin and made a winding path down the side. Anna was about to reach out and touch it, but Cecelia grabbed her hand.

"What the hell do you think you're doing? His flesh slips inside your body, Anna, and gives repulsive images of his hideous crimes."

The flesh dripped from the bottom edge of the coffin. Long, lingering droplets fell to the floor and seemed to reshape.

"He's getting out of the coffin, Cecelia."

Both women watched as the pace of the dripping increased. The ancient vampire threw a leg over the side of the coffin. The leg elongated until the foot touched the mossy ground.

"He can move on his own, Cecelia." Anna stood agape, watching as the ancient vampire oozed his way out of the coffin.

Cecelia grabbed Anna's hair and dragged her to the hot wall.

"Wait for me, children. I am coming."

There was instant laughter in the room. A single cackle above the rest seemed recognizable to Cecelia.

"Get up and walk," she screamed at the coffin.

A coffin near the women sounded with a loud pounding until a brass eagle broke through the lid.

"A cane," Cecelia murmured, reaching out to grab the eagle. She pulled a sword from the base of the cane. Instantly the lid of the coffin flew up and smashed into the two women.

Chapter Seventy

A matron's dress, Marie thought as she held up a steel-gray dress before her. Not a stitch of lace, no stitched-in curve, no sudden plunges or slits rising up. A plain old maid's dress. A dress a nun could wear. Louis evidently wanted her dressed as his mother-in-law. The dress zipped up the back. No buttons fronted it.

She looked down at the bloody dress she was wearing. The dress stank, and bits of the material had hardened with blood.

Nothing would change Louis's mind. Her ranting never had made an impression on him in the past, and now that he wanted her destroyed . . .

She flung the dress to the floor and began to stamp on it.

* * *

Marie gracefully walked down the marble staircase barefoot. Each marble step felt as cold as her own flesh. Blood speckled each foot. Andre's blood. She heard the high pitch of false laughter, the nervous tinkle of crystal, and smelled the food and alcohol, simple bait for the primary meal.

At the foot of the staircase she stopped. A tinge of blood circulated in the air around her, but it didn't come from the banquet. Marie walked over to a set of double doors and opened them. The room was dark. No fire lit the fireplace. No candle or electric light brightened the room. Shelves of books looked like hulking monsters watching some unspeakable terror taking place. As she walked deeper into the room the blood smell grew.

In front of her was a massive leather sofa; three matching leather chairs were huddled together, but all were empty. To the right of them she saw an ornate antique desk. Figures were carved into the legs. The figures rose up from flames they could never escape. A gargoyle sat atop each leg, enjoying the images of pain beneath it.

A soft moan and lapping sounds broke the silence. She touched the desk, and a familiar wetness made her hand skid. She raised her hand and smelled the liquid: blood. Her tongue had reached out to taste the manna when she heard the guttural sounds of death behind her. She turned and saw Sade folded into a curtain.

"Louis," she yelled.

Sade dropped the body to the floor.

"You couldn't wait for me to start the meal."

"She was merely an appetizer. Nothing like the main course, to which I am especially looking forward." He smiled at her, and she could barely see his teeth, so covered in blood were they.

"It's not polite for the host to start without the guests."

"And it is not polite for guests to intrude into parts of a home to which they weren't invited."

"I'm more than a guest, Louis; I'm family."

"Yes, and I have shared so much with you already, Marie. My blood gives you existence. My wife abandoned me to follow your wishes. And my sons were brought up under your tutelage. What more can I offer you? Perhaps a room filled with victims?"

"Are you trying to make nice with me?"

Sade laughed and stepped over the body that lay at his feet.

"You look lovely, Marie."

"I won't have to worry about staining my clothes," she said as she spread out her bloodstained skirt. "I wouldn't wear the horrid dress you left for me. But this dress is so much more appropriate for the occasion." She twirled around.

"And suits your temperament so well. Shall I escort you into the banquet?"

Chapter Seventy-one

Justin stood in the middle of the fires he had set. Lottie had managed to collect everything burnable into heaps set all around the cathedral. She had even used the altar cloth.

He looked in her direction and saw that she watched the flames reaching out for her. Briefly she looked back at him with a smile on her face. Justin almost moved forward to save her but didn't.

"You are at fault," he yelled at her. He doubted that she had heard him because of the crackling fire engulfing her. The remaining wooden statues began to break apart, spilling debris onto the flames.

Smoke was filling the air, and the heat made Justin sweat. He wiped his forehead with the back of his hand, wanting to keep his eyesight clear. He blinked rapidly, trying to drive the smoke from his eyes.

Howls rose up all around him. The vampires knew flames were at work. The cries settled into whimpers, and for the first time the walls of the church reverberated with pounding fists. All were seeking a way out of the dark corridors that might have already filled with smoke.

"Cecelia," he yelled, and he was answered by a crumbling wall in the wooden chapel. Bits of finely carved wood rained down upon Lottie. He could barely see her body.

"Mama," screamed a young woman who appeared to fall from the crumbling wall of the wooden chapel.

"Mama."

Still alive, Lottie brushed debris from her shoulders and half sat up. Justin guessed that she was blind because her hands flailed in the air, trying to touch someone.

"Anna." The whisper of the name floated through the cathedral, attracting the young woman. She ran into the flames surrounding Lottie. Her dress instantly caught fire, and as she ripped the cloth from her body, Justin watched her fall atop Lottie's body. They hugged, their hair alight, their clothes disintegrating, their skin melting into each other's, fat dripping from their bodies.

Mother and daughter were together again briefly, he thought. He knew that Anna's soul couldn't even follow her mother's into hell, so strong was the binding of vampire and earth.

A grinning, dried-out body walked from the flames. His clothes were dated from centuries past. In his hand he carried a black stick that he used to push debris out of his way. As the body moved closer, Justin noticed the cracks in the face. Now Justin doubted that the being actually was grinning but was instead disfigured by centuries of decay.

Justin could barely open his eyes. His tears did nothing to wash out the residue of the fire. He wouldn't be of any help to Cecelia if she revealed herself now. Hoping he remembered correctly, he spun himself in the direction of the door and ran. Screams seemed to be all around him, and he could feel other bodies bumping into him or rushing past. The vampires were free, and he was powerless to prevent their flight.

He sensed a draft in front of him, a draft that he hoped would lead him out of the cathedral. He took a deep breath when he could smell the night air. Fleeing bodies jostled him until he finally fell down the cathedral steps.

He felt blood slip down his cheek where he had hit one of the steps hard. Hands felt his face. He quickly batted them away. Something dropped down next to him, and he felt a tongue lick his face. He used his hands to push back against the body and sensed that it easily fell backwards.

The vampires are weak from decades, centuries, without nourishment, he reminded himself. Justin made it to his feet. His eyesight was beginning to return. He ran in the direction of the well that serviced the caretaker's house and pumped furiously with one hand while using the other to flush his eyes. Something jumped onto his back, and he had to stop pumping long enough to pull the thing off him.

The body hit the ground, but when Justin looked down he saw no one. The vampire had wasted no time; he had fled to find weaker prey.

Justin looked at the steps of the cathedral and saw torches running down the steps. Each vampire torch became disoriented after it had either fallen from or run down the steps. He could see the agony it suffered as its skin blackened and the terror of extinction dawned.

Chapter Seventy-two

"Thank you so much, child, for waiting."

Cecelia lay beneath the coffin lid, slowly regaining her senses.

"Anna," she called, but there was no answer.

She heard screams and the dreadful slushing noise the ancient vampire made as he came closer to her.

"I will help you escape, child. Depend on me and you will be saved."

Cecelia pushed herself out from beneath the coffin lid and tried to gain the strength to stand.

The other vampires were pounding on their coffins, searching for a way out before the flames could reach them.

She smelled the ancient vampire before she saw him. He reeked of decayed flesh mingled with the dusty odor of age. He leaned on a coffin just a foot away from her. Her arm began pulsing where his flesh had touched her before.

"I knew you would come back for me, child. My memories filled your head with pleasure. You saw my life and knew it had to be yours."

She looked around the room but didn't see Anna— only a gaping hole in the wall from which tendrils of fire leaped.

"Come closer to me, child. The strength in this body is ebbing, but my brain flourishes with dreams of our future together."

"What happened to Anna?"

"She dashed out into the flames. I, on the other hand, can show you the safe way out."

"I know the way out," Cecelia said. As she spoke, visions of men and women tied to posts rushed into her mind. She saw the fires set in the bundled twigs at their feet. She heard the women scream and the men yell for forgiveness. Their skin blackened and peeled into ash.

Something stung her good arm, and she remembered the flames so near her. But flames weren't winding about her flesh. No, the ancient vampire's decay had attached itself to her.

"You will never taste the fires, child. I will make sure of that. We will drink our fill, sate our desires, and keep our freedom. No more lying in a coffin dreaming of the world. We can now be part of the world and all its vices."

Choked off inside her throat, her own voice shimmered a distance from her mind. She grabbed for a single word, for a syllable.

She attempted to turn away from the vampire. She stared out into the fiery cathedral, and upon the far wall, yet untouched, was the fresco of the Last Judgment. The naked sinners gathered together, their eyes bulging, their mouths opened in silent screams. They looked so real. The flames caught onto the right lower tip of the painting and fed on the oils. The sinners instantly turned to dust as the fire climbed.

Chapter Seventy-three

Madeline felt out of place at the hedonistic party. But she was there to plead for Justin's life. *We'll go away to America; leave this country and all of surrounding Europe to Monsieur Sade.*

The sound of giggles and people nudging each other made her turn to the doorway. Sade stood erect, his head held high, and the simple smirk that she deplored stretched the flesh around his mouth. At his side was a woman, in her thirties, Madeline guessed. The woman held herself with equal dignity, but the dress she wore appeared covered with blood and the smell in the room confirmed that impression.

"A guest from the States," Sade said. "Via Paris. We met one night when we both were in betting

337

moods. So far the odds are in my favor. Isn't that so, Marie?"

The woman smiled politely, and as she did, her eyes took in the entire room. Madeline could have sworn the woman was choosing her next victims.

"But if I lose, Monsieur Sade . . ." As she spoke, the woman took an appetizer from a passing waiter's tray. "I will lose sated, and knowing that I can try again."

The woman looked out across the room and flung the appetizer over her shoulder.

As the woman walked through the crowd, people sniffed their displeasure at the sight and smell of her. The woman Sade had called Marie didn't seem to care.

Remembering why she was there, Madeline looked around the room, trying to locate Sade again. He seemed to have disappeared the moment Marie released his arm.

"What kind of people has Monsieur Sade taken to inviting to his parties? The woman looks like a street person, one who has passed her time in cheap brothels and smelly alleyways. I wish I had known he was inviting someone like that."

"Would you have stayed away, Monsieur Landron?"

With a smile on his face, the first speaker whispered something in the ear of his companion, and both broke into laughter.

Boldly Madeline went up to the pair and asked whether they knew what the party was celebrating.

Both shrugged.

Madeline watched the people fill themselves with rich, creamy foods and drink flute after flute of champagne. Some became ill and hurried from the room. None seemed to return. A few people began to wander out of the big room to look for friends or acquaintances who were missing.

She saw a blond woman with shaking hands search the room, looking into each face, memorizing each stance.

"What are you doing?" Madeline asked.

The woman nervously flipped her chin up to stare into Madeline's eyes.

"We're locked in. I tried to find my lover. I tried the front door, and it's locked. The doors to all the other rooms are locked. He wouldn't have left without me. He felt ill and left to use the bathroom. I thought maybe he went outside to get some air. It's very stuffy in here."

"There are no windows in this room," Madeline said.

"What? There are curtains all around us."

"They cover walls. The room has been sound-proofed."

"How do you know?"

Madeline blushed, remembering the orgies she had participated in.

A loud crash interrupted the conversation.

A woman had collapsed onto a table, tumbling the dishware to the floor. She writhed in pain on the carpet, closing her body into a fetal position. Her hair covered her face, but Madeline could see a blue tinge begin to cover the woman's flesh.

Madeline rushed into the mob crowding around the woman and noticed that a fresh tureen had been knocked to the floor.

"Oh, my God, he's slowly poisoning everyone," Madeline said.

"Poisoning? What are you talking about? Why would he poison us? She just ate too much. Look at the flab on her body. Obviously this woman is a ravenous eater," said a man next to Madeline.

The crowd took up the nursery rhyme of the piggies.

"And this little piggy ate it all up," the crowd shouted in unison while pointing at the woman, who had begun to choke on her own vomit.

"No, we must help her. She is seriously ill," Madeline said.

"Seriously rotund, I'd say." Another man laughed.

"Oh, but the smell is oppressive," said a woman with a pale pink handkerchief held to her nose. "Shouldn't we remove her before she ruins our fun?"

Several large men lifted the woman and carried her into the hall, where they deposited her on the marble floor. On their return they closed the doors behind them.

"Ah, the dress is as beautiful on you as I had imagined it would be," Sade whispered into Madeline's ear. The breeze of his cold breath sent a chill through her body. She faced him and saw his eyes alight, as if he had been drinking too much. There was no alcohol smell on his breath, only a hint of coppery blood.

"You mean to feast on us. That woman; she is the same as you."

"The feast has begun." Sade touched her cheek with his hand and stroked the softness of her flesh. His fingers were ice.

"Justin?"

"Haven't seen the charming young man. I had hoped he would escort you to this feast. I'll not waste my time looking for him, though. There is an intimate feast going on in the library." He offered her his arm. "Let me take you there, Madeline."

Madeline looked around for the woman he had called Marie. She was no longer in the room.

"You look so pale, Madeline. It's the heat in this room. No windows, but you know that from past occasions. The library has large French doors that look out onto the gardens. Perhaps we may take a final stroll through them."

"No!" she screamed, backing up into a couple that had begun to copulate on their knees.

Sade grabbed her wrist, preventing her fall. Several people took notice, though none came to her assistance. They turned their backs on her and broke out into uproarious laughter.

Chapter Seventy-four

Cecelia collapsed onto the cemetery dirt. Her hair was melted to her skull. Her hands were singed and shapeless with the excess flesh of the ancient vampire. She tried to touch her face, but sensation had gone from her fingertips. Her torn dress was smudged with soot and the brown stain of flame. She looked down at her legs and saw how bloated and blackened they were, with veins almost breaking free of the flesh.

The ancient vampire had lied. He had no safe way out. She had been forced by his energy to run through flames that crisped her body in agonizing pain. She wanted to cry, wanted to scream, wanted to destroy what was left of herself.

"Child, we are together now. I will not permit you to die. We will journey to Sade. Won't he be surprised by us, conjoined as we are."

"I don't want to exist like this."

"You will heal, though your features may be slightly altered and your body will need time to become accustomed to the additional mass."

"Why not take my body completely and free me?"

"I would, but I don't know how. I have gathered much wisdom over the years, had time to ponder all sorts of problems. If I destroy you, I destroy myself. I need your energy, your desire to live and seek vengeance."

"I have no strength to give you, no desire for life."

"It is there, child, buried under your despair. Vengeance will carry you through this night. At dawn we will rest in Sade's own coffin."

"The soil . . ."

"I am French and need this soil. It will work for you also, as long as I am with you. We are intertwined closer than any lovers could be, child."

Chapter Seventy-five

Justin dropped down on his knees, and for the first time he prayed. He prayed for the givers and receivers of pain. He prayed for the absolution of those who would ravage the world, and he prayed for the suffering souls who met God stainless.

A flare-up of the fire made him look once again at the cathedral. A cross stood at the top of a spire, backdropped by an almost full moon. Smoke clouded the night sky, blurring his view of both cross and moon.

He stood and noticed that he could see flames in among the trees, probably caused by the fleeing vampires. It had been dry for several weeks. He knew this meant danger for the town and the destruction of the forest.

Sparks floated in the air, some landing on the roof of the caretaker's house. Most burned out, a few took hold, and he saw the flash of fire light one end of the roof.

"There's that stranger!" a nearby voice yelled.

The town was coming to life. The sound of fire engines shattered the silence. Justin couldn't explain his presence at such a scene. He ran into the woods and toward the mansion.

Chapter Seventy-six

Cecelia ran through woods she didn't recognize, found paths she never knew existed, and memories she'd never had came to her.

She broke out of the woods, and there was Sade's mansion, gleaming with lights, yet somber. The ancient vampire allowed her to pause only briefly. Her body ached, and she felt the death sleep coming on. The smell of Sade came to her, riding above the smoke and burnt flesh.

"He's there, child, waiting. Waiting for us. Vulnerable as never before. I can tell by the amount of blood in the air. An orgy of death is taking place, and it stimulates my senses, refreshes my ability to outwit Sade."

Cecelia found herself running again. She didn't

346

remember moving her feet, didn't remember why she ran.

"You run into the arms of your lover, child."

"My lover. He sent me away."

"You are returning to fling yourself into his arms and ask for mercy. But we will have none for him."

There were noises in the distance. Squeals. Cries. Sirens. Her mind raced with the energy building all around her.

"The door will be barred to us, child."

"The mansion is lit up. He must be having a party. The door will be open."

"Not this night, child."

"Death is locked inside Sade's mansion?"

"Death cannot be locked in or out of any place. Death forces its way into lives that are both robust and weary. Death can never be sated. It is hungry all the time. I can feel it leaking through the cracks of the mansion and finding its way to the cathedral. It stops briefly to pick up a life here and there in the woods. A tree turned to a black husk. An animal loses its home and litter, or perhaps its own life."

"You take special glee in this," she said.

"Not glee, child. I have envied those who can die. Sometimes I have stared in awe at the amount of pain a body can take before losing the fight. I have watched tears flood anguished eyes. Death will end the suffering. Death will take the soul home. What about us, child? Our home is destroyable. Our home isn't always beautiful."

347

"Then why not die in the flames?"

"Because I live to defeat death."

Cecelia's hands touched the front door. She attempted to open it, but the ancient vampire had been right about it being bolted.

"Around to the right side of the house, child. There are double doors. I remember peering from them at night when soft, girlish bodies would tend the flowers. I would choose a morsel and have her before dawn. The French doors on the right side of the house. Hurry!"

Chapter Seventy-seven

Justin trod upon a carpet of colorful flowers. He never noticed the path that zigzagged through the garden. Never smelled the perfume of the garden. He smelled only fire and blood.

The French doors hung smashed and open. A body lay on the threshold, fear frozen on its face, limbs mangled and blood spattered. A rodent crept softly, gingerly, atop the hulk, pausing occasionally to sniff the air.

Justin rushed toward the body and lifted the rodent high into the air. It nipped at several of his fingers, but he didn't release it. He flung the rodent out into the trampled garden, where it lay, limbs splayed, in shock.

He stepped over the body and entered the library. The smell overwhelmed him for a few moments. He saw nothing but darkness until his vision cleared and his senses became accustomed to the odor. Bodies lay scattered over the carpet, some in piles, others isolated where they had initially fallen. He recognized none of the faces. He recognized only the slashes on flesh that Marie would have made.

"Marie," he called. "Marie, I know you're here. Have you gotten what you came for, or have you decided to once again join forces with that fiend Sade?"

A book fell off a shelf, startling Justin. Quiet returned. Some of the victims had obviously used the books as weapons, throwing them about the room, leaving the books on the shelf in precarious disarray.

The doors to the library were open, and from where he stood Justin could see the carnage that had occurred in the stately hallway.

He lost his respect for the dead and shoved bodies out of his way to reach the staircase that led up to the bedrooms. Vomit speckled the staircase, and at the top several bodies seemed huddled together on the brink of falling back down.

On the landing Justin could see that every door had been opened. Some doors had been ripped off their hinges.

"Marie!"

She didn't answer. No one answered.

He made the rounds of the bedrooms and found more dead bodies. One room had practically been painted with blood. The final room wavered in front of his tearing eyes.

A slurping noise alerted him to life in that room. "Marie!"

What would he do if his mother's form was dripping with blood and Marie's spirit continued to drain a victim dry? He spied a spindly table and broke off one leg to use as a stake.

He almost called to his mother. Instead he called once again to Marie.

The marble floor rang with his footsteps. His right hand tightened around the stake. Sweat dripped from his face, staining Madeline's father's shirt with his fear, not of his own death, but of his mother's final moment.

He stood in the doorway and called Marie's name.

"Cecelia," a voice called back.

He dropped the stake when he recognized the voice.

"You escaped the cathedral." He moved faster now, eager to see Cecelia.

A remarkable tangle of flesh lay on the floor behind the giant canopied bed. He recognized Cecelia's blue eyes and a hint of her former profile. Otherwise she was singed, sooty, and burned, with massive deformities spread across her flesh.

"Justin," she said, smiling up at him. She licked her fingers and used her teeth to pick flesh from under her fingernails. When she was done she offered her hands to Justin.

He reached out for her, and she instantly pulled back her hands and took the pose of an animal protecting its prey. She snarled.

351

"Cecelia."

The light of recognition brightened her eyes.

"Cecelia, let me help you."

From under the bed he heard a moan.

"You have someone hidden from me. Cecelia, let me see who you have."

"He says I should allow you to join me on the floor."

"Sade?"

She shook her head. "I don't know his name, but he wants your blood, Justin."

"Where is he?"

Cecelia spread her deformed arms wide before Justin.

"The thing has taken possession of your body."

"He says he shares." Her face crumpled into such a sadness that Justin fell to his knees and hugged her close to him.

He felt her fingertips play with the skin of his neck. Her flesh churned with life. Slowly he pulled away and watched waves flutter through the deformity, finding its own separate life.

"You wouldn't harm me, Cecelia."

"No." Her voice was weak; the word vibrated on her tongue.

Cecelia reached under the bed and pulled out a body clothed in a pale dress covered with pearls. Madeline's face slid into view.

"Is she hurt?"

"Drugged. Sleepy. Waiting." Cecelia giggled.

He reached for Madeline, but Cecelia ripped at his arms and snarled furiously.

"She's waiting for me, Cecelia."

"No," she whispered. "She's in place of you." Cecelia got to her knees and leaned over Madeline's body. "Her blood for yours."

"I'd rather give my own blood," he said.

Cecelia's head tilted so she could look at him.

"It's I you would die for, Justin."

"She is human."

Cecelia flung her body back to rest on her calves. "And I am a vampire."

"I would spare you whatever pain I could."

"Would you separate my head from my shoulders? Can you do that, Justin? Would you take away what little pleasure is left to me? Or perhaps silence me, as you did your mother? You wanted me, Justin." Cecelia looked at the body on the floor before her. "She's beautiful, unmarked, and her hair glows from fire." Cecelia ripped at Madeline's neck.

He heard Madeline cry out in pain even in her drugged state. He dove down onto the floor to protect her.

Cecelia licked Madeline's blood from her nails.

"She's tasty too." A smile only made her deformed face look more frightful.

"She's innocent," he said.

Cecelia sniffed. "She smells from Sade's touch."

"He abused her. You must understand that, Cecelia."

"What was that song you sang in the cemetery back home?

"All Christian men, give ear a while to me.
How I am plung'd in pain but cannot die;
I liv'd a life the like did none before,
Forsaking Christ, and I am damn'd therefore."

Her eyes took on a dreamy softness and she rocked back and forth to the memory of the song's tune.

"Let me help you, Cecelia. Let me take away the pain."

Her eyes squinted back at him. One of her hands reached inside her tattered garment and pulled out a stake. She laid it on the floor between herself and Justin.

Madeline became conscious and called Justin's name. Opening her eyes, she threw her arms around him. Cecelia went mad, ripping the two apart and sinking her teeth deep into Madeline's neck. He grabbed the stake, raised it high, and stabbed it into Cecelia's back, driving it through her heart and out the front of her body, nicking the pale material of Madeline's dress. Cecelia howled and fell back, reaching at the last moment for Justin's hand. He didn't touch her flesh, didn't cry tears for her, didn't wonder at his cruelty. Instead he grabbed Madeline into a hug.

"Sade is here with a strange woman," she said.

"No, there's no one else besides us. I've searched each room."

"Where have they gone?"

"I wish it were to hell. My fear is that Marie has reunited with Sade. I'll take you home."

"No, let my family think I died here."

"They'll find no body. You don't understand the pain they'll live through. Losing . . ." Justin's voice faltered. "Being robbed of a dear one hurts so much."

"You loved Cecelia."

And my mother, he thought.

"Wait in the hall for me, but go no farther."

"What are you going to do?"

"Give Cecelia her final peace."

An hour later a body burned on the gravel drive.

"They'll think it's me," Madeline said.

"No, they'll look for some form of identification."

Madeline slipped off a pinkie ring and tossed it into the fire.

"That ring was given to me by my father on my twelfth birthday. It was too big for me then. Now it barely fit."

Her naïveté made Justin smile. He knew a simple ring wouldn't serve as final identification.

Take her home, he told himself.

She took his hand and led him to an antique Rolls. The carved wood of the dashboard gleamed with polish. He had no idea how he had come to sit in the passenger seat. The engine started, and Madeline took the turn away from Albi.

Quenched

MARY ANN MITCHELL

An evil stalks the clubs and seedy hotels of San Francisco's shadowy underworld. It preys on the unfortunate, the outcasts, the misfits. It is an evil born of the eternal bloodlust of one of the undead, the infamous nobleman known to the ages as . . . the Marquis de Sade. He and his unholy offspring feed upon those who won't be missed, giving full vent to their dark desires and a thirst for blood that can never be sated. Yet while the Marquis amuses himself with the lives of his victims, with their pain and their torture, other vampires—of Sade's own creation—are struggling to adapt to their new lives of eternal night. And as the Marquis will soon learn, hatred and vengeance can be eternal as well—and can lead to terrors even the undead can barely imagine.

___4717-9 $5.50 US/$6.50 CAN

Sips of Blood

MARY ANN MITCHELL

The Marquis de Sade. The very name conjures images of decadence, torture, and dark desires. But even the worst rumors of his evil deeds are mere shades of the truth, for the world doesn't know what the Marquis became—they don't suspect he is one of the undead. And that he lives among us still. His tastes remain the same, only more pronounced. And his desire for blood has become a hunger. Let Mary Ann Mitchell take you into the Marquis's dark world of bondage and sadism, a world where pain and pleasure become one, where domination can lead to damnation. And where enslavement can be forever.

___4555-9 $5.50 US/$6.50 CAN

Dorchester Publishing Co., Inc.
P.O. Box 6640
Wayne, PA 19087-8640

Please add $1.75 for shipping and handling for the first book and $.50 for each book thereafter. NY, NYC, and PA residents, please add appropriate sales tax. No cash, stamps, or C.O.D.s. All orders shipped within 6 weeks via postal service book rate. Canadian orders require $2.00 extra postage and must be paid in U.S. dollars through a U.S. banking facility.

Name_____
Address_____
City_____State_____Zip_____
I have enclosed $_____ in payment for the checked book(s).
Payment <u>must</u> accompany all orders. ☐ Please send a free catalog.
CHECK OUT OUR WEBSITE! www.dorchesterpub.com

WOUNDS

JEMIAH JEFFERSON

Jemiah Jefferson exploded onto the horror scene with her debut novel, *Voice of the Blood*, the most original, daring, and erotically frightening vampire novel in years. Now her seductive, provocative world of darkness is back.

Vampire Daniel Blum imagines himself the most ruthless, savage creature in New York City, if not the world. He once feasted on the blood of Nazi Germany and left a string of shattered lovers behind him. But now the usual thrill of seduction and murder has begun to wear off. Until he meets Sybil, the strange former stripper whose mind is the first he's ever found that he cannot read or manipulate. . . .

___4998-8 $5.99 US/$7.99 CAN
